*For Teachers
everywhere*

Miss Madeira

Published by Deckle Press, Vancouver, BC Canada
www.austin-gary.com

This novel is a work of fiction. Any references to real people, events, organizations or locale are intended only to give the fiction a sense of reality and authenticity, and are used fictitiously. All other names, characters and places, and all dialogue and incidents portrayed in this book are the product of the author's imagination.

Photograph by Kim Ballalance.

Printed in the United States of America

ISBN 978-0-9877-821-0-6

Miss Madeira

A Novel

By

Austin Gary

PART ONE

One need not be a Chamber—to be Haunted—
One need not be a House—
The brain has Corridors—surpassing
Material Place—

Far safer, of a Midnight Meeting
External Ghost,
Than an interior confronting—
That cooler Host—

Far safer, through an Abbey gallop,
The Stones a'chase—
Than unarmed, one's a'self encounter—
In lonesome Place—

Ourself behind ourself, concealed—
Should startle most—
Assassin hid in our Apartment
Be Horror's least.

The Body—borrows a Revolver—
He bolts the Door—
O'erlooking a superior spectre—
Or More—

~Emily Dickinson

ONE

In the fall of 1917, the Prospect School had an enrollment of 187 pupils—116 in grades one through eight and seventy-one in high school; had war not been raging half a world away, a handful more would have graced the upper hallway. Five local boys waived their senior year to join the army—hoping to aid the allied forces on the Western Front, where it was reported the war's end was imminent. Such mundane occurrences had a major impact on Prospect, a small farming community, seventy-five miles southwest of St. Louis.

Four days prior to the beginning of the new school year, the superintendent, W. O. Johnston, learned that the newly hired English teacher was in the building. "*Here*...now? Do you know what's she doing?" he queried his secretary, Mrs. Dean.

"Said she had to ready her room. Been working all morning."

"You did tell her school policy doesn't permit her to be in the building without prior authorization?"

"I told her, of course."

"And?"

"Said that was an idiotic rule. 'Mrs. Dean,' she says, 'that's like asking a shopkeeper to arrive at the same time as his customers. There'd be no fire in the furnace. No stock on the shelves."

"Said that did she?

"Actually, she said 'arrive simultaneously.' Likes big words, that one. 'An *ambiance* of inhospitableness would prevail,' she says, 'and the entire enterprise would fail.' I asked the meaning of the word and she grabbed a dictionary and had me look it up. Thought certain she was going to require me to use it in a sentence."

"The new school year doesn't begin 'til after Labor Day. Teachers are expected to be here prior to students' arrival and long after they depart. That's more than enough preparation time."

"Miss Orton once told me, 'Saying Amelia Madeira's strong-minded is like calling a tornado a gust of wind.' And that's when she was only a freshman in high school."

"Rules are rules, and they apply to everyone…especially *neophytes*."

"Atmosphere…mood."

"*What?*"

"Ambiance…its meaning."

"Mrs. Dean, I will not have a teacher, let alone a first year teacher, dictating policy."

"I'm just a secretary, Mr. Johnston. I leave enforcement of school policy to you men."

"Indeed!" he snorted—charging past her into his office. Yanking open his middle desk drawer, he removed an envelope and slid it into the pocket of his suit coat. "I'll show her strong-minded."

He dashed out of the office and down the hallway towards the English room, where he discovered her busily inventorying textbooks. Earnestly engaged in that task, she moiled like an industrious worker bee, all the while radiating an oddly regal demeanor. Fascinated, he observed her for nearly a minute before she noticed him.

"*Oh*…Mr. Johnston! You startled me."

Amelia Madeira had made every effort to appear older than her twenty years. Her brunette hair was piled high. She wore a dark blue blouse with a broad lace collar and matching skirt that hung to the ankles of her high-button shoes. Wire-rimmed glasses provided a look of severity, masking the real Amelia, who more often resembled a wounded deer—vulnerable and slightly dazed. However, those who came to know her soon realized her unassuming appearance in no way reflected any diffidence when it came to her abilities.

"I knocked, but you were so engrossed you failed to hear me," he said—chuckling in a way that made her stomach clench. "When Mrs. Dean mentioned you were here, I was quite surprised."

"In what way?"

"To find anyone working on an unpaid Friday before the school year commences Tuesday. Labor Day being Monday." He waited for an explanation; none came. "I'm not accustomed to having teachers in the building on holidays," said Johnston, whose hair lay in oily strings, carefully raked across and plastered to his balding pate. One twisted strand had worked its way loose; she tried desperately to avoid the distraction of the flapping mesh. "In fact, it's highly irregular," he added—adjusting his pince-nez, which had slipped to the tip of his sloped nose.

"It's just that there's so much to do…planning, preparation, readiness. Those are important, wouldn't you agree? Surely there's no objection to being prepared for the first day of school?"

"Yes…I mean *no*…no objection."

"Was there something more?"

"No…er, *yes*." He reached into the pocket of his suit coat and removed the envelope, which he presented like an indignant process server delivering a summons. "Miss Orton wanted whoever assumed her teaching duties to have this."

She took the letter and pressed it to her bosom.

"I'm certain she had no idea when she wrote it the position would be filled by one of her former star pupils," said Johnston, who, having previously served as principal at nearby Graniteville, was in his second year as superintendent at Prospect High School.

They stared at each other for a few uncomfortable seconds.

"Would that be all then?" she asked, somewhat dismissively.

"Yes…that's all." He turned to leave and then turned back. "As you know, when Miss Orton retired to pursue her interest in orenthology—"

"*Orni*thology," she blurted—correcting him before she could stop herself.

"Orenth…ore…*bird watching! S*he left you some very large shoes to fill. Very large."

"I've been made most aware of that. I quite remember Miss Orton's shoes…petite, yet commodious. I shall do my best to occupy them with dignity and grace."

"I didn't mean to suggest you aren't capable. Your academic record speaks for itself; however, you must know it's rare a first year teacher is given such an opportunity. The very thought of entrusting the English curriculum to anyone without the highest standards is unthinkable. Normally, we would have chosen a proven professional from the elementary ranks, and were planning to do so before receiving your last-minute application."

"Knowing that, I'm even more honored to have the position." Her large brown eyes glistened—which they seemed to do whenever she was being facetious. Having been a student under all but one of Prospect's elementary teachers, she wondered which of them he thought capable of handling the position. Though she believed some of them competent enough to instruct young children in the basics, it was her opinion none was suited to teach high school students, because each lacked the most requisite skill—the ability to inspire.

"Now, if you'll excuse me, I'm curious to discover what words of wisdom Miss Orton had to impart." She waggled the letter.

Johnston produced a tepid smile. He started towards the door.

"Oh, one other thing, sir…"

He paused in mid-step.

"I'll need a key."

"All teachers have keys," he said—resuming his departure.

"Not a room key, sir. A key to the building."

He turned to confront her, his face twisted and perturbed. Sweat beads dotted his forehead and the sebaceous flap of hair drooped like a misplaced queue. "Teachers have no need of a building key...except for the coach, of course."

"But I'll need to work in my room over the weekend."

"Miss Orton was an outstanding teacher. I'm quite certain she never darkened her door on weekends."

"Everyone knows she spent her weekends bird watching, a noble pursuit. But she also taught here for thirty years from the same texts, using the same lessons. I'm trying to update the process."

"Update the process, Miss Madeira, or upset the apple cart?"

"To prepare my students to excel in college and in life. To introduce them to the immortal poetry of Emily Dickinson and Walt Whitman and to usher them into the 20th century."

"Our young men need preparation for *war* not poetry. And, if I may be so bold, our young women need to learn how to keep the home fires burning. Neither of those things can be accomplished with *poesy*."

"But, sir, education is the only—"

"Don't be so impudent as to explain education to *me*," he huffed. "I've been in the business of education for thirty years. You've yet to begin."

The business of education! Amelia started to protest, but thought the better of it.

"Teach the classics and forget the moderns. Grammar, spelling, penmanship. That's all that's required. Now, meditate on the words of Miss Orton and learn."

She watched him go—waiting for him to cross the threshold before she allowed herself to exhale. *What a ridiculous man! I will not cry. His ignorance demands pity not tears.* Besides, she thought, his dictates were mere piffle compared to the daily demands of her ailing father.

Needing more light and hoping to catch the slightest flicker of air, she moved towards the open window; mid-morning, and the heat and humidity were already oppressive. Removing a monogrammed handkerchief from her sleeve, she patted her brow. *Caniculares dies...the dog days of summer.* 'If the weather doesn't break, the students will suffocate.' She tucked the handkerchief back into her sleeve.

"Words of wisdom from Miss Orton. Whatever could they be?" she wondered aloud. She recalled the many times she'd butted heads with Miss Florence Orton, whom she considered a congenial person but a barely adequate teacher. Whenever she questioned her interpretation of a poem or the theme of a short story, her teacher would nervously launch into a long, often implausible explanation. As a result, Amelia coined a portmanteau her senior year—one not truly appreciated by her peers. She called the process of pretending to listen to an Orton screed, "Ignortoning."

The running joke among students was that you could mouth an answer to "Orton," who was virtually deaf and apparently too embarrassed to acknowledge it, and not run the risk of further questioning. At times, students' answers were hysterically inappropriate, but unless she detected laughter or disconcerting looks, she would nod approvingly.

Many students found this charade a respite from actual learning, but not Amelia Madeira. There was something in her that yearned to acquire and share knowledge. She felt compelled to inform her classmates—resistant though they often were—of her latest insights into poetry analysis, comparative literature and the symbiotic relationship between art and life. She didn't care if they were actually interested, only that they be exposed.

Ironically, it was Miss Orton who predicted she would make an outstanding teacher one day. 'I would have loved to have seen the look on her face when she found out who her replacement would be.'

Sliding an index finger under the envelope flap, she removed and unfolded three sheets of linen stationery, immediately recognizing the familiar cursive predating the Palmer Method—a

Spenserian style she found self-indulgent.

> To Whom It May Concern:
>
> You have been given the great privilege of teaching the youth of Prospect the very basics of a good education: the English language. You will inherit three of my classes and introduce the new freshmen to your own methodology. I leave you with not only a great privilege but also an immense responsibility.
>
> I am writing to you, principally, to alert you to the needs of one particular student in your senior English class. His name is Chester O'Malley. Chester is one of those delicate, rare birds—like the nearly extinct marshland bittern—that must be nurtured and protected. His sensibility and insight far surpass his contemporaries. In the whole of my teaching tenure, I have encountered only one other student with his perception and intelligence, but her gifts were diminished by impertinence and a willful bearing.

Amelia looked up with a wry smile. 'So that's how she thought of me. I wonder if she knew what I really thought of her?'

> Chester O'Malley will most likely be one of only two graduates of the Class of 1918 to pursue a post-secondary education. Since he comes from a family of modest means, he must be given every bit of encouragement and support to leave his intemperate father and his emotionally destitute mother. University will be his salvation.
>
> Chester is a gifted writer, whose essays and poetry sing like those of Emerson, Arnold and

Tennyson. Do not permit his classmates to mock him or denigrate his talent. He is too shy to read his work aloud to the class, but promise to be his Cyrano—sharing his compositions with his classmates in hopes they might prove inspirational.

Amelia rolled her eyes and sighed with mild disgust. Suggesting Cyrano was merely the mouthpiece for Christian's ideas was typical of the inaccuracies for which she used to chide Miss Orton. 'Impertinent and willful, indeed!'

I entrust him to you like one of the bejeweled, fragile eggs Faberge' artfully crafted for the imperiled Russian czar. Chester O'Malley is such a delicate treasure.

Sincerely,
Miss Florence Orton

P.S. This winter, please go to the meat counter at Rainey's and ask Joe Shanks to save suet for the birds. If you look out the window, you'll see the little wooden stands where I feed the finches, cardinals and sparrows. Fasten the suet to the spikes. Be so kind, won't you? They've come to expect it when a cold wind blows, and such loyalty demands attention.

A bejeweled, fragile egg? Amelia barely recalled the O'Malley boy. He would have been a freshman her senior year. She remembered him being physically immature, *a delicate, rare bird—* unlike the farm boys, who all seemed older than their years.

"Artistic" was the epithet most often applied to Chester.

9 MISS MADEIRA

Though no one said it, everyone knew what that meant.

TWO

August 18th, 1917

Ypres, France

Dearest Sis,

Am only now able to write you. Seat yourself for what I am about to say will upset you no end. Not a week after my last letter announcing our triumph at Messines Ridge the Germans shelled us with gas. It was a dark yellow vapor ~~rimanisant of~~ like the wild garlic bordering your spring garden. Remember the dry puffballs we found that autumn day in the woods and how when we stomped them a mustardy powder exploded? Imagine the air choked and poisoned with it. It was not a direct strike on our trench and thank the Lord the wind carried the thick cloud away from most of my comrades but there was enough to blister my face and damage my lungs and please dear Sis do not despair...cause blindness in my left eye. In Dutch Ypres means "leper" and for the past three weeks I've looked like one. At my lowest someone spoke of the Portuguese wine "Madeira" saying how hardy (fortificado) it is. That little reminder of our heritige (sp?) sparked my recovery. But know it is my Love for you Sis that always sustains me. With it all I was one of the lucky ones. A young British officer named Alex Easterly died from exposure to this poison. I watched my best buddy die a horrible death. His commanding officer gave me Alex's pistol ~~in rememberence~~. I shall keep it always. We have all lost much and are determined to succeed whatever the cost. A wounded animal is the most dangerous! Allied forces are only months away from Victory. Can't come too soon. <u>So much death</u>! The sounds echoing through the hospital day and night torment the soul. French nurses are a comfort but conditions bad. Supplies running low and surgical staff exausted. Tell Papa Portuguese and Dutch make big contrabutions to the War effort. Lied when asked of our dear Mother's nationality. Said Dutch not German. How's Papa? Black days still upon him? Think he'll ever forgive me? And what of your teaching duties? So many questions but the long days of idelness torture the brain. Tell me everything and pray in your own way for a speedy end to this war. Celebrated my 21st birthday in a hospital.

> Love always,
> Karl

P.S. "Miss Madeira," please excuse my

grammer and spelling errors…and HAPPY BELATED BIRTHDAY DEAR SIS!!

*   *   *

"Clara…Clara, *a minha irmã* (my sister)!"

In less than four hours, Amelia needed to be at school. Day One was crucial: first impressions, command of subject, proven competency. For the second time that night her Papa had awakened her—calling out from his tortured sleep.

3 A.M. I must get some rest. It was a futile plea and she knew it. 'Other teachers have pressing personal problems, yet they manage. They come to school, day after day, and carry on,' she told herself.

"Millie! Clara! *Podes me perdoar?* (Can you ever forgive me?).

Over the years, like an ingenious jigsaw puzzle solver, Amelia had pieced together Fredo's biography from his random musings and reassembled them into a sketchy portrait. These fragments appeared without logical, let alone chronological explanation. Even as a child, she was curious to know more. Throughout her Papa's fractured history, she looked for repetition, patterns—hoping to illuminate his shadowy past.

From the first two decades of her life, the following represents the sum total of what she had gleaned and reassembled in a journal:

> Fredo (Fred) Madeira—born Godofredo Karel Madeira in San Leandro, California in 1869—the son of Portuguese and Dutch immigrants who, lured by rumors of gold rush riches, sailed from the Azores in 1858, across the Atlantic and around Cape Horn to California. Failing to discover some version of El Dorado, they settled in the village of San Leandro on the San Francisco Bay, where they

joined Portuguese fishermen, to become farmers in the fertile fields.

In 1886, with no aspiration to be a cherry picker, a seventeen-year-old Godofredo boarded a transcontinental train in San Francisco and headed east—carrying with him only a few personal items. For no apparent reason, he disembarked in Ada, Ohio—claiming it as his new home. Unable to find work, he headed south to Cincinnati. A week later he was employed in the Holderon Paper Company, where he learned to operate a roller press. A year to the day, he traded that job for one with Jouvance Funereal Artworks, a company specializing in hand-carved, mildly erotic cemetery statuary: nude mourning women, sleeping women with erect nipples piercing thin gowns, virginal putti, winged cherubim and majestic seraphim with exposed genitalia.

Following a year of lugging slabs of limestone and marble on wooden sleds, he commenced a 10-year apprenticeship with the renown, Jean François Jouvance, a protégé of French master, Henri Michel Antoine Chapu.

Seven years into the process of becoming a master stone carver, he was introduced to Millicent "Millie" Gerbacher, a beautiful German girl, whom he met while attending a fall festival, "Old Michaelmas Day"—honoring Saint Michael the Archangel. Five Sundays later they were married in Holy Cross Cathedral. Fredo was twenty-six, Millie, sixteen. Scarcely nine months preceded the birth of a son, Karl, thirteen months later, Amelia.

Before Amelia reached her second birthday, her mother died from complications of a third pregnancy. Eight months after her burial, Jouvance Funereal Artworks placed a large limestone statue of a young girl in mourning on Millie Madeira's grave. It had been carved by Jovance himself. Members of the Gerbacher family were offended by the statue, which they considered indecent and an affront to God.

A week later, without a word to anyone, Godofredo Karel Madeira packed a few possessions—including his tools and his two young children—into a horse-drawn wagon and traveled two miles into Cincinnati, where he purchased a train ticket to St. Louis. He had learned from Jean François that statuary was being carved on site for the 1903 Louisiana Purchase Exposition. He abandoned the horse, the wagon— everything except the valuable stone carving skills he had acquired.

On a beautiful April day in 1900, Fredo Madeira and his two children settled in a four-family flat on Arsenal Street near South Grand Boulevard in St. Louis. It took several weeks before he located the company contracted to build the cascades and exhibition halls for the Exposition. He was told to return in a year when most of the construction was scheduled to begin, but when he explained he could carve statues for the fountain arcade, he was hired by the famed sculptor, Bela Pratt, who knew of Monsieur Jouvance's reputation. Pratt, operating out of New York, had received several commissions and was looking to shore up his crew. For a moment it appeared Fredo's new life was on the ascendant, but when he saw the staid, lifeless statues Pratt proposed for the fountains, he complained and was fired before chisel touched stone.

"Clara! O que e que eu poderia ter feito? (What was I supposed to do?).

'Papa, *please*...not again.'

It had been more than three years since Fredo suffered a debilitating head injury when a huge chunk of limestone fell—fracturing his skull. Hearing someone had vandalized his recently completed sculpture of the archangel, St. Michael, the magnificent warrior perched on a limestone pedestal near the bandstand in the middle of the Prospect town square, he had rushed to determine the extent of the damage.

Unbeknownst to him, a passerby happened along in time to frighten off the vandals and prevent the entire statue from being destroyed. Still, hundreds of hours of glorious work came to naught; the statue's sword, shield and genitals—barely detectable beneath the sweep of sheer drape—were demolished. Clearly, it had been difficult for the defacers to reach the wings, though the wingtips themselves were obliterated.

Enraged and in a drunken stupor, he scaled the statue's base. In an effort to pull himself to his feet, he lost his balance and launched himself onto the angel's massive wing. He hung there in mid-air, struggling to maintain his grip, before falling. The pinion, already fractured where it joined the scapula, cracked completely and plunged with him.

It was nearly an hour before Luke Phillips, owner of the town's only barber shop, discovered Fredo lying in a pool of blood—encircling him and the shattered limestone wing like a crimson aureole. His fractured skull left him with what came to be known as the "3 D's": diplopia (double vision), dysphasia (impairment and comprehension of speech) and disinhibition (difficulty controlling urges).

It seemed everyone in the community had orchestrated his own version of the incident. The preacher at the Baptist church referred to it as the "Revenge on the Angel of Destruction"—assuring his parishioners it was God's response to idolatry. Several 'Concerned Citizens' wrote anonymous letters to the editor of the *Prospect Banner*—criticizing both the Iron County Historical Society, which had financed the project, and 'that depraved dago.' Jokes flew like spittle in the local pool hall.

'Ya gotta be crazy to wrastle an angel.' 'Not even an archangel could defeat ol' Satan without his family jewels!' Other comments were more profane.

At the time of the incident, Amelia was set to begin her senior year of high school; Karl had recently departed for the Army —leaving her to face the ignominy alone. The humiliation she suffered was palpable. Still, it did not prevent her from defending her father in the newspaper.

Dear Editor:

I'm writing in response to the recent destruction of my father's sculpture of the archangel, St. Michael, in the Prospect town square. Fredo Madeira created the sculpture in tribute to a city he considers his adopted home.

Like a poet, the artist "dwells in possibility." Contrary to the prose writer or craftsman, the poet-artist is unencumbered and his vision unlimited, unlike the narrow-minded who would destroy or applaud the destruction of his Art. The Artist Life is a difficult one and is often misunderstood by those whose mundane existence involves no risk, no Soul bearing and no outlet for self-expression.

The loss of time, energy, artistic effort and subsequent injury caused by the desecration have left my father in precarious health and a state of *tristeza profunda* (profound sadness). The language is Portuguese—not Spanish, not Italian nor Puerto Rican. Fredo Madeira is a proud, first generation Portuguese American and the equally proud father of a son serving his country in the United States Army.

Many thanks to those who have expressed condolences. Shame to those who would applaud this heinous act of ignorance and destruction.

Sincerely,
Amelia Irmelinda Madeira

Her ringing indictment appeared to bring closure to the calamitous event, but as anyone with an intimate knowledge of the workings of small-town America knows, episodic memory is the bailiwick of barbershops, beauty shops and pool halls.

By the time she was ready to leave for college, he had recovered enough to care for himself; yet, his behavior had become even more bizarre in the final days before she departed. He began calling her 'Clara' or 'Millie'. Once, when she was checking on him at bedtime, he awoke from a nightmare and grabbed her so savagely that, as she struggled to pull away, his fingernails left deep bloody scratches in her forearms.

Away at college, though continuing to worry about his well being, she was relieved to be temporarily free of the burdensome responsibility. Disencumbered, she relished her new life and her new friendship with Sarah Jamison. The two eighteen-year-olds met while registering for classes at the Missouri State Normal School in Cape Girardeau in the summer of 1915. Both were seeking Teacher Certification—a 2-year program.

Due to the war, there was a mad rush to replace male

teachers with single females. Not only were men needed for military service, it was determined single women could live cheaper because most lived at home with parents; thus, school systems could save money by offering lower salaries. Married women were rarely employed to teach unless deemed incapable of bearing a child. It was not simply a matter of having to replace a pregnant teacher mid-year.

"A female teacher must be *chaste* if she's to be permitted to instruct America's youth," Dr. Phineas Martin announced to a class of prospective female student teachers.

"Males and their insipid vestal virgin fantasies," whispered Amelia. Her hand insistently pierced the air.

"Question or comment?" He struck a match, lit his pipe—disappearing in a smoky haze.

"Both, actually. I'm curious. How exactly will a women's chastity be determined? By the school board? In a public forum? Need we all be Persephone to impart wisdom?"

There was a ripple of varying responses that included some audible gasps. One or two smiled broadly. Some stifled laughter. Others reacted as if they had been personally scandalized.

"Your name…Miss…?" asked Dr. Martin, whose southern drawl dripped with contempt.

"Madeira. Amelia Madeira."

"Oh, yes…of course. I must say I found your essay on the need for *kindergarten* in America rather *pro-German*, Miss Madeira. Just as I find your comments…highly inappropriate." He took several short puffs on his pipe, and arched one of his bushy eyebrows.

"Well, Dr. Martin, I find the concept of one's chastity affecting one's teaching ability ridiculous to the extreme," she countered. "After all, we're studying to be teachers…not nuns. Though I admit becoming a teacher is very much like taking a vow of poverty."

A young woman on the far side of the auditorium let out an involuntary guffaw. She quickly covered her mouth, lowered her eyes and mumbled, "Sorry."

"Those constraints aren't mine," said Dr. Martin—ignoring the interruption. "Though I must admit, I agree with them. If you find them ridiculous as you say, perhaps you should choose another profession."

"Perhaps, I shall," she said, with complete assurance.

Again, there was a mixed reaction—some shocked and others clearly admiring of her outspokenness. When the students' attention finally returned to Dr. Martin, she leaned towards Sarah and whispered, "Old fogey."

Sarah Jamison grew up on a farm near Valley Ridge, Missouri, eighty miles southwest of Cape Girardeau, on the Arkansas border. When she was eight, her father was killed instantly from a mule kick to the head. She had never told any stranger the truth surrounding her father's death because she was embarrassed by the circumstances, nor had she ever mentioned how much she despised her father, who was drunk at the time of the fatal *coup de grace*, for leaving her, her two brothers and their barely thirty-year-old mother saddled with the hardship of maintaining a farm. These secrets she readily revealed to Amelia.

"What a horrible way to die. If I'm correct, didn't Lincoln once get kicked by a—"

"Believe me, Jack Jamison was no Abe Lincoln. I loathed him when he was alive…and I despised him for dying. I know it's wrong to hate, especially a parent. But, he was an irresponsible drunkard and his death, while a calamity, wrecked our lives," she explained on one of their late-night confessionals.

"There have been times in the past when I resented my mother for dying and leaving Karl and me alone. That sounds absurd when I say it aloud," said Amelia, "but that's how I felt. For years I was angry with Papa for always being gone…for never really being there even when he was home. Having a creative mind is no excuse. Somehow, that kind of abandonment felt worse than if he were dead."

It didn't take them long to discover they shared many other

commonalities. Both currently had an older brother in the war. Both loved literature, especially poetry. Both elected to become a teacher, though for Amelia, writing would have taken priority over teaching had she been afforded the luxury. Neither had a desire to marry since neither had ever been interested in boys—finding them rather callous and irksome.

"Clara...a minha irmã...por favor perdoa-me!"

She hoped to avoid going into Fredo's bedroom; however, once the delirium began, it often took hours to get him calmed and back to sleep.

"Por favor perdoa-me!"

Of late, this was a common refrain. 'Forgive him for what?' His relationship with his younger sister had insinuated itself throughout her childhood. 'Ioiô, you are so remind me of your Aunt Clara.' How many times had he repeated those words to the young Amelia, his *Ioiô,* his "little love?"

All she really knew of her aunt was that she had never married—dedicating her life to caring for others. Of all of her father's siblings, she was the only one he ever discussed at length. The two were "Irish twins," born eleven months apart. As children, they had been inseparable.

"Por favor perdoa-me!"

She had to quiet him. Hurrying into his bedroom, she found him clawing at his cotton nightshirt. "It's all right. You're having a bad dream... *só um sonho*...only a dream, that's all. Go back to sleep, *por favor.*"

The room reeked of sweat and urine-stained bedclothes, liniment and the perpetual stench of human waste no chamber pot could conceal; the bouquet of dried lavender she kept on the bedside table proved ineffectual.

"Um sonho?"

"Yes, just a dream."

"Demasiado quente!" The more delirious he became, the more he reverted to his native tongue.

"I know it's hot. Stop struggling and let me dry your brow." She dabbed at the perspiration with a cloth she retrieved from the tarnished metal headboard.

"*Quente!*"

"Shhh...the neighbors will hear. I can't do anything about the heat. Calm down now and go back to sleep, *por favor. Dormir.*" Before exiting, she considered emptying his chamber pot, but decided to postpone that unpleasant task until daybreak.

'Karl, I would trade places with you in an instant.' It was Amelia's contention that in any conflict, the real warriors were those who were left to battle life on the home front.

In the dark, she slowly made her way down the creaking stairs. Like St. Lucia, she shuffled along—blindly feeling her way towards the dining room table. Her knee bumped against a chair, which scraped the floor and rapped sharply against the table. As always, the noise startled her.

She brushed her hand across the lace tablecloth—reading the Braille of its intricate design—until her fingers found the tin holder. Sliding a match from it, she struck it against the metal container. A spark flew from the tip, the bright flame causing her to squint. She lifted the glass globe on the kerosene lamp and quickly lit the wick. Lowering the globe, she adjusted the flame and picked up the lamp. A shimmer of light in the window caught her eye, and, for an instant, she was spooked by her own ghost-like image; she audibly gasped. Annoyed by her timidity, she ushered the lamp into the kitchen—casting familiar shadows.

She held her hand just above the cast iron stovetop— checking for warmth. Nothing. She set the lamp on the warming shelf, reached down into the firewood box and picked out two small pieces of white oak and some kindling. Sliding the coiled wire handle into the grooved slot, she removed the heavy, round stove lid and dropped the wood onto the cold ash. She crumpled a sheet of old newsprint and wedged it between the pieces of oak, before arranging the dry tender. Striking a kitchen match on the stove, she lit the paper in several places. Once again, a wisp of sulphur floated into her nostrils. She waited until she heard the kindling crackle before replacing the lid.

Grabbing the handle of a dull copper teakettle, she carried it to the screened-in side porch, where she filled the kettle half-full of water from a metal bucket that sat, along with a wash pan and a scrubbing board, on a wooden table covered in faded red oilcloth. She took a sip of the well water, metallic and tepid, then dropped the dinted tin dipper back into the bucket with a 'plunk'—the handle scraping the side as it bobbed up and down before sinking.

Oh, Sarah...how long before I see you again...?

With a sigh, she returned the teakettle to the stove.

Recalling a line from *Lalla Rookh*, she quoted it aloud: *"I knew, I knew it could not last—'Twas bright, 'twas heavenly, but 'tis past!"* 'No! We *will* be together!'

"We must!" exploded from her lips, the words hanging in the night air like thick smoke.

Moving back to the porch, she glanced out towards her garden...her sanctuary. It was only then she became aware of the plaintive sounds. A few locusts were droning their last summer chorus, greatly diminished from the full-throttle symphony of June and July. All had shed their thin, outer skeletons—leaving brittle amber shells clinging to tree bark, porch screens and windowsills.

'How fortunate to be able to leave one's old self behind,' she thought.

The moonlight danced on the water in limestone bird feeders. The yard—including a dozen hand-carved statues—was bathed in shadows. Over the years, Fredo had carved the miniature angels (*anjos*) as gifts to his children. The weathered statuary, obscured by a thin patina of moss, was a haunting reminder of her childhood, the details of which she had faithfully recorded in journals and poems written in the style of her literary heroine and "spiritual sister," Emily Dickinson.

Summer was closing fast. Most of the flowering plants had withered weeks ago; a few straggly marigolds, geraniums and impatiens were all that remained of her annuals. She had recently planted petunias and anemones to accompany the colorful winter cabbage—knowing they would survive only until the first hard freeze that usually appeared weeks before winter's official arrival. Because the moribund garden had pleaded for one final touch of color, she granted its entreaty with splashes of purples, yellows and clumps of feathery greens, violets, magentas and pinks in pots, placed, strategically, around its borders.

She was relieved Fredo no longer ventured out. Where once he would have applauded her '*polegar verde*' (green thumb), now he would chide her for '*tal desperdício!*' (such waste!).

I hide myself within my flower... Like her beloved Miss Dickinson, she cherished her garden, and in imitation of the reclusive poetess, had, for years, pressed flowers in scrapbooks and presented nosegays of the dried blossoms as gifts to her teachers and friends. *...that, fading from your vase, you, unsuspecting, feel for me almost a loneliness.*

Poetry had long been a part of her inner monologue. Only occasionally did she acknowledge how she much preferred it to her own thoughts.

Returning to the kitchen, she retrieved the lamp and carried it into the dining room. She sat down at the table and picked up her cherished book of Dickinson's poems, sent last June by her dear Sarah—pressing it to her breast, tenderly, as one might a beloved infant.

'What is it about your poetry that resonates so deeply? What is it about your solitary life that mirrors my own?' Holding it prayerfully, the book fell open to:

> *If I can stop one heart from breaking,*
> *I shall not live in vain;*
> *If I can ease one life the aching,*
> *Or cool one pain,*
> *Or help one fainting robin*
> *Into his nest again,*
> *I shall not live in vain.*

Under this verse, she wrote:

> *If I can one Soul inspire—*
> *With Language white hot searing—*
> *Words of Truth ignite Desire—*
> *All Darkness disappearing.*
> *Then Lightning cannot blind the eye—*
> *Nor Thunder faze the hearing—*
> *Like Language white hot searing.*

'That is the life I desire. That is the life I have chosen,' she told herself.

In the hallway, the clock struck once on the half hour. 'This is going to be a very long day.' Suddenly, the elevating shriek of the teakettle caused her to leap to her feet. She rushed to remove it from the stove.

At only twenty years of age, Amelia Madeira had tired of all shrill sounds. What she longed for now was silence.

THREE

The Madeira home stood half a block from the new school; that block and the next on West 6th Street were affectionately known as "Old Maid Row." Four elementary teachers and one other high school teacher lived along the row, all but one former teachers of Amelia's. The exception was Bessie Sweeney, who, along with her widowed mother, had recently moved next door. An expansive side yard and flower garden separated the two homes.

A lifelong resident of Ironton, Bessie, a vibrant young woman with shocking red hair and an explosion of freckles, had been hired to teach first grade. She and Amelia agreed to meet the first day and walk together, the beginning of thousands they would make over the next thirty-five years.

In 1917, most students got to school on "Shank's pony"—a euphemism for "by foot"—sometimes as far as up to four miles one-way. Superintendent W. O. Johnston had recently discouraged parents from allowing their children to come by horseback, still the favored mode of transportation to rural, one-room schools throughout the county.

'Prospect High School is moving into the modern age,' Johnston was quoted in the *Prospect Banner*. 'Hitching posts have been removed from the school grounds. Horses and buggies, carriages and wagons are means by which you may deliver and retrieve your children, but by no means expect the school to board these conveyances while students participate in the business of education. It is neither feasible nor prudent to continue this outmoded practice—the cost of removing horse manure, alone, being prohibitive.'

For weeks there was an out-pouring of "Letters to the Editor." The following represent both the articulate and the obtuse:

Dear Editor:

I am withdrawing my sons, Lloyd and Floyd, from Prospect High School. First, we hire someone from outside the community to over-see (superintend) the education of our children, (a mistake indeed). Now, rather than vouchsafe a longstanding tradition, he has deigned to make it impossible for those children to transport themselves to that very school building! For shame!"

Yours sincerely,
Wilma Dean (Alexander) Rogers

To the editor:

Graniteville knew what they was up to when they got rid of W. O. Johnston. Just like President Wilson he makes up his own rules and runs ruff (sic) shod over everyone. I got three

kids who ain't going to be
coming to his school in the
distant future.   Take it from
me.   This horse buisness (sic)
ain't over yet!

Marion (Bucky) Brashears

Johnston stood his ground, and by a vote of 3 to 2, the school board supported the new "no horse" regulation. By the time school opened, few attempted to test the ruling. One was Wendell Robertson, principal, math teacher and athletic coach. He insisted Johnston leave a hitching post near the south entrance to the gymnasium so he could secure his horse.   Robertson was a no nonsense disciplinarian. His features were rugged and his manner unflinchingly combative. He was a stocky brute-of-a-man with marcelled, iron gray hair; his thick mustache was an attempt to cover the ghastly scar from a cleft lip and partial cleft palate, both crudely sewn together when he was an infant. His underbite resembled a bulldog's, one that had been ravaged in a fight. The moustache did little to improve his diction.

"Dhammit, Johnshon! I've ribben tha horsch a school efry day hor the fas fiffeen ears. If hue wan an afhwetic fhrogram, ish tha horschorme!"

An allowance was made. The school board later amended the declaration to exclude faculty—eliciting even more editorial protests.

Another exception was a senior boy, Willie Stansbury, who had ridden "Ol' Paint" three miles to school every day since sixth grade when he transferred from the old Sager school near Granville Ford. With an air of defiance, Willie and Paint would trot into the schoolyard. Aware of his audience, he'd dismount with a flourish, carefully fasten the rein to the saddle horn, and, with a friendly smack on the rear end, send the steed galloping back home. By the time he arrived on foot in late afternoon, Willie could count on Paint, still saddled and bridled, to be patiently waiting in his barn stall.

By previous arrangement, Amelia and Bessie agreed to leave at 6:30 A. M.—giving them nearly an hour before the school day began. Though she had awakened hours earlier, Amelia failed to arrive until 6:40. She found Bessie sitting on her front porch swing.

"My...just look at you. I simply adore your hair," said Amelia.

Bessie had swept back her abundant red hair and pinned it into a casual style covering her ears—ears, which she proclaimed, made her look 'monkey-faced.'

"I was beginning to worry," she said—ignoring the compliment. "I thought I saw your lamplight earlier this morning."

"I would have been here on time, but Papa needed something."

Bessie joined her on the sidewalk. "I know how demanding parents can be."

At first, Amelia looked as if she concurred, but then she appeared impassive. Sensing her discomfort, Bessie quickly changed the subject.

"Is that lavender?" she asked—referring to a large bouquet of dried flowers Amelia clutched in her left hand.

"Yes...and statice, larkspur, baby's breath and delphinium...for you," she said—thrusting the bouquet towards her. "Thought it might help brighten your room. I've several arrangements in mine."

"How lovely...and so thoughtful. Thank you, dear."

Amelia smiled, but she appeared preoccupied.

"Look at us," exclaimed Bessie. "Carrying lunch pails...like two carefree school girls!"

"Actually, I'm feeling rather—"

"Nervous? Me, too."

"*Armado e pronto!*" Noting Bessie's quizzical expression, she translated. "Armed and ready!"

Up ahead, two young boys climbed down from a horse-drawn wagon and bolted for the playground equipment. Early arrivals were customary, as some students had been up for hours doing chores.

The two-story brick building was only two years old. There had been a general outcry when a school-tax levy was first proposed. However, the previous superintendent, Hayden Caruthers, through a series of Town Hall meetings and with assurances from the Iron Mountain Railroad that Prospect would remain a viable stop, managed to garner enough support that the levy passed on its third and final attempt.

Though Caruthers lived to see the building completed, he died of heart failure one week after it opened in the fall of 1915. Wendell Robertson served as temporary superintendent until Johnston was hired for the 1916 school year. Robertson believed the superintendent's position should have been his permanently. Secretly, he blamed the "fhivical encumrance of thich dahm harewib."

A dozen children were scattered about the playground when the two young teachers arrived. Two hopped off the swings and ran towards them.

"Which of you's the new first grade teacher?" trumpeted a girl of about ten.

"I am," said Bessie. "I'm Miss Sweeney."

"This here's my sister, Adeline. I'm Dorothy. I'm in fifth. She's in first." Both girls wore dresses that suggested a long succession of hand-me-downs.

"Hello, Adeline," said Bessie, warmly. "What's your last name, dear?"

The little girl continued to suck her thumb.

"Galbraith," answered Dorothy—reaching down and dislodging the thumb, which shot back into Adeline's mouth as if it were spring-loaded. "Stop being a baby!" she commanded—yanking the thumb out her sister's mouth and twisting her arm behind her back.

Adeline let out a yelp.

"Now, now," said Bessie. "That won't do."

Adeline began to cry.

"Dorothy, stop that immediately!" ordered Amelia.

She let go of Adeline's arm but snapped back, "She's *my* sister!"

"Another reason why you shouldn't hurt her."

"Come with me, dear," said Bessie—taking the child by the hand.

"Wait," demanded Amelia. "Dorothy, apologize to your sister."

"Huh?"

"Tell Adeline you're sorry you hurt her."

"…"

"Apologize *now,* or I'll paddle you myself."

Bessie looked at her in disbelief. Miss Madeira, stern-faced, fixed her eyes on Dorothy.

"I'm…I'm sorry," said the crestfallen girl.

"Sorry for…? Tell her *why* you're sorry. "

"For hurtin' you."

"Very well," she said—turning to Bessie as if nothing unusual had transpired. "I believe we have a meeting in the library at 3:30. See you there."

Bessie offered a weak smile. Clearly, she was shocked by Amelia's unyielding demeanor.

In truth, that brief playlet set the tone for what was to become her over-arching reputation. By the end of the first week of school, word spread that Miss Amelia Madeira was a taskmaster who suffered no fools and brooked no foolishness. Many students admitted to fearing her; others were put off by her high standards, which seemed not only inflexible but also downright unfair.

"What does Lizzie Borden think this is…*college?*"

"Homework every night this week. Don't she know I have chores?"

"I cain't understand half of what she's sayin'. Must be Spanish blood."

"My sister went to school with her and says no boy ever

looked at her twice."

"I don't get it. 'I'm *nobody*. Who are you? Are you *nobody*, too?' Madeira and Dickinson are both a couple of crackpots if you ask me."

However, one student lived in steadfast anticipation of Miss Madeira's senior English class. Not surprisingly, that student was Chester O'Malley.

FOUR

The Prospect School was a two-story, rectangular brick building with a small gymnasium attached by a covered walkway. In the basement were the furnace room, utility room, music room and the boy and girl's dressing rooms. The first floor housed grades 1-6. On the second floor was the superintendent's office—including a large outer-office for his secretary—next to a small conference room fronted by French doors, three classrooms, (two for 7th and 8th graders), restrooms and the library on one side of a long hallway and four classrooms on the other. At the end of the hall were the principal and librarian's offices.

Miss Madeira's room was third on the right—adjoining the library; located on the backside of the building, it overlooked the backyards of homes along Willow Street. Her room contained five rows of sled-desks, the cast-iron frames attached to wooden runners, six desks to a row. The tops of the dark wood desks were stationary—each containing an inkwell—with a small storage area underneath for books and supplies. The tilting seats were attached to the desk fronts, so that each row had an extra seat in front and an extra desktop in back. The pine floors were still relatively new and had not yet begun to creak. Slate blackboards lined the wall to the right of the student desks, with four large windows and two modern coal-fired steam heaters to the left. The back wall contained a series of bookshelves of varying heights and framed portraits of her two favorite poets, Emily Dickinson and Walt Whitman. Facing the five rows stood Miss Madeira's modest oak desk. Scattered around the room on the tops of bookcases and filing cabinets were vases of various sizes and colors, each brimming with nosegays of dried flowers from Amelia's garden.

Though she looked forward to the challenge of her other classes, Amelia cherished her English IV class. She discovered she could confront them and expect something in return—unlike the freshmen, who were not only green but also slightly uncivilized. True, they were now in high school, but they seemed fearful of their new status. Rather than reticence, their fear manifested in a sort of vulgar incivility—coupled with an abhorrence of anything remotely intellectual—which provided a challenge she relished.

Freshmen girls were more mature than the boys as a whole, yet they, too, seemed anti-intellectual to a point where Amelia was often offended to be in their presence. It wasn't enough to correct improper grammar, she felt obligated to lay bare their nescient lives and force-feed them bits of knowledge in hopes they might eventually transform into someone worth knowing. Though she met resistance, she was determined to remake them anew.

"Imagine sitting across a dinner table from someone for the next forty years without a single thing to discuss. The tedium…the sheer *ennui*. Please, I implore you, learn as much as possible so your lives will have meaning. And *do not*, I repeat, do *not* let me hear you say how 'stupid' something is when it's obvious you don't comprehend its meaning. That epithet applies only to those who make no effort to do so."

The sophomores thought themselves superior to the freshmen. Still, there was something in their bearing which betrayed that belief. Perhaps it was the realization they existed in a sort of limbo; regarded as neither child nor adult, they seemed to lack any true identity. She was determined to give them one.

In general, the juniors were intellectually superior to the sophomores. She attributed their swagger to the belief they would soon "rule the roost." However, by the end of the first week, she'd managed to clip their wings in an attempt to replace their bluster with something more substantial in the way of knowledge—not to prevent them from "flying," which, in the very best sense, she encouraged.

The intriguing thing about the seniors was they seemed to suddenly realize that in nine short months they were to be unleashed on the world, and the very thought made them more receptive to learning as much as they could as quickly as possible. Though she had been in their position only three years before, she felt ancient in their presence, and when she discovered how little they actually knew—not only of literature but also of the world in general—she was determined to sharpen their perspicacity. She had no need to be loved, but she demanded to be taken seriously.

On the blackboard behind her desk, she had written:

A Secret told—
Ceases to be a Secret-then—
A Secret—kept—
That-can appall but One—

Better of it—continual be afraid—
Than it—
And Whom you told it to—beside.

~Emily Dickinson
(1830-1886)

As students entered, they were instructed to: "Copy the poem in your tablet, and when you've finished, put down your pens."

Of the dozen members of Miss Madeira's English IV class, eight were girls; oddly enough, those eight females contained two sets of twins. The five army volunteers left the senior class particularly devoid of males. Of the four who remained, three were farm boys; only Chester O'Malley lived in Prospect proper.

As she closed the classroom door, she overheard Maisy, one of the McDowell twins, complain, "Not more of that *weird* poetry."

There was a mild twitter among the students until they

noticed Miss Madeira's expression. The atmosphere of the room quickly chilled as she approached Maisy, who sat directly behind her sister.

"*Weird*, you say? Please share with us the meaning of weird, Miss McDowell." Her tone brought immediate silence.

"Which Miss McDowell?" asked Daisy, the older of the two by nine minutes.

"A meaningless question. Your sister, of course."

Maisy McDowell smiled nervously. "You know… weird… *crazy*." She looked at the Shepherd twins and grinned before exchanging smiles with Daisy.

"Yes, *I* know, but the question is…do *you*?"

"I…well, it means…sta-strange," she stammered— appealing to her sister for confirmation her answer was sufficient to end the interrogation. For a moment, she seemed self-satisfied.

"Actually, it means unearthly or uncanny…fantastic or bizarre. That's its meaning, Miss McDowell." She walked toward the windows and then sharply pivoted to face her.

"Now…please share with us the *etymology* of the word weird."

"Eta…mology? I…I…don't—"

"Yes, etymology…the *origin* of the word…its derivation. If you're going to casually throw out a word, it helps to know how the word originated so you can fully grasp its meaning, and thus determine if it's the word you intended. As you will learn, intention is the basis of all creation."

She returned to the blackboard behind her desk and wrote e-t-y-m-o-l-o-g-y. "Etymology. The origin of the word weird, Miss McDowell. I'm waiting…"

"I…I don't know." Maisy's erubescent cheeks radiated a florid blush that grew darker with each embarrassing second.

She wrote, 'wyrd' under etymology. The chalk broke as she put too much pressure on the downward stroke of the "d." If there were an impulse to laugh, it was squelched.

"W-y-r-d.   It's Old English…meaning its origin is

somewhere between the 5th and late-11th century in the region now known as England. As an Anglo-Saxon word, it's often represented as w-u-r-d, w-y-r-t, w-u-r-t and u-r-d. Wyrd meant fate or destiny…a Norse concept. Germanic tribes hailed the Goddess Wyrd." She scanned the room to see if any of this were registering. Convinced she had their attention, she slowly stalked up and down between each aisle.

"In the modern sense, w-e-i-r-d developed in Middle English—beginning with the Norman Invasion of 1066 and running to the late-mid 15th century—and refers to the three *fates* or the *weird* sisters…the goddesses who controlled *destiny*. They were often depicted as odd-looking or frightening. Thus, Shakespeare portrayed the weird sisters in *Macbeth* as witches. Does that explanation satisfy you?" she asked—pausing in front of Maisy.

"Y-y-es." Her eyes glistened with tears. "I only meant—"

"I'm not interested in what you meant, only in what you said, which it now appears was inaccurate. Do you understand?"

"Yes, Miss Madeira."

"Good." She continued on to her desk where she paused to address the entire class, still frozen in an attentive tableau.

"Now, if *your* fate or destiny is to pass senior English, perhaps you should quickly finish copying Miss Dickinson's poem, which is neither fantastic nor bizarre, and be prepared to answer a few simple questions."

Daisy McDowell passed a handkerchief to her sister.

Amelia waited patiently. For the next minute, the only sounds to be heard were pens tapping the sides of inkwells and metal tips scratching paper.

"Finished? Good. Who can tell me the meaning of the poem?"

No one volunteered.

"No one? Mr. Miller…the poem's meaning, please."

Raymond Miller was a big, raw-boned farm boy with rounded shoulders and a thick lower lip that protruded into a perpetual pout. Though he appeared sullen, he was actually rather pleasant, with a playful sense of humor. "It's, uh...something about...uh...something about if you should keep a secret or tell somebody."

"Should you tell someone a secret or not?"

"Well...it kinda depends on what it is."

Madeline Jones raised her hand—waving it with an anticipatory flutter. She was vying for the position of Miss Madeira's "pet." What she had yet to realize was that her teacher had no intention of establishing such a position, and if she eventually deemed it desirable, Madeline, whose voice would unnerve a saint and whose persona was so saccharine it threatened to imbalance one's blood sugar, would be far down the list of eligible candidates.

"Miss Jones?"

"I believe it means that if you tell a secret, then it loses its...confidentiality." Her smile was self-congratulatory.

Miss Madeira stared at her in disbelief. "Care to delve a little deeper?"

"I...I..." The smile faded.

"What do you think *Dickinson's* opinion would be...based on the text? Everyone has a personal opinion, I'm sure, but always refer to the text for clues to the author's intended meaning. Madeleine...? Anyone...?*"*

A variety of answers were offered, 'Something about being afraid.' 'Secrets are scary.' 'How are we supposed to know the answer when she doesn't even tell what the secret is?' 'It don't *(DOESN'T)* matter what it is. If it's a secret, then ya can't tell nobody *(ANYbody)*. Or it ain't a secret...*(ISN'T)*...isn't a secret no more. *(ANYmore)*.'

"I'm looking for an answer based *on the text*." Her eyes fell on Chester.

"Mr. O'Malley. What are your thoughts?"

Chester O'Malley had an epicene face, cleft chin and light brown hair. Like many of the boys, it had been cut at home using a bowl—leaving the top longer than the sides. He had made an attempt to part it in the middle, but it hung in wavy strings over his brow. He nervously swept it back from his forehead—revealing large hazel eyes and long thick lashes. The eyes were not the eyes of a young man but someone older, wiser—knowing. One couldn't help thinking they revealed a certain sadness—bordering on disappointment.

"Uh...I..." He took a deep breath and exhaled audibly. Then, as if trying to stifle the sound of his own voice, he emitted a sort of moan.

The two sets of twins exchanged glances. Willie Stansbury fidgeted.

"I...I think Dickinson...was talking about something deeply *personal*. Something, if shared, that might embarrass...or, as she says, appall." He paused for a moment in an attempt to free himself from the stares of his classmates. He'd learned over the years that when he looked directly at them, they instinctively looked away as if they'd been caught spying.

"She says...it's better to keep the secret to oneself...rather than...contaminate another person with the knowledge of the secret, or have to live in fear the person you told would ever use the knowledge of the secret against you." His eyes slowly closed, his head fell forward and his shoulders slumped.

"Good answer. Thank, you Chester. How many of you think that's what Dickinson was trying to say?" Most of the students raised their hands. "How many of you have ever told a secret, and then feared the person you told might later use the secret against you?" Again, there was general agreement. "Now, how many of you've had a secret told to you that you later wished had *not* been told to you?"

"Like what?" asked Willie.

"Like they killed someone or somethin'?" asked Melvan Rucker.

"You're goofy, Melvan," said Raymond.

"Why do you say that?" asked Amelia.

"Because that's a goofy thing to say. Ain't nobody gonna go kill anybody and then *tell* somebody about it. And, nobody's gonna wish they hadn't been told a secret. Everybody likes secrets."

She started to correct his grammar, but instead asked, "Have you heard of Oedipus?"

"Eddy *who*?"

Some of the class giggled.

"Oedipus," she repeated—writing the name on the blackboard.

"What kinda name is that?" asked Willie. "It looks like octopus."

"Exactly. Both are Greek."

"That's Greek to me!" exclaimed Raymond.

The class roared.

"We read that in *Julius Caesar* sophomore year. When I don't understand somethin', I pretend like I'm Brutus and say, 'That's Greek to me.'"

"That's nearly correct. The actual quote, spoken by Casca in reference to Cicero's speech in Greek is, 'It *was* Greek to me.' Now, who can tell me what secret Oedipus learned he wished he had not?"

No one answered.

"Young women?"

Madeline Jones raised her hand but quickly withdrew it. When no one volunteered, all eyes drifted towards Chester.

"Do you know what secret he learned he wished he had not?"

He squirmed in his seat and raked his fingers through his hair. It was then she noticed what appeared to be a bruise on his left temple.

"Come on," said Melvan, "you know everything."

Willie looked at him as if to say, 'Sorry, friend, you knew this was going to happen.'

"Yeah, what was the *big* Greek secret?" prodded Raymond.

He glared at them, then appealed to Miss Madeira with his eyes—imploring, 'Please don't ask me this.'

"Do you know the answer?"

"Yes," he finally said, in resignation.

"Well, what the heck is it?" demanded Raymond.

Apparently, there was no avoiding it.

"Oedipus is uncertain of his birth parents...until he discovers a shepherd who knows his true origin. He makes the shepherd tell him who gave him up when he was a baby." He paused, as if the explanation suddenly exhausted him.

"That's it?" bellowed Raymond. "That's the big Greek brouhaha? I don't get it."

"No, Raymond, the big *brouhaha* was...when Oedipus and his sister are told the secret of his birth, she hangs herself and he scratches out his eyes."

There was a rumble of disgust.

"That's the dumbest thing I ever heard of! Why would they go and do that?" asked Melvan.

Again, Chester's expression was an entreaty, 'Spare me this.'

"And why did they do that?" she asked, with an empathetic smile.

"Because they realized the prophecy had been fulfilled."

"What prophecy?" asked Melvan.

"Yeah, did somebody predict this lunatic would blind himself?" asked Raymond—emitting his high-pitched hyena laugh.

"The prophecy that Oedipus would kill his father...and marry...his mother."

Raymond was suddenly dumbstruck, his eyes as wide as two shiny bits.

"Aaaw, what the devil? That's sick!" said Melvan.

"Marry his *mother*? What kinda crazy story is that Miss Madeira?" demanded Raymond, his face now rumpled up like a washrag.

"Sinful, that's what!" hissed Daisy McDowell. All of the girls around her nodded in agreement.

"If you ask me, them Greeks were *pre*verts," declared Melvan. Suddenly realizing what he'd uttered, he looked apologetically at Miss Madeira. "Sorry, M'am, I misspoke."

Without expression, she walked back to the blackboard and pointed to the poem. "Please reconsider Miss Dickinson's poem.

How many of you would now concur it's sometimes better to keep a secret to oneself...where it can appall but one?" Everyone but Chester raised his hand.

Raymond Miller leaned over and whispered, "You're unearthly *and* uncanny, Chester, you know that?"

FIVE

In 1904, the year Fredo and his children moved from St. Louis, Prospect's population of roughly 1700 was on the decline. Until the previous winter, it had been the home of a Normal School—a school that established teacher's standards or "norms." When it mysteriously burned to the ground, a group of businessmen from Cape Girardeau persuaded school officials not to rebuild in Prospect but to join forces with the Missouri State Normal School in Cape Girardeau. It was rumored the "persuasion" was accompanied by $100 bills.

The town square, a tree-filled park with a bandstand, croquet court and a Civil War cannon, was surrounded by businesses, including: the Bank of Prospect, City Hall, D. Denham's Fashion, the Law Offices of W. R. Clayton, Jones Dry Goods, Luke's Barber Shop, Rainey's General Store, Prospect Pharmacy & Sundries, Dr. Simpson's Office, O'Malley's Metalworks, Müller's Lumber and Agriculture Supply and, southwest of the square, the Granite Quarry Hotel. On the edge of Prospect's north city limit, less than a mile from High Ridge cemetery, was Hoffman's Missouri Red Monuments, an offshoot of the Iron County Granite Company that operated several quarries in Iron and St. François counties.

Deposited in the pre-Cambrian age, most of the quarry's barite was dark red, due to high hematite content; however, some veins were pink, white and even transparent. Although the quarried stone was shipped from California to Massachusetts, most of the granite was used architecturally in St. Louis—including the pillars for Eads Bridge. Stones too small for building façades were cut into shoebox-sized blocks and used extensively in resurfacing city streets leading to the 1904 World's Fair.

Al Hoffman originally worked in the quarries when it began operation in 1869. As a natural outgrowth, he now owned the small monument company he operated with his son, William. For nearly twenty years, the business produced simple lettered headstones. When customers wanted something fancier, Hoffman's acted as a middleman for a monument supplier in Cincinnati. It was no small irony that the supplier turned out to be Jouvance Funereal Artworks.

Thanks to Al's son-in-law, Harvey Heinrich, Fredo's supervisor at Annan's Funereal Monument business in St. Louis, where he had been employed for nearly two years, a position was created for him. Although initially reluctant, when Harvey explained that Fredo had apprenticed with Jean François Jouvance and could carve beautiful statues, Al Hoffman agreed to hire him on that recommendation alone. However, William wasn't convinced.

"If he's as good as you say, I cain't understand why he'd want to leave St. Louis?"

"He's wantin' to raise his kids in a small town's all," said Harvey. "Trust me, William, you're gettin' a true artist. You and your daddy'll thank me later."

Hoffman could pay only $15 a week until the business expanded, but he owned a small two-story house in Prospect that he offered to Fredo rent-free. Previously, the house, located on West 6th, had been rented to a succession of school teachers; the last, a Miss Murchison, married and moved to nearby Pilot Knob.

The wagon carrying Harvey Heinrich, his wife and the Madeiras arrived on Karl's eighth birthday, July 29th, 1904. The journey had been a tribulation because of torrential rains, which followed a series of tornadoes that ripped through southeastern Missouri. Between the Heinrichs and the Hoffmans, the house at 906 West 6th was partially furnished.

Due to the close proximity of the school, the children could get there without assistance, and Fredo easily navigated to and from work on a second-hand bicycle. The major drawback was that the Madeiras no longer had in-laws, neighbors or housekeepers to supply meals; it was imperative Amelia learn to cook. Fortunately, Miss Minnie Lajoy, a first grade teacher who lived across the street, soon volunteered to instruct the young girl.

On her very first visit, Amelia learned to make homemade noodles. Boiled in a chicken broth with onions, cabbage and potatoes, the noodles became a staple—along with a Portuguese meat stew (*cozido à portuguesa*) she tried to recreate based on Fredo's memory of his favorite childhood dish.

"There's *nothing* to making noodles," insisted Miss Minnie, who had a habit of overemphasizing—believing it lent clarity to meaning.

"Just flour, egg yolk and a pinch of salt. Of course, the *goodness* comes from the *love* you put into it." She floured the board and lightly sprinkled the dough.

"As with anything, you must *love* it for it to turn out right, don't you know."

"May I help roll it out?" asked a seven-year-old Amelia, who stood on an old conductor's stool once belonging to Miss Minnie's brother, a railroader killed when his Missouri Pacific train—headed for the 1904 World's Fair—crashed in Vernon County.

She handed the rolling pin to Amelia, who had difficultly applying even pressure.

"*Thinner*, dear."

When the dough resembled an ochre sheet, she again sprinkled it with flour, rolled it up like a jellyroll and cut it into slender strips. "See, anyone can make noodles, but one must have the *patience* to wait until they're completely dry or they're tough, and that simply won't do. Do you know what *gift* you receive when you learn patience?"

"The thing you've been waiting for," Amelia answered, confidently.

"No, dear, the gift you receive when you learn patience…is *patience*," she announced, certain she'd coined an aphorism.

While they waited for the noodles to dry, she ushered Amelia out into her garden: a panorama of hydrangea, columbine, geraniums, zinnias, marigolds, roses and shrubbery. "You should see it in the spring. The white and pink hawthorns and the lilac are *breathtaking*."

"I love flowers. We went to Shaw's Garden once."

"I've heard it's splendid. You know, your yard is a lovely spot for a garden. A flower garden in the side yard and a vegetable garden in back. If you'd like, next spring I'll give you some starts. Miss Murchison didn't have much of a green thumb, but I'll teach you. Remember, flowers in your garden are a reminder that we're *all* flowers in *God's garden*," she said—dead-heading a geranium.

For the next hour and a half, Amelia helped weed and water—carrying bucketfuls pumped from a well.

"Madeira…is that Italian?"

"No, *Portuguesa*…Portuguese. Papa's parents came from the Azores."

"Oh, *my*…I must…I'll have to check my geography," sputtered the portly woman.

"The Azores is an archipelago in the Atlantic Ocean."

"A what, dear?"

"An archipelago…it's a chain of islands. My grandparents were born on the island of Flores. *Flor* is Portuguese for flower."

"My, aren't you a clever little girl."

"That's what the nuns always said. Sister Mary Alphonse said I was the smartest first grader she ever had."

"Well, remember *modesty* is more important than intelligence, especially in one so young," she admonished—removing lint from Amelia's braid. "So, you're…Catholic?" she asked with a tinge of pity.

"We used to be, but now we're nothing."

"Oh, dear…I wouldn't tell that to anyone." A few moments later, she added, "Maybe your father would allow you and your brother to come to the Presbyterian Church with me sometime."

"I'll ask…but Papa isn't very happy with God right now."

"What a thing to say!"

"Papa says once you make God mad, life is *sem esperança*."

"What, dear?"

"*Sem esperança*…hopeless," she said.   "Are the noodles dry yet?"

In time, Fredo not only permitted Miss Minnie to take the children to church, he occasionally accompanied them. For the next few years, things could not have been better. Amelia's report cards were awash in "E's" for "Excellent" and all her teachers told him what a brilliant daughter he had. He proudly extolled the virtues of his "*a princesinha perfeita*" ("perfect little princess") to anyone who would listen. However, shortly before she turned fourteen, an incident occurred that seemed to alter not only her affable mood, but also her father's perception of her. For two days, she refused to leave her bedroom.

"*Eu estou doente*…I'm sick," was the answer to every inquiry, this coming from someone who, in the past, never missed a day of school, not even when she had a fever or a chest cold.

Concerned, Fredo insisted she unlock the door. She refused. Karl was enlisted; she stubbornly ignored his entreaties. Finally, Fredo sent for Doc Simpson. At first, she rejected Doc's plea, but when she read the note he slid under her door, she acquiesced.

Following a lengthy conversation, he emerged – explaining that Amelia was no longer a child. "Her body's changin'. The changes frightened her, that's all."

"What now can I do?"

"You don't have to do anything. It's perfectly normal," said Doc. "She's just missin' her mama's all. Give her some time."

Before leaving the neighborhood, Doc summoned Miss Minnie Lajoy, who brought food to the house. She stayed with Amelia all afternoon—comforting her and insisting she eat chicken broth and soda crackers. She also prepared and served a medicinal tea made from juniper berries and raspberry leaves.

"It's disgusting!"

"I know, dear, but it relieves the ache...and that's a very good thing. Mama used to make it for me. Drink it all down. You'll feel better."

"I hate this! It's unfair that only women have to suffer."

"Though plenty of men suffer *because* of it," countered Miss Minnie, with a chuckle.

"What do you mean? How do men suffer?"

"It's only a *joke*, dear. Just a little humor to lift the *gloom*." When she departed, she took a bundle of soiled bedclothes and sheets she washed and returned the next day.

Neither Fredo nor Karl spoke of the incident, though for days after, Amelia rarely left her room. When she did, it was only to hurriedly prepare a meal for them. Eventually, things returned to normal. However, whenever "the curse" was on her, her congenial nature disappeared. She appeared irritable and was not above telling both her father and brother to fend for themselves.

She abhorred everything about menstruation: not only the physical pain and the inconvenience, but also how it altered her moods. Throughout her life, she would refer to "it" in her journals. The theme first emerged in a poem she composed in her fourteenth year.

> *When thorny Perle d'Or first appeared*
> *In panic and in Haste—*
> *The pungent red Grant rose I feared*
> *Would flood my Garden Gate—*
> *I locked the Door, I hid my head*
> *A sickness gripped my Soul—*
> *O' Mother dear, did it take Death*
> *To abdicate the role—*
> *Of one who comforts, calming Fears*
> *Usurping all the Pain—*

Of womanhood, of Childhood tears
Now hidden in the Rain—
Is this the Price when Innocence
Is shattered from Within—
Is Blood the only Recompense
When Sinners pay for Sin?

Prior to this incident, Fredo had always favored Amelia. Perhaps because Karl was not a scholar and showed little interest in the arts, his father thought him *"uma pessoa comum"* (an average Joe) and attached little value to his true passion—athletics. When it came to sports, whether baseball, football, track or basketball, he transcended all his peers. He exhibited a natural grace and an intense competitive drive that had recently garnered the attention of several college coaches.

As a result of Karl's success or because he felt more distanced from Amelia, whose physical maturity unsettled him, he began to take an interest in his son's achievements. In the fall of Karl's senior year, Fredo attended his first and only football game; he also promised to see him play basketball in the regionals if Prospect won the conference title.

"You really coming?"

"Si."

"Promise? Papa...*a promessa*?"

"Não abuse da sorte." (Don't push your luck).

As was the custom, Karl rode to the ballgame against county rival Ironton with Max Nixon, also a senior. Max drove a Fliver, his father's Model T Ford. For this critical game against archrival, Ironton, Bobby Allenby, a senior reserve guard and Karl's best friend, rode with his two teammates instead of traveling with the team convoy.

Following their narrow 3-point victory, they celebrated by downing two pints of corn whiskey furnished by Max's uncle, who operated a popular still. This led to some traditional mischief that entailed turning over more than a dozen outhouses—including at least one that was occupied.

On the way back to Prospect, Max pulled off the road. Both he and Bobby had to urinate. It had begun to rain and the sky opened up.

"Goddamn! Come on, boys!" yelled Max—running towards a nearby barn. The two joined him there to smoke another victory cigar and wait for the rain to dissipate.

"Think we can beat Po...tosi?" asked Bobby, who was smashed.

"Hell yeah," said Max. "They're better than they was last year, but so are we.

"They got three...players...over six feet! "One... is siiixthree," slurred Bobby—taking another swig.

"Better slow down," said Karl. "You've had enough."

"That's Simpkins. Saw him against Caledonia," said Max—grabbing the jar of moonshine from Bobby. "He's tall...but runs like he's got bricks in his shorts." He took another gulp. "Anybody want this last little snort?"

"Not me...I'm copasetic," said Karl.

Out on Route 21, an old Model A Ford slowed down and stopped. Its weak headlamps barely illuminated the rain—whizzing past the lights like a barrage of shiny bullets. The temperature had dropped in the past hour and the rain appeared to be turning to sleet.

"That's Beverly Brown's dad," said Karl, who had taken Beverly to a church social junior year. "Probably thinks you've had a breakdown."

"Another pint of Uncle Jimmy's white lightnin' and he'd be right," said Max, with a loud sonorous belch.

The car slowly pulled away.

"I ain't feelin' so good," said Bobby.

"That's 'cause ya drink liquor like its cider," said Max—flinging the empty glass jar into the darkness.

"What was Robertson yellin' about the last two possessions?" asked Karl. "The crowd was screamin' so loud I couldn't make out a word."

"I can't understand a damn thing that mush mouth bastard says half the time anyways," said Max.

Karl took some short puffs on his cigar. "Give me another light will ya?"

"Hey, guys, I *mean it*...I ain't feelin' so good," groaned Bobby.

"I ain't feelin' nothin' and that's good," said Max—striking a kitchen match on the metal clasp of his overalls.

"Aw, ooh...bwaaah..." Bobby covered his mouth and staggered forward a few steps—spewing vomit through his fingers.

"Aw, Jesus! Here...watch your hands," said Karl—grabbing his arm to keep him from stringing it all over himself. "Keep 'em away from your clothes, will ya? Help me, Max!"

Max flicked the match aside.

"Let's get him back to the car," said Karl.

"I can make it...by my-s-self," said Bobby, who then tripped over his own feet—falling to his knees.

"Dammit, Bobby! You ain't gettin' back in daddy's car smellin' like puke. Wipe that off your hands," said Max—scooping up a handful of straw."

"Come on, *get up*," said Karl—flipping away his cigar butt. "We gotta get home before the road gets so bad we can't."

The three of them staggered back to the car.

Shortly before midnight, Karl stumbled into the house. Fredo slept in the downstairs bedroom just off the kitchen. The bedroom door barely muted his thunderous snoring. 'Wonder how Mama ever slept next to that?' he thought—heading up to his room. The stairwell was lit by a dim glow from under Amelia's bedroom door.

She's reading...or writing in her journal.

Halfway up the stairs, her lamplight was extinguished. Slowly, he continued to climb—one step at a time. Thinking he had reached the top, he stepped forward, tripped over the riser and crashed to the floor. He lay there, laughing, until he heard Amelia throw the latch on her bedroom door.

"Aw, don't worry little Sis," he mumbled. "You're safe..."

Three days later, superintendent, Hayden Caruthers, knocked on Miss Orton's door. He whispered something to her. She peered back into the classroom a moment before summoning Bobby, Max and Karl, who figured it had something to do with the upcoming game with Potosi. Caruthers led them to his office where a bear-of-a-man dominated an old leather chair.

"Boys, this is Sheriff Larson. He wants to ask you some questions."

Larson had thick bushy eyebrows and a nose as porous as a sponge. He wore an old light brown Stetson, the crown encircled with a dark sweat stain. His uniform consisted of a khaki-colored shirt and pants; his belly ballooned over his leather belt.

"Whacha boys do after the game with Ironton last Friday night?" he inquired in a deep tobacco rasp.

"Drove home," said Max, with a look of pure defiance.

"I'm asking you whacha did *before* you drove home...and you might as well know at least two people've come forward sayin' they saw you all turnin' over privies."

"Didn't know tippin' shitters was such a big crime."

"Watch your language," said Caruthers.

"Heck, kids from Ironton pushed over dozens here last year," interjected Bobby, who couldn't stop fidgeting with his shirt collar. "It's tradition. My daddy says—"

"I ain't talkin' about turnin' over no toilets. I'm talkin' about burnin' down a barn just past West Madison Street."

The three exchanged glances.

"I 'spect you didn't do it on purpose," said Larson. "If you had, you probably wouldn't have been dumb enough to leave a jar from your Uncle Jimmy's still behind, Max."

"A jar's a jar Sheriff...don't prove nothin'." He looked at Supt. Caruthers for assurance.

"He's right, you know."

"Son, Vern Brown said he saw your daddy's car pulled off the side of the road...right across from where the barn burned. That proof enough?"

"Sheriff Larson, I swear to you...we didn't know we started any fire," said Karl. "We stopped so Max and Bobby could take a leak. It was rainin' so hard we ran into the barn for shelter." He glanced at Max.

"Don't look at me. It was probably that cigar you tossed."

"Or your match."

"I know I didn't do it," said Bobby. "I don't smoke...'sides, I was too busy pukin' up my guts!"

"A fine way for our best ballplayers to behave," said Caruthers. "Not much of an example by boys headed for the conference championship."

"Won't none of 'em be playin' no more *ballgames*."

"Oh, come now, Sheriff. It was clearly an accident."

"The game against Potosi's for the conference title," said Karl. "We're defending champs. If we win, we're in the regionals again. I got college coaches comin' from Columbia and Cape."

"I don't think you understand the seriousness of the crime, son."

"*Crime?*" mocked Max. "An accident ain't no crime."

"There were two work horses trapped in a back stall. Both of 'em burned up alive."

"Aw, no-o-o..." moaned Karl—sinking into a chair.

"And the worst part is...Lester Denham got burned up pretty bad hisself tryin' to git 'em out of the barn. Second and third degree on his hands, arms and face. Done lost two fingers on one hand and one on the other."

Karl's head slumped forward.

"I *repeat*...I was out of it," said Bobby.

"You little chickenshit!" snarled Max. "If you could hold your liquor none of this would have happened!"

"That's enough out of you," said Caruthers—springing to his feet. He glared at the boys as he moved from behind his desk.

"So what are you saying, Sheriff? Are they being charged with something?"

"Arson…property damage and bodily injury."

"That's a crock! It was a *goddang* accident and that ol' barn ain't worth a *goddang*—"

"Not another word!" Caruthers fumed.

"Son, you was trespassin' on private property. You burned down a barn and kilt a man's only two workhorses. Plus, that man ended up in a hospital over in Fredricktown. Ya need to know Denham's filed charges agin all three of ya. Better be gittin' yerselves a good lawyer."

The hearing took place six weeks later in Ironton. The circuit judge found in favor of the plaintiff. Bobby was placed on probation for two years and ordered to pay $500 in restitution. Max and Karl were given a choice: three months in jail, three years' probation and a $1000 fine each. Or, they could pay the fine and serve the probation but forego jail by joining the Army immediately upon graduation. Both chose the latter.

SIX

October 13th, 1917

Dear Sis,

My wing of the hospital destroyed.
Moved to temporary shelter. Barely survived
but dozens of wounded killed. Can't take much
more! Remember Papa's saying, '*Quem tem cu
tem medo*?' He was right! Anyone with an
asshole does have fear! Now the really great
news. Being shipped home in November and
with luck back in Prospect by end of month.
Honourable Discharge due to my eye but also
because bouts of the most terrible headaches.
Like metal spike being driven into my brain.
Only relief is to find dark room and take to bed
with cold compresses on my forehead and pray
for sleep. Germans continue to pound city but
resistance strong. Letter from Bobby saying
Max got shot up and sent home. Always wished
something bad would happen to him cause he's
the reason I'm even here. Sorry now. Just
reread above and see I haven't asked about you
or teaching. How are you? How's teaching?

Bet you have them trained by now. Last letter about Papa's nightmares and ~~detreorating~~ health upsetting. Get morphine or something like it from Doc Simpson to help him sleep. Thanks for sharing my address with Sarah. Got some wonderful letters from her. Can't understand why you keep warning me not to get my hopes up. Case this letter don't reach her before you write her again please tell her good news about my homecoming.

> *Com Amor Eterno*,
> Karl

P.S. Warning! Patch over left eye. Last letter before leaving this Hell Hole.

*   *   *

Only seven weeks into the school year, Amelia was already experiencing a weariness bordering on exhaustion. It wasn't just the demands of teaching, the preparation and the countless hours spent reading and grading papers, it was the sheer onslaught of the students' frenetic energy.

Most boys were like clumsy calves—careening and bellowing in the hallways and tripping over their own feet, or bear cubs playfully pawing and wrestling; a few, the older ones, huddled in packs—leering, whispering and elbowing one another. The girls resembled clutches of barnyard hens, pecking and scratching, or frightened rabbits—scurrying from one hutch to another as if pursued. Each class had a least one queen bee attended to by a bevy of conciliatory worker bees, who felt privileged to bask in her popularity—competing for her favor by supplying bits of gossip and compliments on hair, clothing and her innate ability to attract mindless drones.

"The fatal mistake any teacher can make," she told Bessie,

"is letting them see your fear. Great teaching requires great acting."

"You're joking, of course."

"Wild animals always attack the weak. Remember, vulnerability has no place in the classroom, unless one is seeking martyrdom."

Bessie started to offer a rebuttal, but instead replied, "Fortunately, my babies have yet to develop claws and incisors."

Amelia stared at her a moment. "Go ahead...make fun, but mark my words. Someday the attitude of today's high schoolers will filter down to your little darlings. Perhaps then you'll be more empathic."

"Oh, I do hope you're wrong."

"As do I. But, I am right about this...good teachers are like ideal parents. We give children the skills to make better, informed choices. We try to instill a desire to expand their horizons, to live a better life...hopefully an authentic one. And in the end, we prepare them to leave us. That's the one thing I can state categorically. No matter what void we fill or what bonds we form...they will *all* leave us."

"Perhaps that's a good thing," said Bessie.

This particular Friday had been punctuated by an especially disturbing episode—occurring in her third period freshman English class—when Billy Patton purposely dipped the tip of Paulina Heiser's pigtail in his inkwell. Just how he thought he'd escape the incident, unscathed, seemed not to have occurred to him. Several of those who witnessed the act were stifling snickers when she entered the classroom.

"What exactly is going on in here?" demanded Miss Madeira, who had been summoned to the library, where she served as librarian when not teaching English. Because of their immaturity, she had reluctantly agreed to leave the freshman alone, engaged in silent reading.

"When I am out of the room, I expect you to conduct yourselves with decorum." She scanned the room, her eyes settling on Billy Patton. As she moved towards him, she spied the tip of

Paulina's pigtail resting in his inkwell.

"*Billy*...what have you done!"

Paulina Heiser turned around suddenly, and her long queue showered a black semi-circle on the floor. When she saw her pigtail dripping ink, she emitted an anguished cry and burst into tears. "Aww...*der Schweinehund!*"

"Nancy Rainey...please help Paulina to the restroom and try to keep the ink from ruining her clothes."

Carefully, Nancy lifted Paulina's pigtail away from her blouse, but the damage was done.

"Cecil, run and get Mr. Stokes and tell him to bring a pail of soapy water and some rags."

Cecil, a gangly redhead with a large overbite, glanced at Billy and smiled.

"And wipe that insipid smirk off your face!"

"Yes'um."

"Did you hear what that Hun called me?" Billy said with a sneer. "A *pig*, that's what."

A few students tittered.

"*Silence!* Not another word!"

"But Miss Madeira, you can't be on her side. Your brother's in the war. Why, none of them Heiser's even speaks English. They say her daddy fought with the Kaiser. My daddy says—"

She grabbed his ear and pulled him straight up out of his chair.

"OW! That hurts!"

"I told you...not another word. Come with me."

"Okay...OW...okay, but you're tearin' my ear off!"

"*Silêncio!* "

He looked askance at her.

"You heard me...silence!" She marched him out of the room, down the hall and into Mr. Robertson's office.

"This boy needs to be paddled."

"Whaa ha he dhuun?"

She quickly gave an account of Billy's egregious act. When Robertson tried to explain he would send the boy home with a note justifying the day's suspension, she was incensed. "I insist you paddle him...now."

"Meh Mahdeirah, bhoys whill be bhoys, dohn hu nhoh." He glanced up at Billy, who smiled.

For a moment, she felt the urge to scream. Instead, she took a deep breath. "Students of German origin make up nearly twenty percent of the student body of this school. This was an inexcusable xenophobic act and I will not permit it. You can either paddle him right now...in my presence, or I will do it myself."

Robertson started to protest but then relented. Since the beginning of the school year, he had been engaged in several verbal skirmishes with her, and frankly, he had come out on the short end each time. Besides, he had no idea what a xenophobic act was, nor had he any wish to have its meaning or origin explained to him by Amelia Madeira. Reluctantly, he spanked Billy while she looked on.

"Now, you may send him home with a note," she said, before returning to the classroom.

Word of the incident spread through the school like the Spanish flu would do in six months. However, unlike that pandemic, which would claim the lives of over seven dozen residents of Prospect, this virus seemed relatively benign until its ramifications were felt throughout the community. In the next few months, several homes of German families were desecrated with painted, hate-filled threats. Two families—the Grunwalds and Heisers—would move to Cape Girardeau and Poplar Bluff, respectively.

As the sugar maples along West 6th began to blaze bright oranges and reds, Amelia embraced her weekends with the ardor of a ship-bound sailor—longing for the sight of land. This particular Friday, perhaps due to the inkwell incident, her yearning was even more profound. As the clock neared 3:15, she seemed as anxious as her students to hear the day's adjournment announced by the ringing of Robertson's brass hand bell.

A Friday afternoon ritual had already been established. She and Bessie would meet by the first floor landing precisely at four o'clock and walk home together. While Amelia nearly always carted home an armload of papers and essays in need of grading, Bessie was free to carry both of their lunch pails.

"I envy you grade school teachers. You almost never have to bring any work home. For the second time this week, I have a good ten hours of grading ahead of me."

"You have my sympathy, but many's the time I would gladly trade grading for cleaning up vomit, wiping runny noses and repeating instructions a dozen times for every little thing," she answered in her own defense—a talent she had heretofore lacked, but one Amelia had encouraged her to cultivate.

"Actually, some of my students still need to learn to wipe their noses," said Amelia, with the sarcasm for which she had a well-deserved reputation.

"Yesterday, I looked back and saw Melvan Rucker's sister, Violet, shoving her dirty anklets into her mouth. The poor thing is a simpleton…nine years old and still in first grade. On the playground, she picks up sticks and bright bits of paper and chews on them. Please explain to me how we are preparing that child for any kind of life?"

"Sending her off to Farmingdale would be worse," said Amelia, who seemed distracted.

"Oh, I forgot to tell you. Birdie Davis came to school yesterday without undergarments. I hadn't noticed until a group of boys gathered to watch her on the teeter-totter."

"Okay…you win. I promise to stop complaining."

"I didn't mean to be so adamant," she said—smiling. It was rare she felt Amelia's equal. A moment later she remarked, "I heard about Billy Patton."

"I swear, when Robinson started in with that 'boys will be boys,' I nearly exploded. He actually looked at Billy and gave him a wink. That male arrogance really galls me. And, Paulina…you should have seen her…poor child. I must stop by the Heisers tomorrow and apologize."

"I heard her parents will not allow English to be spoken in the home."

"Wherever did you hear that? She says her father has several degrees from the University of Heidelberg. He speaks *five* languages—including fluent English. How do these rumors get started?" For a moment, she thought about her own father and the circumstances that brought them to Prospect. "Why they ever settled here is a mystery. He can't find a decent job. He's completely overqualified."

"I'm told he sells some kind of elixir from a horse-drawn carriage. I'm not exactly certain what it is."

"It's a liniment. *Dr. Peter Fahrney's Therapeutics.* I bought a bottle from Paulina for Papa. It claims to be a panacea....more likely a nostrum. Contains all sorts of oils. Camphor. Sassafras. What else? Oh, yes, turpentine. Even oil of chloroform. His bedroom reeks of it." Immediately, she was drawn to the thought of what might be awaiting her at home. They walked on in silence until they approached Bessie's house.

"What are we to do about all this anti-German sentiment at school?"

Amelia looked at her and smiled. They had established an unwavering rule: they could exchange a few anecdotes about the day's events, but once they reached the Sweeney's front stoop, all talk of school ceased. "I guess we'll have to solve that problem on Monday."

"Yes, of course. See you in the garden."

While Bessie disappeared inside to put on water for tea, Amelia retrieved the mail, then hurried in to check on her bedridden father—bringing him fresh water, helping him use the chamber pot and change into a clean nightgown, the exact routine she had performed earlier that afternoon. Though Johnston had initially disapproved of her rushing home during the lunch hour to attend to Fredo—following an incident where she found him lying on the bedroom floor in a puddle of urine and feces—she had insisted, and was begrudgingly granted permission.

'The room does reek of liniment. Wish it were stronger.'

"We got a letter from Karl. I'll read it to you at supper."

"Karl...*onde está o meu filho?*" he mumbled, his voice raspy and weak.

"Still in France...but he's coming home soon," she said—smoothing his pillow.   She kissed his bearded cheek before taking her leave. In the past several weeks, she'd given up trying to shave him.

She dashed into her bedroom. Pouring water from a pitcher into a large porcelain bowl, she washed her hands and splashed water on her face. After blotting it with a hand towel, she gave herself a spritz of rosewater from an atomizer and checked her hair in the mirror. The visage staring back at her revealed a woman who was now older than her own mother had been when she died in childbirth.

'Only twenty. To die so young. Was the sole purpose of her life to be a daughter, a wife...a mother? Did she come into our lives, briefly, so we could forever feel her loss?' "*Porque?*" she asked aloud.

She rarely permitted herself to think about her mother. It suddenly occurred to her that part of her anger towards Billy Patton's treatment of the Heiser girl was connected to her feelings for the German mother she barely remembered; as always, those feelings were conflicted. True, she felt empathy for a young girl who spent half of her teenage years pregnant, yet she couldn't help but feel anger because Millie permitted herself to yield to Fredo's constant demands and because her death bequeathed that burden to a child.

She descended the steps, grabbed a small tray of cookies and sweet biscuits from the kitchen cupboard and ventured out into the garden to await Bessie and the tea. In moments like these, she wished Sarah could join her there. Although she enjoyed Bessie's company, she longed for the sound of Sarah's voice and the pleasure she derived from her embrace. Since their first meeting, something told her they were meant to be together.

In spite of present circumstance, she still believed in that inevitability.

SEVEN

One memory was almost too painful for Amelia to revisit; yet, on days when she missed Sarah desperately, her mind carried her back to the spring day the two walked from their rooming house on College Hill in Cape Girardeau to the banks of the Mississippi. Inseparable for two years, but with graduation looming, the spectre of estrangement created an atmosphere of unspoken dread. However, the first signs of spring had temporarily elevated their spirits.

"I know…let's take a picnic lunch to the river," said Sarah.

"Oh, yes! I can't remember the last time I went on a picnic."

They packed a simple lunch and strolled, arm-in-arm, down Normal Avenue past Academic Hall, where they'd first met. The domed structure contained light fixtures from the World's Fair.

Like tiny green propellers in freefall, maple seedlets twirled to the ground—cushioning the sidewalk. Pink and white dogwood exploded on the hillside, blanketed with daffodil, dandelion, clover and violets. A gentle breeze ruffled leaves on the giant elms, and the sun defied clouds to block its rays—bringing warmth too long denied by an unusually cool and rainy April.

"Dear Emily would adore this. She so loved her flowers. *Flowers – well – if anybody can the extasy define—half a transport – half a trouble –with which flowers humble men: anybody find the fountain from which floods so contra flow – I will give him all the daisies which opon the hillside blow…*"

"I'll swan, sometimes I think you've memorized every Dickinson poem."

"Nearly," she said—grabbing Sarah's hand as they continued on.

The muddy Mississippi 'lapped the miles' only a half mile from the campus. Other than the Third District Normal School, Cape Girardeau was virtually indistinguishable from many other river towns between St. Louis and Memphis.

On North Street, they passed by modest, two-story wood frame houses and occasionally, a large Victorian home, girded behind a wrought-iron fence—dominating a corner lot. As they approached the river on North Park Drive, the houses grew shabbier: patchwork boathouses built on stilts, some little more than shacks. Suddenly, Amelia stopped. "Listen…the river. Hear him?"

"Him?"

"The Mississippi's commonly referred to as him.   The Missouri River, her."

"Well, with all the rain we've had, *he* must be engorged."

"Engorged? My...how *sanguine* of you," giggled Amelia. "Who knew Human Physiology would make you such an expert on the male anatomy?"

"Tch, tch, tch…you're terrible."

They found a lovely spot near an old boat dock and spread a blanket on the ground. The river was running bank full. The whistle from an Anchor Line steamer moaned in the distance. A tugboat pushing a barge filled with coal, slowly chugged along—fouling the air with dark billows of sulphur dioxide. For a long time, they sat in silence, Sarah's head resting in Amelia's lap, as they watched the muddy water, turbid with roiled sediment and flotsam, rushing by.

"It's never the same river."

"It's the muddy Mississippi…the same river that's been snaking its way to the gulf for thousands of years."

"Yes, but it's *always* moving…changing. Every day another river runs by. It's the perfect metaphor for life."

"You see everything as analogy," said Sarah. "You were

born to teach literature."

Amelia leaned down and, without hesitation, kissed her. There was an electric cathexis—a riveting exchange of pent-up psychic energy. They kissed again.

"I was born...to be with you," she whispered.

"Amelia—"

"Wait, let me finish," she said—pressing her fingertips to Sarah's lips. "We both agree we've never known anyone who understood us as completely as we do each other. True?"

"True," she said—sitting up.

"And, we've never been as comfortable with another person as we are with each other. Isn't that so?"

"Yes, dear one, that's also true." She unwrapped a sandwich—handing it to Amelia. "I know in three weeks you have to return to Valley Ridge to spend some time with your mother...just as I have to go back to Prospect and make sure Papa is doing well. But, after that, we simply must find a way to be together."

Sarah reached in the basket and removed another sandwich. "I would love that, but the truth is mother is struggling right now with my brother gone. She really needs my help on the farm."

"Let your younger brother do it. Did you just complete a teaching degree so you could milk cows and slop hogs? Seriously, you can have a teaching career now...and you'll not be dependent on any man...ever again."

Sarah continued to look lovingly at her.

"What...?"

"Do you remember once when we first met, how I told you about that little frightened girl you have inside you?"

"Yes, but how does that figure into your plans to put yourself out to pasture?" Her head dropped. "I'm sorry. I don't mean to be so acrimonious. It's just that I—"

"Our separation feels like I'm abandoning you, and it's triggering a lot of fear. Whenever that happens, the little girl in you gets scared...the way you did when Karl first left for the military."

"That was *different*," said Amelia—growing more agitated.

"I was only sixteen. Karl and I had always been together…with only each other to rely on. Then, not long after, Papa had the accident and I was left to care for him alone. Of course I was frightened, but we're talking about you and me…*us*. We share a deep and abiding love, do we not?"

"You know I love you…more than anyone. That shouldn't be in question. But until I can help mother get things worked out at home, I have no other choice. She needs me."

"*I* need you," she said—taking Sarah's hand and pressing it to her breast. "I need to be with you. I'm happier with you than I've ever been in my life." She held out her arms in an attempt to embrace her.

"We, each of us, must find a way to be happy without relying on another person to make it so."

Amelia sprang to her feet as if she'd been scalded. She hurled the sandwich to the ground, grabbed her bonnet and parasol and started away.

"Where are you going? Don't leave."

"You're a good one to talk. People are always leaving me. First mother…then Karl…now y-y-ou," she said, her voice breaking. "I thought you'd be different."

"Amelia, please come back!"

The next two weeks were strained. It was only at the moment of their final goodbye that things altered. At Amelia's insistence, Sarah vowed to write 'everyday' and to come to Prospect for a visit as soon as possible. They held each other in a long embrace and parted with a tearful kiss.

Peering out of their second story bedroom window, Amelia watched as Sarah boarded a carriage bound for the train station. She tightly gripped herself as wracking sobs shook her whole body. When the carriage disappeared, she collapsed onto Sarah's bed—drawing her knees to her chest. Perhaps Sarah was right…for inside, she heard a child's anguished cry from the heart, *'Please, oh please…don't leave me alone.'*

*   *   *

Journal Entry: 2 October, 1917

> *Her breast is fit for pearls*
> *But I was not a "Diver."*
> *Her brow is fit for thrones—*
> *But I have not a crest.*
> *Her heart is fit for home—*
> *I—a sparrow—build there*
> *Sweet twigs and twine*
> *My perennial nest.*

Dearest Miss Dickinson,

I know not to whom you addressed those passionate words, but this I do know: I love Sarah Jamison…and your words might very well be my own, for she has built a perennial nest in my heart and it is hers alone. Every stirring, every heartbeat reminds me of my dearest Love. Could I but be the pearls, pure and virginal, draped above her lovely bosom, then true happiness would be mine.

If absence does indeed make the heart grow fonder, it is difficult to conceive mine could yearn more intensely, for fear it might consume itself with the searing heat of passion and the ache of longing. Such longing! There are moments, while standing before a classroom of eager faces, when I am so overcome with thoughts of the lovely Sarah, so drawn into the memory of her tender embrace—time is suspended and I am back in her arms. Today, while reciting Whitman's, "A Kiss to A Bride"…

> *O sweet Missouri rose! O bonny bride!*
> *Yield thy red cheeks, thy lips, to-day,*

Unto a Nation's loving kiss

...I caught myself blushing. I'm certain some students noticed, though none acknowledged it. If I allow myself to remember her parting kiss, to experience, once again, the honeyed-lips and petal-soft skin, I must fight back warm tears of abject sorrow which linger still...and the utter despair forged by that painful 'goodbye.'

Yet, sometimes, a tear escapes as it did only last week. 'Is something wrong?' a student asked. 'Oh, child,' I wanted to say, 'something is so very wrong when you are separated from the one who holds your heart, from the one who gives life meaning and makes its demands palatable.' Instead, I brushed away the tear and returned a wistful smile. Sarah Bernhardt and Ellen Terry would have been proud.

So, dearest Emily, I, too, know the ache your tender words expressed in "her breast is fit for pearls." Who was she? A secret lover? Did you ever reveal your true feelings? Or, did you carry the secret of your love to the grave...a secret cloaked in a cryptic paean? Not I, dear muse. For someday soon, Sarah and I will be reunited.

Someday soon, the sparrow will return wholeheartedly to the nest I keep warm with old tears of longing.

Your admirer,

~Amelia

EIGHT

"Miss Madeira...you wanted to see me?"

Chester O'Malley waited until he was certain most students had left the building before appearing at her classroom door.

"I *did*...and still do," she said—glancing at the clock. "But first, I'll need you to follow me down to the library. I must secure the lockbox and tidy up a bit." She smiled as she moved past him. "I thought possibly you'd forgotten. It's been nearly half an hour since school dismissed."

"No, I...I was talking to Willie...outside," he said—trailing behind her.

"Willie...Stansbury? I didn't know you were two were *friends*. By that, I just mean... "

"You're surprised we have anything in common."

"Well, yes, frankly. You're so studious and Willie is...Willie." She unlocked the library office door. "Come on in." She walked directly to the checkout window and pulled open a sliding drawer. Removing a small metal box, she flipped the latch and peered inside.

"A penny a day. Those late fees are adding up. Soon I'll be able to purchase a set of encyclopedias. Won't that be nice?" She replaced the metal box and locked the drawer. "Safety first. There can't be more than three dollars in there, but one can't be too careful."

"Miss Madeira...is something wrong?"

"I wanted to talk about the essay you wrote. Have a seat, won't you?"

He sat down in the cane-bottom chair next to her desk. Chester was five foot ten and weighed a hundred and forty pounds. Though he gave the appearance of being somewhat frail, he had worked off and on in his father's blacksmith shop since he was young child and was surprisingly well developed.

"First of all, I must tell you I was taken aback to discover you spoke French. However did you learn it?"

"I'm not very conversant, *Je parle un peu, français,* but I am able to read and comprehend *avec un certain degree de compétence.* Mother taught me. Her family was among the first French settlers in St. Louis...French Canadian.   Her great-great-great-great-great-great-*great* grandfather...was that seven?"

"I believe so."

"Anyway, he was a trapper and sold furs to a trading post located right where the Old St. Louis Cathedral stands today."

"I remember going to the Old Cathedral when just a young girl."

"I've only been to St. Louis once. My father works so much it's rare we ever go anywhere. My aunt, mother's sister, Clarisse, lives there. She's the one who gave me the copy of *Du côté de chez Swann.* Aunt Clarisse thought I'd love Proust. She was right. She and her husband came to visit us when I was eight and they took mother and me back with them on the train. We stayed for a month. I didn't want to come back. There's not much to do here in Prospect, and I really adore the city...the Art Museum and Forest Park where they held the World's Fair."

Amelia had never heard Chester utter more than a few sentences at a time. She marveled at how relaxed he appeared.

"We lived in St. Louis for almost five years...until I was nearly seven. Papa took my brother, Karl, and me to the fair. It's the most wonderful thing I've ever seen. I still have a commemorative glass, etched with a picture of the Ferris wheel. We were on the giant wheel when it broke down. People were screaming. We clung to each other. It took hours to repair. Papa was furious."

He couldn't remember ever seeing his teacher so carefree. He wished some of his classmates could see her now, the way she acted away from the classroom.

"Miss Orton loved the aviary in the park. She always brought me something back whenever she visited."

"She was so very fond of you, Chester. You were her prized pupil."

"I loved Miss Orton, but she wasn't...the best teacher. Well, you know...you had her, too."

"It wouldn't be very professional of me to say so...though she was rather..."

"Old-fashioned?"

She looked at him and then broke into a grin. "Yes, old-fashioned. She had a certain facility for grammar, but contemporary fiction and poetry weren't her forté."

"Longfellow was as contemporary as she got. *The Village Blacksmith. 'The smith a mighty man is he, with large and sinewy hands.'* Made me memorize it freshman year. Thought my father would enjoy it."

"Did he?"

"Not really. My father and I don't connect...at any point."

She stared at him for a moment, but said nothing. He repositioned himself in his chair. Clearly, the silence made him uncomfortable.

"May I ask you something personal? You can say, 'no.'"

"What is it?"

"Does your father ever...hit you?"

"Why would you ask me that?"

"Several weeks ago, I noticed you had a faint bruise on your left temple. I couldn't help wondering if—"

"Oh, *that!* No, no. Willie and I were just messing around and he caught me with his elbow."

"Well, that's a relief. I'm sorry to have asked you, but I know fathers aren't easy." She continued to study Chester's eyes.

There was something about the way he'd stumbled that made her doubt his explanation.

"Your father," he asked, "...is *he* easy?"

"No, although he was better before the accident."

"Guess he's lucky to be alive."

"Yes..."

They sat in silence for a moment.

"About your essay...Proust introduces some very controversial subjects, wouldn't you agree?"

"Controversial, yes, but Europeans have a more open attitude about everything."

"If I'm correct, his homosexual themes were controversial even in France and still are...with the church, especially. Look what happened to Oscar Wilde. Jailed for gross indecency."

"I wouldn't expect you to shy away from controversy. It's one of the things I admire most about you. I still remember the letter you wrote to the *Prospect Banner* when you were in high school, the one defending the statue your father carved for the city park. I used to sit and appreciate how magnificent it was...before..."

"It was desecrated."

"Your article championed art and shamed those who would, out of ignorance, destroy it. People around here are so provincial. Michelangelo's *David* wouldn't last five minutes in the park."

"I always thought it interesting how he created the statue with hammer and chisel and someone else...a coward, too ashamed to take responsibility, destroyed it with the same tools."

Chester's mind flashed to '*you can hear him swing his heavy sledge, with measured beat and slow, like a sexton ringing the village bell, when the evening sun is low.*'

"The parallel you draw—"

"*What?*" he asked, startled. "I...I beg your pardon?"

"I say the parallel you draw between Proust and Whitman is intriguing; however, I'm not sure your assertion about Whitman's sexuality is based on solid evidence."

Though he would never have initiated so intimate a

conversation, he felt comfortable talking to her. *"I sing the body electric...the armies of those I love engirth me, and I engirth them.* It seems pretty obvious he embraced the sexuality of both males and females."

"I see your point, but I'm not certain it's one of his best." Seeing his chagrined look, she quickly added, "Though I do love the critical thought it stirred."

"You have to admit his Civil War poems are highly erotic. It's as if he's writing almost from a feminine perspective, from the feminine, nurturing part of himself."

"There *is* a gentleness one almost never finds in male poets."

"The way he describes wounded soldiers...sensually, yet with such compassion—embracing them without the slightest thought of how anyone would view him. That's what I value most...a sort of naïve recognition that all sexuality...whether between a man and a woman, or two women or two men...is normal. He reveals an astonishing capacity for sympathy...no, an *empathy* for human suffering." As he spoke, his eyes blurred with tears, but he wasn't embarrassed.

"What is it, dear?"

"I'm sorry, Miss Madeira. I just get emotional. I'm an emotional person. It's what my father hates most about me."

She leaned forward and placed her hand on his shoulder. "I understand," she said. "Believe me, I do understand." Removing a handkerchief from her sleeve, she attempted to wipe away a tear.

"Miss Madeira, what's happening here?" Supt. Johnston stood in the doorway.

She quickly removed her hand from Chester's shoulder. He sat up straight, dabbed at his eyes and glanced towards Johnston.

"Chester and I were just having a conversation...about an essay he wrote."

He studied them both for a moment. "Well, I suggest you finish locking up. And Chester, you should run along home. Conversations about essays need to be confined to the school day, and the school day ended an hour ago."

She stared at him with veiled animosity. "Yes, of course," she said—her voice deadened.

"Chester," he said, gesturing. "Come now."

He started towards the doorway. Then, he quickly swung back. "*Merci beaucoup*, Miss Madeira. *Pour votre empathie et votre compréhension.*"

"You're very welcome. We'll resume this discussion another time."

"Hurry on," said Johnston.

"*Bonsoir*, Monsieur Johnston," he said, without a hint of sarcasm. "*Jusqu'à demain.* Until tomorrow."

Johnston looked nonplussed as he watched him exit. "What's wrong with that boy?" he said, when he was certain he was out of earshot.

"Whatever do you mean? Chester's brilliant...the most intelligent and talented student I have. Would that there were others even half as bright."

"When the board hired you, I feared your age might be a concern. It's critical students not see you as a contemporary."

"That's not a problem, I assure you."

"It isn't wise to counsel students, Miss Madeira. Seasoned teachers know this."

"I wasn't counseling. We were discussing his essay and he got emotional explaining something to me."

"I *repeat*...leave the counseling to Mr. Robertson and myself. You were hired to teach, and it would be best if you confined your teaching to the classroom between 7:30 and 3:15."

That evening after supper, Amelia sat at the dinner table and wrote in her journal:

> *I felt your Pain as if my own—*
> *Your Sadness cleaved my joy—*
> *'Twas if a mirror reflected now*
> *An essence of my Self—*

Vain glory lies within the realm
Of all who seek themselves—
In others—like Narcissus' pool
Will drown in futile Desire

The next day in English IV, she copied the poem on the board—presenting it as if it were another Dickinson poem.

Willie Stansbury tapped Chester on the shoulder.

"Hey, Chet, your sadness cleaved my joy. Perk up, buddy. Why so unhappy? Afraid Madeline's gonna be valedictorian or somethin'?"

"No."

"Then what's wrong?"

He studied Willie. They had grown up together. Played together. Wrestled each other.   Defended one another. Their friendship had long been an unspoken love.

"Nothing."

He glanced up at his teacher. *Twas if a mirror reflected now an essence of myself*.

Those words were no accident and Chester knew it. And, what's more, he knew that she knew he knew it.

*   *   *

Chester's bedroom was near the head of a narrow stairway, accessible from the kitchen. The attic remained unfinished, except for a cramped 7'x 9' "room" Blackie O'Malley had cobbled together years ago from random pieces of pine and rock lath given to him by Herb Müller, who owned the lumberyard on the south side of the square. The house, a simple, four-room box, was one of the oldest in Prospect. It sat, weathered and forlorn, tucked in behind O'Malley's Metalworks, the last blacksmith shop in the county.

Until he was six, he slept in a cramped storage closet— under the attic staircase —next to his parent's bedroom. Due to a childhood fraught with ear and throat infections, respiratory congestion, catarrh and asthma, his mother insisted he be within earshot so she could minister to him whenever he struggled to breathe. That arrangement lasted until young Chester suffered through a protracted bout of pneumonia, one she feared might claim her only child. Kept awake by the coughing, his father finally erupted.

"That's it…goddammit!" he fumed—sitting up in bed.

"Shhh… Why are you yelling?" She whispered as she crawled in beside him. "He's finally stopped coughing and, mercifully, fallen asleep."

"I'm glad someone's gettin' some rest. Ain't slept through the night in weeks. Hell, years."

"Doc Simpson says we're lucky this time, but he's still not out of the woods."

"Oh, stop it. Anytime the boy gets sick, you act like he's gonna die. All he has to do is sneeze, and you fly in there like he's at death's door. It's gone on long enough."

"What do you mean?"

"I'm tradin' some work with Herb Müller for lumber, and I'm fixin' him a bedroom upstairs, where maybe his hackin' won't wake me every five minutes."

"In that drafty attic? No, Frank, it's freezing up there, and in the summertime, it's like a furnace."

"This ain't a discussion. If you want, you can move up there with him. Can't remember the last time we had a moment alone in this bed without you jumpin' up to check on him. Think I can't hear you in there hummin' them silly French songs at all hours of the night? I'm done with it."

After a protracted silence, she whispered. "Is that why you spend nearly every Friday and Saturday night at the hotel?"

"What now?"

"Think I don't' know what goes on there…with those women brought in by the railroad?"

The room to which Chester had been exiled at age six quickly became a sanctuary, where he could not only lose himself in the classics but also create a world that shielded him from the harsh reality of his father's drinking and the utter poverty and abuse it propagated. Eventually, he overcame the illnesses that ravaged his childhood, and the years he spent bedridden served as a prelude to a lifetime of reading.

By the time he entered high school, he had devoured practically everything in the school library. Every teacher was keenly aware that Chester O'Malley, though introverted, possessed an encyclopedic knowledge and an amazing facility with the written word. For years, his poems regularly appeared in the *Prospect Banner*—funneled by one teacher or another. Unlike Blackie, who seemed embarrassed by them, Pearl took great pride in her son's accomplishments.

Even more remarkable, a short story, "The Enigma," was reprinted in the Sunday magazine accompanying *The St. Louis Post-Dispatch* when he was only fourteen. Heartened by the Italian sonnets of John Milton, he extemporaneously composed a Petrarchan sonnet about a Venus Flytrap, which he compared to the "armless" *Venus de Milo*, for Miss Orton's English III final examination:

> *Oh rare, exotic, egocentric snare!*
> *Celestial goddess cloaked in leafy frill,*
> *Your luring beauty expedites the kill*
> *Of those, transfixed, who spider through your hair.*
> *Death's caress your spiny lips could spare*
> *The weak Achilles, who, against his will,*
> *Cannot resist the venom chlorophyll*
> *Venus, you spurn your namesake without care!*
>
> *Did god give you no arms out of respect*
> *For your alluring, all-embracing smile?*
> *Disarmed, your ruby-lips secrete neglect*
> *Which suffocates your ill-starred lover while*

You grow leafy absorbing the "insect."
Your beauty barely transcends the Death Vile!

Entitled, *Dionaea Muscipula de Milo*, it was later reprinted in *Monroe's Anthology of Sonnets, 1916-1924.* Clearly, neither his teacher nor Monroe's selection committee comprehended the vaginal symbolism, which amused Chester.

All through high school, Miss Orton had encouraged him to pursue a college education, but it wasn't until Miss Madeira appeared that he actually believed writing could afford him a career. And, it wasn't until he saw Amelia Madeira again for the first time in nearly three years that he acknowledged any interest in females. Until then, his only sexual feelings had been reserved for his boyhood friend, Willie Stansbury. Knowing Willie as he did, he'd carefully repressed those feelings for years.

Early on, there had been several occasions where the two had been physically close. One such August night, the summer after eighth grade, a month before entering high school, they were lying on a blanket in Willie's backyard—watching a meteor shower. "Sleeping out" was common practice in the Midwest due to the insufferably hot and humid weather that made it nearly impossible to sleep before the midnight air began to cool.

Willie's parents and sister were resting on cots on the front porch. He and Chester were stretched out on an old quilt twenty yards away, behind a cluster of lilac bushes. Both had stripped down to their shorts. They'd been counting "shooting stars" for nearly an hour and were nearing seventy.

His head was resting on the crook of Willie's arm as he counted, "Sixty-eight. See it...? Must have lasted three seconds. I *love* the intensity, the momentary brilliance." He glanced over to see Willie's eyes glistening with tears.

"What's wrong...?"

Willie shook his head and turned away. Finally, in a pain-muffled voice, he whispered, "I hope I die before you do."

That was the closest either of them ever came to mentioning love.

Throughout high school, the two remained close; however, Willie had recently turned his attention to Sandra Shepard. Though he knew it was completely natural, Chester was irritated when Willie sat with her and her twin sister every lunch period, and the last time he'd spent the night, he talked about nothing but his feelings for her. Then, today after school, Chester questioned him about the future and, once again, it all revolved around Sandra.

"So are you thinking about marrying her or what?" he finally asked—pointblank.

"Yeah, thinkin' about it...why?"

"Because I thought we'd decided to get out of Prospect when we graduated."

"That was before. You're for sure goin' off to college, and I'm gonna be workin' on daddy's farm. I'm a farmer. Wish you'd get that through your head 'cause that's all I'm ever gonna be."

"That's why we talked about you earning a degree in agriculture at the university. You and me, roommates...remember?"

"Ain't got the smarts and you know it."

"Who do you think goes to university to study agriculture? Farm boys just like you. Why, you could learn about soils and erosion and crop rotation. There are new breakthroughs in fertilization and food production. Massive improvements in agronomy and animal husbandry."

"No idea what yer even talkin' about."

"Listen, if you don't want to go to Mizzou, I'll go to School of the Ozarks with you. I don't care where we go. I just want us to be together."

"With your smarts...you can go anywhere. But me and Sandra...we're homebodies."

The conversation quickly deteriorated into blame-filled accusations.

"I thought we cared about each other. That's what I thought," said Chester—his face flush with anger. It was the first time in all the years they'd known each other that he'd raised his voice to Willie. "Have I just imagined all this time we had a special kind of friendship?"

Instantly, Willie's eyes brimmed with tears and his chin quivered. "I... gotta go... See ya, tomorrow."

Chester stood and watched until he finally disappeared over the hill by the Catholic Church, three blocks away. The next thing he knew, he was sitting in Miss Madeira's office—revealing his innermost thoughts.

What is it about her? He'd never known anyone who shared his enthusiasm for knowledge, for words and ideas like Amelia Madeira; never had anyone challenged him to come out of himself the way she did.

While they talked, scattered bits of his conversation with Willie reemerged. It wasn't just Whitman's compassion for young soldiers that brought tears to his eyes. It was the realization that he and Willie would never be together.

"Oh, Chester, what is it, dear?"

"I'm sorry, Miss Madeira. I just get emotional. I'm an emotional person. It's what my father hates most about me," he heard himself telling her.

NINE

The Soul selects her own Society—
Then—shuts the Door—
To her divine Majority—
Present no more—

Unmoved—she notes the Chariot's—pausing—
At her low Gate—
Unmoved—an Emperor be kneeling
Upon her mat—

I've known her—from an ample nation—
Choose One—
Then—close the Valves of her attention—
Like Stone—
~Emily Dickinson

Madeline Jones carefully printed the poem on Miss Madeira's blackboard. When she finished, she addressed the class.

"I chose this particular Dickinson poem because it expresses how I feel."

"How exactly does it represent your feelings?" asked Miss Madeira, seated in the back of the room. Knowing Madeline was free to select a work from any contemporary poet, Amelia was amused at her blatant attempt to curry favor.

"You know, sometimes you just feel you're *special*...not like everyone else. I don't mean to sound vain, but I've always felt special...different. Like I was meant to be somebody."

The McDowell and Shepard twins whispered among themselves. Daisy McDowell laughed out loud, then quickly covered her mouth.

"Quiet please!" Miss Madeira glared at Daisy and the rest of the quartet. It was obvious Madeline had missed the whole point of the poem, but she was determined to hear her interpretation before dismantling it.

"Let's stop right there a moment. Can you adduce where in the text you think the poet's talking about feeling special. Please be specific."

"Well, the first part...stanza...describes her as a majority of one. That makes her feel special. And then, in the second stanza, a chariot comes for her and a royal figure bows before her, which shows she must be special. And the last stanza is about...how...how the whole nation chooses her, which is like a metaphor...er, a simile...*no*, a metaphor...for how special she really is. And finally, her especial fate is sealed in stone."

Her especial fate? Amelia glanced at Chester, whose look mirrored her own. Perhaps if the two sets of twins had not already attempted to belittle her, she might have questioned her further, but instead she dismissed her with a faint smile. "Thank you," she said— rising and taking her place in front of the classroom as Madeline returned to her seat.

"Would anyone else care to offer another interpretation? How about you, Daisy? I'm sure you have your own opinion."

Daisy narrowed her eyes but said nothing.

"Sandra? Anyone else who found her interpretation lacking?"

"I think she's correct," said Maisy McDowell.

The Sheppard twins nodded in agreement. Chester raised his hand. It was rare he volunteered.

"I think Dickinson is saying that a soul chooses only a few

select companions to become a part of her inner consciousness...excluding everyone else. As the second stanza shows, there is no compromising this position...not for chariots, not even for emperors. To make the point even stronger, in the third stanza, she says that a soul has been known to choose only one other person from an entire nation. I think it's implied Dickinson feels that letting one person into your personal adytum...where no outsider is ever permitted entry...is a rare and precious thing. Or, as Madeline might say, *especial*."

It was moments like these that made Amelia thrill to the idea that words and ideas made life not only bearable but something to be cherished. She laid no claim to Chester's intelligence or his insight, but she relished the knowledge that she had made her classroom a haven where he felt safe enough to express it. Knowing she would not permit mocking and encouraged self-expression, he was slowly emerging from his self-imposed cocoon.

His reticence had given way to self-assurance, a newfound confidence that bolstered his courage. For the first time in his life he'd stood up to his father, whose nightly drinking made him not only insufferable and belligerent, but also consumed much of his paltry income. The incident began with Blackie's comment about the evening meal.

"Not potatoes and cabbage again! Can't we ever have a bit of ham or a sliver of beef? I sweat my balls off over that hot forge every day, and when I come home, I'd like somethin' to eat besides colcannon!"

"It's all we have. I've no money to buy meat. It's a luxury we can't afford."

"Well, where the hell'd it all go? I'll tell ya where. If you didn't spend every last cent on your goddamn son, I could sit down and have a real meal. The boy needs another writin' tablet like I need a longer day."

Chester had heard versions of this conversation for years. 'You bought *him* shoes? *I* need shoes.' 'I quit school in the sixth grade 'cause I *had* to get a job.' 'Your baby's too good to work, but he ain't too good to keep askin' for money for every little thing.' 'Son, me and your mother go *without* so you can have things we never had!'

Blackie reached into his back pocket and pulled out a pint. He uncorked it and poured whiskey into a water glass. He took a swig and continued the diatribe. "All the boy ever does is sit up in that room and read them goddamn books. Wish I could sit around and read me some books, but somebody's gotta earn money to buy oil for the lamp he keeps burnin' half the night. When I was his age, I had a job. What kinda seventeen-year-old boy reads all the time anyways? A mama's boy, that's what kind. You've made him soft, Pearl…and he ain't ever gonna amount to nothin'."

As he often did, Chester sat on the top step—listening. It was the last allegation that finally pushed him to defend himself. He flew down the stairs and into the kitchen. "You don't read…because you *can't* read."

"What did you say to me?" Blackie O'Malley was a bull of a man, and when he drank, a mean one.

"You heard me."

"Think you're big enough to talk to me like that?" he said—pushing his chair back from the table.

"Now, *stop it* you two!" shouted Pearl, who rarely raised her voice. "I mean it…stop this right now!"

For a moment, Blackie backed down, but Chester was determined to not let it end there.

"I'm sorry you had to quit school and pick up chunks of coal along the railroad tracks to heat your home. That you had *so many* brothers and sisters you got stabbed with a fork in the back of the hand—reaching for the last piece of fatback. But, none of that is my fault." Before Blackie could respond, he continued.

"You said yourself you always hated school. Well, I don't hate school. I love it. And because I do read and because of what I read, I'm going to go to college and make something of myself."

"Just how many horses am I gonna have to shoe and how many plows am I gonna have to sharpen to pay for your big college?" He shook his head in disgust and took another gulp. "Son, you know nothing about the real world."

"It won't cost you a penny. Miss Madeira says I can get scholarships to pay for everything."

"*Miss Madeira says?*" He chuckled to himself. "You mean crazy Fred Madeira's daughter...that odd duck? What nonsense has she filled your head with now? Told you you're gonna be a big success has she?"

"Yes, as a matter of fact. She also helped me understand that there's more to manhood than swinging a hammer and forging steel. Having the courage to face who you are sober is what makes you a man. Being able to express my humanity is what will determine if I'm a success."

Blackie stared at him with contempt.

"In the meantime, if you'd stop drinking up every dime you earn, maybe mother could afford to buy some meat. Because, and this may come as a revelation, but every now and then we'd like to have some goddamn meat, too!"

Though the meal ended with Blackie threatening to take Chester down 'a peg or two'—before bolting out the door—it didn't put a halt to his drinking; likely, it helped accelerate it. However, it was clearly the beginning of Chester's emancipation from feeling like a disappointment to feeling like a young man whose intelligence more than compensated for any perceived lack of masculinity.

In his journal, he referred to the turning point as *"un coup de foudre"*—a thunderclap. He stayed after school and stood by while Miss Madeira read it. Though she applauded his courage in standing up for himself, she said there was a Portuguese expression for what occurred that day, *Em casa onde não há pão, todos ralhao e ninguém tem razão*: 'in a house where there is no bread, everyone shouts and no one is right.'

Four Years Earlier

Pearl O'Malley waited for Blackie's return. Following a

heated exchange on whether or not Chester was "too sensitive" to survive the brutal realities of the world, she feared her husband's agitated mental state would provoke another dramatic episode. He'd slammed out the door—his usual way of exiting an argument—only to disappear into his shop next door. She prayed that's where he'd remain, even if he spent the rest of the day drinking.

Oh, merciful heaven...what now? She pressed her face against the kitchen windowpane and peered into the early morning dusk. She could barely distinguish what he was carrying as he emerged from the shop, but she thought it was a pipe or a forging hammer—what he called his "helve." As she watched him disappear across the street towards the park, she feared the consequences. Their argument, as it often did, revolved around his obsession that Chester's artistic bent was a sign of weakness—resulting in his inevitable ruin.

"Last week, I caught him sittin' in the park...starin' at that goddamn monstrosity of Fred Madeira's," he recalled with disgust. 'Son, what're ya doin'?' I asked him. 'Admirin' the craftsmanship,' he said. 'A damn eyesore's what I call it.' 'That's because you have no appreciation for art,' he says to me...and the damnedest part was he got all teary-eyed like he always does. 'The man who carved this is an artist,' he says...'and that's what I am, but you wouldn't understand.' 'Oh, I understand all right. I understand this thing ain't fit for no decent people to see. It's supposed to be some kind of angel, but that crazy dago bastard gave it a cock and balls!' 'What's wrong with you?' he asks me. 'What's wrong with *me*? ...with ME?' I tell ya Pearl, the boy ain't gonna make it."

"Why do you keep saying that, Frank? With his mind, he can do anything he wants. Miss Orton told me he's the most talented writer she's ever had. Better than some of those in school books."

"Why do you listen to them old maids? Ever since the boy entered first grade, one or another of them's been fillin' your head and his about how smart he is. Fairy dust, that's all it is. Sprinklin' him with fairy dust and fillin' his head with shit. Let me ask you somethin'...can he *shoe* a horse? *Dig* a ditch? *Plow* a field?"

"He's going to be a writer, Frank, not a laborer. Chester's gift is his mind. My sister says—"

"Your sister's married to a man who makes hats! How in Sam Hill do you think he's gonna support himself writin' books? Artist, my ass. I tell you what *art* is...it's forgin' wrought iron, shapin' a scythe's blade, sharpenin' the scissors used to trim the bristles on an artist's brush...not words on a page. All this talk about him bein' an artist is just puredee shit."

As she waited for his return, the morning light began to bring night shapes into focus. 'Someone's certain to spot him...Herb Müller or Luke Phillips. Someone heading to work early,' she thought to herself. 'What then?' She wasn't sure how much more she could endure. 'Once Chester's gone,' echoed in her head. Once Chester's gone, just you wait, Frank O'Malley!

He was back in ten minutes, but he stayed in his shop the rest of the day—drinking.

"Is something wrong?" Chester asked his mother as he sat eating breakfast later that morning.

"No, hon...I'm just tired."

"Where's dad?"

"In the shop."

"I heard you two going at it early this morning."

"Just a little disagreement," she said—busying herself with the dishes.

"Did he touch you?"

"No...*no*, of course not. Now eat your breakfast. You'll be late for school."

TEN

Perhaps it was her talk with Chester, but that night Amelia lie awake remembering her childhood in St. Louis: the two-room flat, the hours spent alone with Karl while Fredo searched for work, and the constant ache of missing her mother. For the first time it occurred to her that the feeling of emptiness, disconnection and the pang of separation she experienced in childhood was precisely the anguish that gnawed at her, consciously and unconsciously, since "losing Sarah."

She recalled other mother substitutes—including the young teacher, Miss Jenkins, and her elderly mother, who lived next door and who often watched over them when Fredo took a "temporary" job delivering pianos, 'until find work carving stone.' The piano delivery job at Ludwig's Music lasted nearly two years before he was hired as a sculptor for Annan's Funereal Monuments, a company specializing in marble and granite grave markers, headstones and modest family mausoleums.

Meanwhile, Miss Jenkins taught Amelia to read by the time she was four, and even though Karl disdained reading, she managed to teach him some basic arithmetic. She remembered how sad she'd been to leave Miss Jenkins when Fredo moved them across town to Mrs. McCoy's boarding house, a move closer to his new job at Annan's, just off North Kingshighway.

Miss Kathryn Harper, a border at McCoy's, was hired to baby-sit the children, as Fredo frequently failed to return home until long after they were asleep. At first, she loved Miss Harper, but then, "the incident."

She'd called to them twice from the foot of the stairs, "Supper, children!" When they failed to respond, the arthritic old woman climbed the steps and proceeded down the hall to their room. Pushing open the door, she discovered Karl on his knees in front of Amelia.

"Children, supper. Called you twice. What are you doing?" Stepping nearer, she gasped. "Karl! What in the world...?"

He pulled his hand away from Amelia and looked at Miss Harper with alarm. Amelia, expressionless, continued to hold the hem of her dress clutched to her waist.

"Oh, my heavens!" shrieked the old woman, who had never before raised her voice to the children. Her tone and volume frightened Amelia, who began to cry.

"Get away from her you filthy little boy! What do you think you're doing? Answer me!"

"*Desculpe*," he whimpered. "I didn't mean to..." He, too, began to cry.

"Shame on you!"

With great effort, she bent down and pulled up Amelia's bloomers. "Let go," she said—tugging at the hem of her dress. "Did he hurt you?"

She shook her head 'no.'

"Never ever let anyone do that. Ever!"

Struggling to stand, she grabbed Karl by the shoulder. "Don't you ever let me catch you being nasty again, do you hear me?"

A cloud had descended over him.

"Wait 'til your father gets home."

Amelia covered her face and continued to weep.

"Apologize to your sister."

He opened his mouth, but struggled to speak.

"Do it now...or I'll paddle you myself!"

"I'm...I'm sorry, Sis," he said. He reached out to touch her, but Miss Harper grabbed his hand and thrust it away in disgust. As punishment, she put him to bed without supper while Amelia continued to whimper.

"Let's go eat. Supper will be cold."

"Can't Karl come with us? Please..."

"No. He's a very bad boy, and I'm going to have to tell your father when he comes home."

"Don't tell Papa," she pleaded. "*Please,* don't tell Papa..." She began to sob again.

Miss Harper led her downstairs where she gave her a teaspoonful of paregoric to calm her. "There, that's better. Now stop crying. You'll upset the other boarders. Besides, we don't want anyone to know why you're crying, do we?"

"No," she mumbled, as the opiate entered her bloodstream.

Over the years, Amelia tried every means to erase painful childhood memories; however, this one—the old shame-filled movie—had become a part of her knowing. For years, she searched for the appropriate words to describe this conundrum and, of course, she discovered them in Dickinson's poem, *Whether they have forgotten.*

> *Whether they have forgotten*
> *Or are forgetting no*
> *Or never remembered—*
> *Safer not to know—*
> *Miseries of conjecture*
> *Are a softer wo*

Than a fact of Iron
Hardened with I know—

Nothing would ever blot out the memory of her Papa's reaction to Miss Harper's depiction of 'the disgusting' scene she'd discovered earlier that evening. Both children were asleep in the small bed they shared when Fredo burst into the room. In the darkness, he grabbed Karl's wrist—yanking him out of bed.

"*Como e que pôde feito isso com a tua irmã? Para com a tua própria irmã?*" he yelled at the boy, who appeared totally disoriented.

He bent him over his knee and walloped him, repeatedly.

"Don't hurt Karl!" Amelia pleaded to no avail.

Fredo continued to repeat the phrase, ("How could you do that to your sister? To your own sister?").

It was the first time he had ever spanked one of the children, and it terrified the young girl. Even now, years later, she could not understand his violent reaction. Nor could she comprehend how the incident seemed to endear him to her even more, while further alienating him from her brother.

*   *   *

Her fondest memories of St. Louis surround the day her Papa and a beautiful woman, "Miss Anna," took them to the opening day of the 1904 World's Fair, renamed when the 1903 Louisiana Purchase Exposition was delayed. Over 200,000 people flocked to Forest Park the last day of April, and the spectacle of the teeming multitude both frightened and captivated her.

Six-year-old Amelia was mesmerized by the woman's stunning, black silk satin dress with the lily of valley print, the neckline and sleeves trimmed in pink velvet and the intricate jet beading. She marveled at the wide-brimmed black silk hat adorned with black and pink ostrich feathers, and the elegant pink silk parasol trimmed in black lace. She had never been in the company of anyone so resplendent.

"Are you rich?" Karl asked. For nearly two years he had attended a Catholic elementary school, and though it had refined his English, it had yet to improve his manners.

"Very," she replied, matter-of-factly, as if the answer should have been obvious even to a child.

Enid Annan, wife of Fredo's employer, Jacob Annan, and two decades younger than her husband, showed little restraint when it came to her proclivity for the dramatic. Nor, did she intend to hide her attraction for the stone carver, whom she had insisted be hired, based on nothing more than her admiration for his broad shoulders, bulging forearms and thighs, and his doleful eyes, which she regarded as sexy. Everyone at Annan's Funereal Monuments knew of the relationship, even, perhaps, her husband. When she insisted they take his children to "The Fair," at first Fredo balked; however, due to her persistence, she won out, as was her custom.

In the daylight, the view from the crest of the hill overlooking Forest Park was spectacular. Twelve hundred and seventy two acres, nearly two square miles, strewn with nine hundred distinct buildings; fifteen gargantuan neo-classic palaces festooned with electric lights and covering a tenth of the total acreage; towering colonnades reaching fifty-feet in the air, and massive fountains; the wide expanse of the Plaza of St. Louis; the Grand Basin, a giant man-made lake dotted with gondolas; and a virtual sea of humanity. In all, twenty-two countries and forty-four states had erected exhibition halls at a total cost of $45 million, an expenditure of over fifty cents for every man, woman and child living in the United States.

The massive palaces dominated what had become a dreamscape. Of them all, the Palace of Electricity and Machinery was the most impressive, for at night, the luminosity provided by its thousands of electric lights could be seen from as far away as East St. Louis, Illinois; reflected in the Grand Basin, it set the park ablaze. At the moment of illumination, the collective gasp of the spectators resounded throughout the park like a blast of wind—hissing through the giant oak and elm trees.

"Oh, Papa!" exclaimed Amelia. "It's magical!"

The Pike was a mile long boulevard, bordered by myriad amusements and entertainments, unlike anything the world had ever seen. In one, a Negro pianist named Scott Joplin played something called "rags"—buoying the enormous crowds. Karl and Amelia clapped and danced along, much to the delight of their father.

In another, a vast 15-acre spread became the site of the reenactment of the Anglo-Boer War. The two-hour extravaganza featured over 600 soldiers, a British Army encampment and a South African native village. Fredo and the children were enthralled; however, Enid found it 'tiring'—insisting they leave before the "war" was won.

At the eastern end of the Pike, they approached an enormous statue. Fredo immediately recognized it as "Cowboys Shooting Up a Western Town." Hoping to find employment as a stone carver, he had seen it near completion in a large warehouse adjacent to the park. Though his specialty was carving *anjos*, he was awed by the raw power and magnificence of the marauding *vaqueros*.

"Children! Papa see statue before finish!" he boasted. "It made by Remingdon. Reming...ton. *Isto é magnífico!* "

"He's the man who makes those dreadful western paintings and those hideous little bronzes Jacob purchased at Tiffany's. I can't believe they're popular. I simply refused to have them in the house. I made him get rid of all them."

"Who's Jacob?" asked Amelia, innocently.

"Oh, why...he's the man who owns the business where your fa...your papa...works," she said, convinced her explanation had sufficed.

If her disdain for the magnificent sculpture weren't enough, mentioning her husband's name in front of his children plunged Fredo into a deeper funk. He trudged on in silence. Hoping to brighten the mood, Enid bought a mysterious new confection for the children.

"What is it?" asked Karl—tearing a piece from the paper cone.

"Something called, 'Fairy Floss.'

"It's like a pink sugar cloud," said Amelia. "Here...try some, Papa."

"I want to get on that big thing," begged Karl—pointing to the enormous Ferris wheel. Fredo was too detached to protest.

After more than two hours, they reached the head of the line for the giant observation wheel, the world's largest—accommodating up to 1500 spectators at once. Each viewing compartment held thirty-six passengers and an attendant. Enid suddenly announced she was 'terrified of heights'—insisting Fredo remain behind with her while the children rode unaccompanied.

"It's okay, Papa. Don't worry. I'll take care of Sis," said Karl.

As the compartment door closed, Amelia attempted to get off, but was held back by the attendant. Karl wrapped a protective arm around her, and gave his father the high sign.

The massive wheel rotated so slowly it made only four rotations per hour, but from the top, one could glimpse everything in the park. As the car holding the children crested the highest part of the revolution—250 feet in the air—the engine developed a mechanical problem and the wheel ground to a halt. The many thousands who looked on were horrified, and screams of terror resounded throughout the park.

Thinking the children were in imminent danger, Fredo rushed to the ride's entrance, but was blocked by a crush of terrified patrons.

"Folks! There's no need to panic! Everyone's safe!" shouted a carnival barker, who was backed by a muscular trio providing security. "Our mechanics will have the wheel up and running again shortly. Please! Please, be patient. No one's in harm's way!"

After a wait of more than hour, they were informed the repair time might, in fact, be lengthy. Enid insisted they stroll down the plaza. At first, Fredo refused to budge. Finally, she convinced him that waiting would not speed up the repair—adding that if she didn't get something to eat very soon, she might faint 'dead away.'

Stopping at one of the many food stands, she purchased hamburgers and iced teas—both items being introduced to a wide audience for the first time. "I read about these in the *Post Dispatch*," she told him, "Supposed to be all the rage." She took a bite and quickly spit it out. "Why, it's nothing more than a common meat sandwich," she scoffed—tossing it in the trash.

Feeling Fredo's detachment, she hooked her arm through his and snuggled close. "Darling children…especially, Amelia. Though she's a bit of a ragamuffin. Maybe I could take her shopping and buy her some new clothes. What do you say, baby? She'd like that wouldn't she?"

When he failed to respond, she repeated the question.

"Go get children now."

"But look…the wheel's still broken. The man said it could take hours. That gives us more time to be alone. I know, let's take a gondola ride. It'll be fun and it looks so romantic." She grabbed his hand, and he followed along—reluctantly.

As terrifying as it was to be stuck two hundred and fifty feet in the air for nearly four hours, the children could talk about nothing else for days.

"Oh, Papa, you should have been with us," said Amelia. "It was so-o-o scary."

"I wasn't scared," said Karl. "Besides, he was busy. Weren't you, Papa?"

"When will we see Miss Anna again?" asked Amelia.

"Her name's not Anna," said Karl.

"I like her. She's so pretty," she said, totally ignoring him, "...and she gave me the beautiful glass with the picture of the Ferris wheel."

Somewhere between the mention of her husband's name and the gondola ride, Fredo had determined their affair was over; he could no longer risk the consequences. Parading around with Enid Annan was certain to bring trouble. He needed to do something to protect the sanctity of his family. He needed to redeem himself (*redenção*).

He decided to take a job offer in Prospect.

ELEVEN

On Monday, October 22nd, Amelia rushed home during the lunch hour to check on Fredo. First a morning frost, then a brief but heavy downpour left the sidewalks carpeted with wet leaves. Fall's luster quickly faded into drab dissolution. Running late, she entered through the front door and headed straight upstairs to his room. She was horrified to find his bed empty.

Fallen out again! Maybe he's... She cautiously tiptoed to the far side—dreading what she might find. Nothing. 'Where are you?'

"Papa!" No answer. Panicked, she checked her bedroom. Again nothing. There was a small, spare room upstairs, but it served as a storeroom and remained locked. She rushed downstairs.

Fredo's delirium had reached an apogee in recent days: incessant ranting about sin, the need for God's forgiveness, guilt, being 'lost,' Millie, Clara, his father, someone named Enid and an indecipherable bombast about stone carving, art, cowardice and death. He'd been so weak of late Amelia thought him incapable of standing, let alone descending the stairs.

Maybe he's in the kitchen...or his old downstairs bedroom. She checked them both. *No!* Thinking he must have wandered out into the garden, she opened the kitchen door and stepped onto the side porch. "PAPA!" Then she saw it and gasped. 'Who could have done such a thing?' Her mind was riven with disbelief.

I had some things that I called mine—and God, that he

called his—till recently a rival claim disturbed these amities...

The garden was a battlefield. Someone had smashed every one of Fredo's angel statues.

...the property, my garden, which having sown with care—he claims the pretty acre—and sends a bailiff there...

'He must have heard and somehow...but *how?* And where is he now?' She pushed open the screen door and ran to the center of the garden. Frantically twirling in a panicky pirouette, she spotted Bessie's mother staring at her from her back porch.

Mrs. Sweeney was an unassuming woman, self-possessed and not prone to judgment or gossip. Doubtless, through open windows, she had often overheard Fredo's ranting, his fitful cries echoing through the night. Yet, beyond inquiring, 'How's your father, dear?' she never gave the least indication. However, the agonized look on her face was evidence she had witnessed the desecration.

She's pointing. She saw him. She knows where he's gone. Perhaps she—

Then, Amelia heard the sound, and instantly she knew. She rushed towards the shed. As she entered the open doorway, she was accosted by Fredo's plea, *"Perdonami, Clara!"* Again, hammer struck stone.

A large piece of limestone thudded against the dirt floor and a shower of rock pelted her —a shard gashing her cheek below her right eye. "What are you doing? *Pare, por favor!* Please, stop, Papa! *Pare!"*

"Estou perdido, Ioio! Estou perdido!" Clammy with perspiration and gasping for breath, he slumped against the statue.

"You're not lost...you're right here with me."

Years ago he had carved the angel, a massive Seraph with three sets of wings folded forward, as if to embrace the infant cradled in its arms—offering it up to heaven. It had taken him nearly seven years to complete and it was stunning, both in its intricate detail and its sheer size.

On the base of the statue, in letters six inches high, he had carved, 'MADEIRA.' In ritualistic fashion, he brought both children, not yet teenagers, out to his workshop, which were normally forbidden to enter. While viewing his masterpiece, he made them pledge a solemn oath that one day the statue would take its rightful place on his grave.

Though they never discussed its meaning, Amelia often wondered who the angel cradled, if it symbolized the unborn baby who perished along with her mother. Only recently, she'd thought of the statue and wondered how soon it would serve the purpose for which it was created. Now, one set of wings, along with the angel's forearms and the infant, lay shattered on the moldy earthen floor.

*"Deus…nunca perdoa…*never!"

"Forgive you for what?" She felt a trickle of moisture on her cheek; not realizing it was blood, she smeared it with the back of her hand. "Tell me, why do you need God's forgiveness?

"Peca-a-a-do!" he shouted in agony. *"Si-i-i-n!"*

Three days after his destructive rampage, Fredo died of pneumonia. Lacking any form of anti-bacterial, Doc Simpson had administered a mild dosage of strychnine, but his convulsive reaction prevented its further usage. It was torturous watching her Papa drown in his own fluids, and the last hours of his lung-rattling gasps were excruciating.

Though he'd had no affiliation with the local Catholic Church, she summoned a priest from St. Stephen's to administer last rites. Having passed from the delirium of fever into a state of septic shock, he lacked any awareness of the holy ritual. For that Amelia was grateful, since she knew he would rail against the intercession, particularly the Penance. To her knowledge he had never sought absolution, and she doubted he would accept it if he were conscious. Whatever "sin" he had committed, blaming God had taken the place of seeking forgiveness. Within minutes of the conclusion of the Viaticum, he mercifully died.

Foster Mortuary provided a horse-drawn carriage and a plain wooden coffin to transport his body to the funeral home, where it was embalmed with a solution of arsenic. Originally, a simple graveside service had been arranged, but due to torrential rains, a private ceremony was held Saturday morning in the funeral home's chapel. As there was to be no priest or pastor present, the undertaker, Clayton Foster, asked Amelia if she wanted something read. Instead, she insisted on speaking.

Oh, it's highly irregular for a family member to speak."

"Who better than someone who actually knew the deceased?" she countered. "The last thing Papa would want is some stranger telling others about his life or his struggles…or, even worse, some minister using the opportunity to try and save a soul."

"Hmmm..." intoned Mr. Foster, disconcerted by her bluntness. "Still, it can be very difficult...due to emotions, you know." When she failed to respond, he added, "However, if that's your wish, then of course you should say a few words."

"As I'm paying for your services, Mr. Foster, I'll say as few or as many as I choose."

Because of the short notice, the ceremony was attended by only a handful of teachers, Supt. Johnston and Fredo's former employer, William Hoffman and his wife. Amelia approached the Hoffmans, whom she hadn't seen for several years. "So glad you could come. Papa would be pleased."

"Fredo was a fine worker...a talented man," said William. "Daddy would have been here, too, but he's not feelin' up to par. You know, he'll be seventy-five next spring. Sends his condolences."

Just minutes before the service was to begin, Chester O'Malley and Madeline Jones slipped through the back door of the small chapel and took seats next to Supt. Johnston.

"I wasn't aware students were invited," he whispered.

"I'm here representing the senior class," said Chester, rain-soaked and shivering. "I'm hoping to be able to speak."

"And, I'm here to support Chester and Miss Madeira," said Madeline.

Spotting them, Amelia quickly approached. "Chester? Madeline? I had no idea you were coming."

"Knowing how busy you must be making arrangements, we didn't want to bother you," said Madeline.

"The class asked me to write something in hopes I could deliver it at the memorial. Something to honor the living," said Chester.

"Well, I would be—"

Johnston cut her off. "I was about to tell him how irregular—"

"...honored to have you share whatever you've written."

"I only meant—"

"In fact, why don't you deliver what you have first," she said, once again failing to acknowledge the superintendent.

"You mean now?"

"Slip out of your wet coat and come right on up." She smiled lovingly. "I'm so happy you both came."

Turning to the small assembly, she cleared her throat. When

she had everyone's attention, she announced, "You all know Chester O'Malley..."

The teachers smiled at Chester, who had risen and was draping his coat over the chair back.

"...and Madeline Jones."

Again, they similarly acknowledged Madeline.

"My senior English class asked Chester to compose something for the service, and I've requested he share it with us at this time."

Some teachers nodded approval; a few responded verbally with, "Ooohs." Amelia noticed a couple, Goldie Maddox and Sylvia Adams, who appeared to take umbrage.

"Chester," she said—gesturing towards the podium. She resumed her seat next to Bessie, who reached over and gently squeezed her hand.

Attired in a morning coat borrowed from Willie Stansbury's father, he took his place behind the podium. The coat had been worn only once for Willie's sister's wedding. It was several sizes too large and the shoulders sagged. Still, Chester, who hastily slicked back his wet hair, looked handsome, and his former teachers were impressed by how confident the once morbidly shy boy now appeared. His eyes compassed the small assembly.

"I'd like to begin by reciting a poem by Miss Madeira's beloved poetess, Emily Dickinson." He looked earnestly at her as he began reciting Dickinson's most famous poem, *Because I Could Not Stop For Death.* He recited from memory, his voice clear and confident. However, in the middle of the third stanza, he faltered. Panicked, he glanced at his teacher, whom he knew was silently reciting the lines along with him—appealing with his eyes for help. She mouthed, 'the Fields of Gazing Grain.' He repeated the line and continued on. Amelia exhibited no emotion as she listened. She maintained an approving smile that only Chester could see. When he finished, he looked at her—letting his eyes linger—before continuing on with his interpretation.

"I believe the poet is portraying death as something not to be feared but rather accepted...calmly...as one would a welcomed caller. She takes us on life's journey, which leads from childhood to maturity and, finally, to eternity. Those of us privileged enough to be in Miss Madeira's senior English class feel that she, like her dear Emily, is launching us on life's pathway." With each sentence, his confidence grew.

"In just a few short months, she has taken us from our simplistic, childlike understanding of literature...to a more mature comprehension of how words and ideas create the framework for a more meaningful life. Philosophically, she has broadened our understanding of epistemology. What we know and what we *know* about what we know. The truth of our knowledge." He looked at her with obvious affection. "And like another great teacher, Socrates, she is helping us arrive at these truths...not by supplying answers but by drawing out the answers through probing questions. Likewise, she encouraged us to examine our individual belief systems, to question everything. She has challenged us to follow our passion, to be our authentic selves and to not settle for a life of mediocrity. For this and more, we hold her in the highest regard." With those words, his eyes teared.

Several in the audience were deeply moved by his sincerity and offered encouragement. 'It's okay, Chester.' 'You're doing fine, dear.' 'Go on, lamb.'

He took a deep breath and continued. "I regret not knowing Miss Madeira's father, Godofredo Karel Madeira. But, I do know he was an artist...a man of considerable talent."

"Indeed, he was," said William Hoffman.

Amelia glanced back at him and smiled.

"Artists are often misunderstood by the masses," he continued, "but without them our lives would be reduced to the mundane. True artists transform the turmoil and pain of human experience into something lofty and ennobling...something redemptive. That is the kind of art he produced. He also produced a daughter who has elevated the art of teaching and, among her students, the pleasure of learning. For this, the Class of 1918 and all those to follow will be forever in his debt."

His eyes fell upon Amelia, who was visibly touched. He haltingly returned to his seat by Supt. Johnston, who started to say something but seemed incapable of finding the words. Madeline whispered in his ear. He lowered his eyes, then looked at her as if to say, 'Thanks.'

Amelia sat for a moment—collecting herself. Finally, she stood and faced the gathering. Unlike all the other women who wore some kind of hat, either toques or cloches with veils, her unadorned brunette hair was pulled up and back in a way that resembled a

Grecian style currently in vogue, though it had not yet gained popularity in rural America. It was held in the back by a tortoise shell comb that had belonged to her mother, the only keepsake of Millie's not abandoned in Fredo's hurried departure from Cincinnati. Though some were shocked to see her head uncovered, none was surprised.

"Thank you, Chester. That was...lovely. In time, I can only hope to attain the status to which you have prematurely assigned me." With feigned embarrassment, she scanned the faces of her colleagues. "I appreciate all who have come to show your support at this difficult time. I know how precious weekends can be, and I want to thank you for sharing some of yours with me."

Several teachers smiled and nodded.

"Most of you have known me since I entered second grade in the fall of 1904. Miss Belle was my second grade teacher. Papa brought us to Prospect from St. Louis in a horse-drawn wagon, a trek that should have taken no more than three days but required twice that. Countless times, the wagon wheels were stuck in mud two to three feet deep. If it weren't for the help of his former supervisor and his wife, Mr. Hoffman's sister and brother-in-law, the move would have been impossible." Her mouth was dry and she suddenly realized Mr. Foster had failed to provide the glass of water she'd requested.

"Friends are important," she said—glancing down at Bessie and her mother. "Sadly, Fredo Madeira chose to go through life without them...friendless. *Sem amigos...*"

Several of the teachers visibly shuddered; Supt. Johnston loudly cleared his throat, and others shifted in their chairs. Bessie and her mother tightened their grip on each other. The Hoffmans exchanged veiled glances. Fearing what might be coming next, the air was shrouded with a discernable tension.

"Prospect is a small town," she continued, "and we all know that in a small town, people know...or worse, *think* they know, each other's business. That can be both good and bad. Neighbors can come to your aid," she said—pausing again to acknowledge the Sweeneys. "Or, start a spark of gossip that spreads like wildfire through the community." She managed to take in Goldie Maddox without letting her eyes linger. She would never forget her scathing letter—criticizing Fredo's statue of St. Michael—calling it 'a vulgar display.'

"Perhaps because he was Portuguese...and the only one in Prospect, Papa never permitted himself to get close, to trust others enough to let them see what a sensitive, creative man he truly was. Part of his reticence was his resistance to the English language. His refusal to master it created yet another barrier. Lacking the words, at times, he appeared foolish...*ridiculo* ...blundering. But when it came to his passion, his art, he could express himself like a poet. *Um poeta.*"

As she spoke the word, her voice quavered. She paused, took a deep breath and attempted to regain control. "Other impediments were also of his own creation...or products of his imagination. It was almost as if he somehow managed to feel superior and inferior at the same time. For whatever reason, he set himself apart, chose to be an island...to go through life alone..."

At that very moment, it occurred to her that she was describing herself. She paused and turned to Mr. Foster, who appeared to be nodding off. She signaled for a glass of water. For a few seconds, he stood there, slack-jawed. After regaining consciousness, he disappeared inside.

"If a person feels unworthy of success or happiness...or love, then that person must destroy success, obliterate happiness and reject, yes, reject love whenever it is offered."

Small islands of light—floating on a filmy substance over her eyes—suddenly clouded her vision. She felt energy draining from her body. Caught up in the frenzy surrounding her father's death, she'd eaten little the past few days. Belle Armstrong whispered something in Wilma Sager's ear. Mrs. Sweeney clutched Bessie's arm. Chester and Madeline looked anxious.

Amelia raised her left hand and pressed her fingertips to her temple. "I have...a dear friend who says there are no judgments stronger...than those we...than those we make against...ourselves." Her vision suddenly blurred; the room tilted. She gripped the podium with both hands. "Some say guilt...demands...punishment..."

And with those words, she saw the ground rise up to catch her crumpling body.

Following her collapse at Fredo's funeral service, she spent the entire weekend recuperating in bed. Bessie and her mother checked on her from time to time; others brought food. She insisted she did not want people bringing casseroles and pastries—knowing they would surely go to waste. She possessed no appetite, hadn't had one for days.

A note, written by Bessie and attached to the front door read:

> *'Thank you for your kind concern. Miss Madeira is resting. If you've brought something perishable, please take it next door to the Sweeneys.'*

Making funeral arrangements while attending to her classes had totally exhausted her. Against Supt. Johnston's advice and the admonition of some of the faculty, she had missed only a half day of school. Following her fainting spell, Doc Simpson insisted she be confined to bed.

"Not a thing wrong with you good food and bed rest won't cure," he told her. Doc had been general practitioner to the Madeiras since they first moved to Prospect—treating Amelia's infected tonsils, successfully removing Karl's appendix and nursing Fredo's fractured skull. He had a reputation for no nonsense, straight talk.

"Young lady, I've known you since you was a feisty little girl, and though you may be sharper than a tack, it's about time you learned to listen to someone who knows a thing or two about people who overdo," he said with a tone of genuine concern. Uncharacteristically, he pulled up a chair and sat down by her bedside. Instead of hearing the warning behind his words, she focused on the clichés.

"You're a little high-strung like your daddy was, and just because you're young, you think you can burn the candle at both ends, but I'm tellin' you now...it *will* catch up with you. It already has. You're lookin' like the last rose of summer. Heard Karl's been discharged. That right?"

"What? Oh, yes...hoped he'd be home by now."

"Heard he got gassed up and lost sight in an eye."

"But he's fully recovered now."

"'Member Max Nixon, don'tcha?"

"Considering the damage he did to my family, I doubt I'll ever forget Max. Why?"

"Got shot up pretty bad on one of them U.S. merchant ships deliverin' supplies to the British. Nearly died."

"I was sorry to hear of it."

"He ain't the same boy who went off to war and I don't mean physically. His mama says he don't eat much, can't sleep...cries out in the middle of the night. Any loud sound makes him jump like a rabbit. She told me, and don't be tellin' this to no one, but the other night he come in the livin' room with a gun and threatened to kill her, his daddy and himself."

"..."

"Had one heck of a time talkin' him down. His daddy ended up havin' to restrain him. Tied him to a chair. Summoned me hopin' I could give him some sort of medication to bring him back to his old self, but there are no wonder drugs to take care of what ails Max. He's in Farmingdale. Don't nobody know 'cept a few relatives."

"Poor Max..."

The next morning, she rose early. The silence she'd longed for seemed, in its own way, clamorous, a slight echoic buzz in her ears. Any sadness she felt over Fredo's death was diminished by her long-held need for tranquility. The irrationality of his demands, coupled with nightmarish outcries, had conditioned her to live an anticipatory existence. Suddenly, her newfound freedom was offset by her ambivalence over Karl's return—forming a discomfiting stasis. Caught in this odd equilibrium, she began to question her own infallibility—coloring her need to be relieved of all responsibilities save those at school.

Not since childhood had she felt so vulnerable. What began in innocence, familiarity, curiosity, need... She recalled the deep ache of missing her mother...longing to be held...the pink powdery warmth of Millie's skin...her soft, moist kisses...her cold, lifeless lips... the disorientation of being uprooted...the clamor of horse and wagon...the rumble of train tracks...the endless walking...the discomfort of being carried, dragged...the staleness of that room... the fraternal bond with Karl...the fascination of their bodies...the shame.

Always the shame. Shame—the joy killer! *There's no reasoning with shame. No escaping its power.* 'Better to keep it near,' she thought, 'than to let it disappear into the distraction of the present or the fantasy-turned-fear of the future, only to have it return with a jolt, with every flicker of the old movies, from the guilt...the past...'

'Where to find joy? In the classroom. In the refuge of Literature. In dear Emily's words. But grief...oh, that's easy!' Emily had said it best: *I can wade Grief—whole pools of it—I'm used to that—but the least push of Joy breaks up my feet!*

"Why can't Sarah be here?" she suddenly said aloud.

TWELVE

On her way to collect the weekly mail, Sarah Jamison sauntered down the shade-dappled lane—leading to a rut-filled dirt road a quarter mile from the Jamison farm on the outskirts of Valley Ridge, Missouri, "a hoot 'n holler from the Arkansas border." She paused to pull the blossom of a creeping thistle that had sprung up among the abundant chicory. Primrose and a variety of flowering weeds lined the otherwise desolate road with dots of color. Since girlhood, she had favored the electric blue chicory blossoms, often imaging a dress in that vibrant shade. She studied the feathery pink pom-pom of the thistle in her hand.

'I'm the delicate tuft adorning the prickly thistle,' she thought, 'and Amelia's the vibrant blue blossom of the chicory...a tenacious, irrepressible weed if there ever was one!' She tossed the pink blossom aside. When she reached the mailbox, she paused before checking the weekly mail. 'Someone's going to have to do something before it falls down.' Termites had hollowed the post, likely to be toppled by the next strong wind. Her older brother, David, would have repaired it, but he was off fighting in France. 'Rex is too lazy to do anything resembling actual labor,' she said to herself in disgust. 'As worthless as daddy...so, of course, that leaves mother and me.' The role of dutiful daughter and the thought of being stranded on a farm were becoming more and more oppressive. 'Let the thing fall down. Let the whole farm go to ruination for all I care.' For weeks now, she had regretted her decision to return to Valley Ridge. Amelia had been right in questioning why she'd gotten a teaching degree, only to squander it.

She yanked open the rusty latch and was bombarded by an explosion of hornets—causing her to retreat a few yards. In just one week, they had constructed a large nest in the back of the mailbox.

Tiptoeing cautiously forward, she carefully retrieved the mail, wrapped in a circular—featuring a stylish young woman wearing a Tam and a matching plaid skirt. Draped around her and helping her swing a golf club was a handsome "instructor."   The ad bore the slogan, "*There's a delicious freshness to the taste of Coca Cola.*"

"In what universe do men ever really help?" she said aloud. She quickly sorted through the rest of the mail until she spotted an envelope—bearing a splatter of blood-red sealing wax —stamped with a familiar filigreed "M." As much as she anticipated another letter from Amelia, she recalled how she always felt after reading them...*confused.* Confused and something more, something that left her emotionally depleted.

She picked up a stick and forced the rusted mailbox hasp back into place. Tucking the stack under her arm, she broke the seal on the envelope flap, extracted the letter and began reading as she walked back toward the farmhouse.

Prospect, Missouri
20 October, 1917

My Dear Sarah,
Last night, I dreamed we were sitting in the garden glider swing, your head resting in my lap while I gently stroked your hair. That was no mere dream but a remembrance of our last moments together before you made your solitary return to Valley Ridge. What of our vow to write each other everyday? It seems Time's Chariot Wheels have crushed the promise, or at least delayed its execution...

That night, as she lay in bed, she recounted the ease with which the two young women had become friends; she recalled their first evening together when she had taken a sheet of paper and written down Amelia's full name and date of birth—assigning a number to each letter:

AMELIA	I RMEL I ND A	MADE I R A		
1 4 5 391	9 9 4 5 3 9 5 4 1	4 1 4 5 9 9 1		
23 /5	49 /13 /4	33 /6	= 105/6	(Destiny)
16 /7	24 /6	16 /7 = 56/11/2		(Soul's Desire)
August	14th	1897		
8	14 /5	25 /7 = 47/11/2		(Birth Lesson)

$$3 \qquad\qquad 2$$

$$1$$

$$1 \text{ (Challenges)}$$

Intrigued, Amelia watched in amazement as Sarah quickly recorded what appeared to be an elaborate equation. "What's this…some kind of parlor game?"

"If you prefer, you can think of it as such. Actually, it's called The Science of Numbers. An uncle of mine learned it from the famous Madame Blavatsky, who founded Theosophy. I spent part of one summer with him and his wife in New York."

"Never heard of her."

"She was very controversial. Gave readings for dozens of remarkable people. The famous French actress, Sarah Bernhardt, Mark Twain and Sir Edwin Arnold were all clients. It's based on Pythagoras' theories."

"*Geometric* theorems? That Pythagoras? I thought he was the father of math," said Amelia, who rarely met someone who knew things she herself did not.

"He was also an Adept. He believed music could cure what ailed the soul and that reading poetry, before and after sleep, aided the memory. His followers, the Pythagoreans, lived a very strict, structured life."

"So, what does all that have to do with my name and birth date?"

"He believed everything in the universe is alive, pulsating…vibrating to a certain frequency. Those frequencies have numerical equivalents. If you understood their relationship, life is like a big math problem."

"Really...?"

"Likewise, he said the letters of the alphabet are attuned to certain frequencies. Your name and birth date together reveal your destiny and what you desire to experience while in the physical— including lessons and challenges. In other words, your life is also like a math problem. Totally explainable."

Because she found Sarah so captivating, she tried to hide her skepticism.

"So, Madame Sarah, what do all these numbers tell you about me?"

"Many interesting things, but you may have to suspend your belief...since much of this is based on lives from the past, and, those "7s" in the vowels of your name, indicate how skeptical you are."

"You mean reincarnation? I thought only Hindus and Buddhists believed such things."

"Many scholars are convinced Jesus was a member of a Jewish sect, the Essenes, who believed in reincarnation, one of the reasons he was so despised by the Sadducees and Pharisees."

She further explained that the "16/7s" foretold a lifetime of abandonment—karma reaped from many lifetimes, predominantly male, where she had abandoned others. "The thing to remember is you must learn to love the little girl who lives inside you...for in reality, the past, present and future exist simultaneously...and she's still experiencing everything."

"A little girl...who lives inside me?" she repeated—making an effort to stifle a laugh.

"I'm sorry, I don't mean to...it's just that I—"

"A little girl who believes she could have kept her mother from dying had she herself been more lovable. By judging *her* responsible, it is she you've abandoned, and anytime others threaten to leave you, it's that little girl who suffers the anxiety and loss...who feels responsible for everything and everyone."

Amelia grew quiet.

She said that "6" as a destiny number meant Amelia would most likely become a community worker and a teacher—that through teaching she would have the opportunity to love many of those she had previously judged unworthy of love, and from teaching she could, in turn, experience the love she had adjudged herself unworthy of receiving.

"It's not possible to judge something and love it at the same time. That includes one's self. All judgment locks up energy that has to be released through forgiveness and love."

"The 11/2s indicate you'll have the opportunity to receive much recognition in this lifetime, but if you fail to remain positive, your ultimate reputation could be harmed. They also suggest you have much to learn about relationships...that you don't know how to ask for what you need. Leaving clues no one picks up on can be very frustrating. It's okay to ask for what you need, dear Amelia...*without expectation*...then you won't get your feelings hurt."

And finally, she said her "1" main challenge came from a parent or sibling who attempted to control her—thus, her personal challenge was not to control others, but to "focus on controlling yourself...and that's a full-time job for anyone, wouldn't you agree?"

Amelia's mind sifted through each statement—searching for paradox, weighing each anomaly against what, here-to-fore, was an acceptable version of reality. The metaphysical nature of Sarah's words, though peculiar and abstract, seemed to resonate in a way that left her feeling both exhilarated and overwhelmed.

Looking back, Sarah couldn't believe how forthright she'd been—immediately assuming a role of authority simply because she knew something Amelia didn't. 'She acted so different then. Receptive...even amenable.' What she didn't know was that the more she revealed, the more fascinated Amelia became—not only with the accuracy of the reading.

'Sarah Jamison...Sarah Jamison...it's you've I've longed for. What's Emily's line...oh yes. *I have no Life but this—To lead it here.* Life has led me here to you, dear Sarah. And, thus, real life begins.'

To Amelia, Sarah's unusual beliefs were provocative—which, of course, appealed to her natural curiosity. But, it was Sarah's physical being that truly beguiled her. The blonde and blue-eyed Sarah was grace personified. It wasn't only that she admired her flaxen hair, soulful eyes and statuesque figure, she craved them, as one would fine jewelry. She wanted to slip Sarah on and wear her like splendid attire. Before Sarah Jamison, she had never felt a fire burning in her breast, had never experienced anything close to cupidity. Now, Amelia found herself lusting after the sound of her voice, the lavender soap smell of her skin and the warmth of her presence—wanting, in effect, to possess her.

THIRTEEN

In Chesapeake Bay, a steamer carrying Karl Madeira was boarded by a team of doctors, who began examining returning soldiers for trachoma, a highly infectious eye disease—often leading to blindness. Karl was checked thoroughly for trachoma; none was found. And, though it was seldom mentioned in the press, soldiers were also examined for syphilis and gonorrhea.

"The Army's been lax about this," said the young doctor who examined Karl. "Thousands...and I mean *thousands* have been infected by French prostitutes. It's damn near as big a problem as bullets and bayonets."

When questioned, Karl stated he had never visited a brothel or consorted with prostitutes. "There were only two places I saw in France...the battlefield and the hospital." Upon receiving a clean bill of health, he was permitted to disembark in the Port of Baltimore. Following a series of clerical checkpoints, he was taken to the Mount Royal Station and Trainshed where he caught a Baltimore & Ohio train bound for St. Louis.

Most of the tedious trip was a blur; stops in cities and towns he'd never heard of. However, when the coachman called, 'Next stop, Cincinnati,' it was the first time in years he had even the slightest recollection of his early childhood. With his face resting against the white cotton antimacassar that covered the faded plush of his seat back, he stared out the window past his own reflection, as passing farmland dissolved into a visual memory so visceral, so long buried, its excavation caused him to recoil. It was a fractured image, a flicker floating in and out of his dreams for years, that had somehow managed to avoid his consciousness; he suddenly remembered his parents fighting: the shouting, the shoving, the tears.

The altercation must have taken place shortly before his

mother died, because the fleeting image revealed her to be in advanced pregnancy. There was little Amelia clinging to her mother, both of them crying, and Fredo shouting and pinning Millie against the wall. 'Stop Papa, stop!' he heard himself pleading—tearing at Fredo's pant's leg. Then, a powerful blow and…total darkness.

The accompanying emotion left him feeling slightly removed from his own being, as if he had suddenly come back to an existence he barely recognized. Perhaps, it had as much to do with his return from the hellish theatre of war as it did with the disturbing memory.

"Are you all right young man?" asked the elderly woman seated next to him. Since first boarding the train in Wheeling, West Virginia, she had attempted to engage him in conversation multiple times with little success. However, when she discovered he was a returning veteran wounded in battle, she prompted passengers throughout the car in applauding him for his valor and sacrifice. Although embarrassed, he appreciated the recognition.

"Young man?"

"Fine, thanks," he finally answered—hoping to avoid any further exchange. "Just need to rest a few minutes." He turned back towards the window. Squinting through his right eye at his own reflection, he could see the patch covering his left. It was if he were looking at a stranger.

"Well, I'll be saying goodbye now. Cincinnati's my stop. My granddaughter and her husband should be waiting for me. I can't wait to see my new great-grandbaby. Hope you recover from all your injuries," she said—leaning forward and gently patting his shoulder. "I know your father and sister will be so happy to see you. And, I do hope you find happiness with that wonderful young woman you told us about."

When he failed to respond, she looked at the couple facing them, her expression an indication of how pitiful and sad she found him to be. The elderly man nodded in agreement. 'War's a terrible thing,' he'd said to Karl earlier. 'There are no victors…only victims.' Karl ignored the insight, though he agreed with it.

As the train pulled into the Cincinnati Union Terminal, he continued to feign sleep until she departed. Then, in an act of complete impulsivity, he raced down the aisle, grabbed his bags from the storage rack by the entry stairs and alighted the train. He stood for a moment as if assessing his decision, then headed for the station—passing by the old woman, surrounded by a gaggle of family.

Rather than wait for his transfer to Louisville, he commandeered a ride from Union Terminal to the Fleischer Building, which he learned was the temporary home of records for Hamilton County—following a fire in the old courthouse. It was there he acquired the address of Frieda Gerbacher, his grandmother. When it came to the Gerbachers, Karl knew very little. Fredo never spoke of them, and though Amelia had speculated about their mother's relatives on rare occasion, he had shown little interest.

Though no photographs were available, he had managed to acquire a vague description of Millie from Fredo. As for an explanation of what she was like, the best he could offer was: 'good dancer' and 'terrible cook' *(muito mau cozinheiro)*. That was it, the extent of his knowledge of the mother he scarcely remembered. To that he could now add the distressing picture of his parents struggling, the shouting and hysteria unearthed by the simple declaration, 'Next stop, Cincinnati.'

The Gerbacher home was located on Eichorn Avenue, recently renamed Hatch Street because of the anti-German sentiment pervading Cincinnati. It was a walk of a mile and a half. On the way, he passed by Holy Cross Immaculate Cathedral and cemetery, unaware it was the church where his parent's had married and the churchyard where his young mother was interred.

The houses were simple brick homes, all properly maintained and forming a formidable German fortress; yet, even amongst themselves, the division between Catholics and Lutherans still smoldered. The home at 927 Hatch St. was identical to the other five houses on the block. The porch was just deep enough for the little lattice swing. A simple iron crucifix was attached to the front door, just below a small windowpane.

He wondered what reception awaited him. Having no idea what he would say, he hesitated before knocking. A woman, who appeared to be in her mid-thirties, answered the door.

"I'm looking for Frieda Gerbacher."

The woman stared at his eye patch.

"May I say who's calling?"

"Who is it, Hul?" inquired a voice from inside.

"Tell her…her grandson, Karl. Karl Madeira."

"Oh! My stars, you're Millie's boy!" she cried.

"Mama, oh, mama…it's Millie's boy, Karl!"

"What? Millie's boy, *here*?"

The door opened wider—revealing a small woman who appeared to be in her sixties. When she saw Karl, she slowly brought both hands to her mouth and her eyes instantly flooded with tears.

"You're my Millie's boy."

"Karl. I'm Karl, grandmother."

"Come in," said the younger woman. "I'm your aunt, Hulda…your mother's youngest sister."

She eagerly grabbed his arm and led him into a tiny living room crammed with overstuffed furniture. The walls were papered in faded florals. A large framed print of the Sacred Heart of Jesus, a plaster wall crucifix and several porcelain statues of the Blessed Virgin and Child greeted him.

Frieda Gerbacher wore a plain white apron over her cotton housedress. Her hands were smeared with lard and flour. Her grey hair was done up in tight pin curls and covered with a thick hairnet. "I'd give you a hug, but I'd get flour all over you. I'm baking. Oh, this is such a surprise. You're so *tall*…and handsome. Isn't he handsome, Hul? Set your bags down and come into the kitchen. Are you hungry?"

"I'll give you a hug for the both of us," said Hulda. She moved right in and wrapped her arms around Karl, who awkwardly patted her back.   "Looks like his father, don't he, mom?"

"Oh, I don't know. I can see some Millie there, too. What's happened to your eye, dear? How 'bout some pie?"

For the next two hours, questions were tossed back and forth between the two women like clothing in a fire sale. Though overwhelmed, he was also energized. He skirted around 'why' he'd enlisted right out of high school—saying he felt it his duty. He told about digging tunnels for the Battle of Messines Ridge and fighting under the command of General Herbert Plumer. He explained how he lost sight in his left eye and his lengthy hospitalization. However, when it became apparent that talk of Germany and the war was upsetting him, the subject shifted to Amelia: her brilliant academic record, her writing ability and her first teaching job, St. Louis, Prospect and Sarah Jamison.

He wanted more than anything to ask about his parent's relationship. He soon realized any reference to Fredo was unwelcome; not once did either woman refer to him by name. In fact, his grandmother never asked about him at all. Not wanting to waste this opportunity to discover something about his past, he inquired about his mother.

"She was just a girl," said his grandmother. "Too young...for anything."

There was strained silence until Hulda broke it. "Millie was a lovely girl...a wonderful sister...full of life. She adored music...loved to sing and dance. And books...my, how she loved books. Read to you and your sister all the time. Don't you remember, hon?"

"I don't remember much."

"She had a musical laugh, didn't she mom? Like the sun shining through. And, she loved you and your sister more than anything."

The rest involved stories from childhood, nothing earth shattering or psychologically revealing, but he relished hearing it all. Finally, around 6:30, Hulda's husband, Ralph, came home from work. A burly, raw-skinned fellow, he was a foreman in one of several Proctor & Gamble warehouses in the city. He appeared to be a friendly sort. After some cordial chitchat and a couple of beers, he and Karl retired to the porch to smoke while the women got supper on the table.

"These Gerbacher women are tough," Ralph said with a smile. "I was a Lutheran when I met Hulda, but Frieda wouldn't let me in the house until I swore I was willing to convert. Before she'd let us get engaged, I had to promise we'd raise our kids Catholic. We tried, but Hulda can't have any. Frieda says it's because Martin Luther disrespected the Pope. She can be nasty sometimes."

"Papa was Catholic, but we weren't raised in the church."

"Well, don't tell your grandma. She don't have any good things to say about Fred as it is."

"What exactly happened, do you know? I mean, what caused the rift?"

"That was before my time, kid. Sorry, you're a war veteran, so you ain't no kid. All I know is your mama died...something about an infection from a miscarriage. Couldn't stop the bleeding. I don't rightly know. But, I can tell you her family blamed your daddy and there ain't no changin' minds once they're set."

"What are you two yammering about?" asked Hulda—flinging open the door but then quickly closing it to a tiny crack.

"Lordy, it's freezin' out there! Come in before you catch your death. Supper's ready."

Ralph's salary had recently provided the household with a new Kelvinator refrigerator—replacing the old icebox. Karl had never seen one. In fact, he found having electric lights a novelty. "Keeps the beer cold," said Ralph. "Don't know how we ever lived without it."

"Other than the new school, the courthouse and most businesses around the town square, there's no electricity to speak of in Prospect," Karl said. "They're sayin' once they get the new power plant built, almost everyone in town will have it. Then, maybe we can have a refrigerator like this one."

The rest of the meal was peppered with similar desultory conversation, but it was something totally foreign to Karl. People sitting at the table and talking about the day's activities was a novelty. Growing up, meals were a solemn affair. But this! This was what real families did. There was laughter. There was good-natured reproach. He loved it all. By the time dessert was served, it was approaching 8:30.

"Planning to stay over aren't you?" asked Hulda.

"He most certainly is," exclaimed Frieda. "Don't think he's going to sleep in the train station, do you?"

"You can have the sofa bed…it's right comfortable. I put out a clean towel and washcloth."

"I don't want to be a bother. Saw a hotel between here and downtown."

"Might as well give in now. Remember what I told you about these Gerbacher women."

"Don't you be telling him tales, Ralph, or the Gerbacher *women* may not continue to make your life quite so pleasant," said Frieda.

"See what I mean?"

"I'll need to be leaving out of here pretty early. The train for St. Louis departs at 7:15.

"Call that early?" said Hulda. She looked at the others and laughed. "We'll be up and about by four. Ralph goes to work at five. You boys go smoke while me and mama clean up."

"Don't be encouraging them filthy things. You know tobacco killed your daddy."

"Okay, let's don't get into that," said Ralph—signaling Karl to follow.

"I'll make up the sofa bed," said Frieda. "You can turn in whenever you'd like. It's been real nice having my big handsome grandson here."

The next morning, as he was packing, his aunt slipped him an envelope. "Mama's kept this in the family Bible all these years. It came for Fred not long after he took you all away. Believe it's from his sister in California. Mama never opened it. I wanted to so many times, and planned to once she passed on. But, this is better."

He packed the letter inside his knapsack. *A letter from Aunt Clara. Won't Papa be surprised!*

He said his goodbyes. Hulda kissed him on the cheek and made him promise to write. His grandmother, realizing she would most likely never see him again, wept openly.

"Love that little girl for me," she said. "And tell her to write…927 Hatch Street."

"I will," he promised.

They stood on the porch and watched him depart. He looked back and waved goodbye. They smiled and waved. At the end of the block, he turned to see them one last time—his aunt was embracing his grandmother, who stood with her head in her hands.

On the way to the train station, he stopped by the Holy Cross cemetery. Hulda had told him exactly where to find Millie's grave. He spotted the statue almost immediately. 'Millicent Gerbacher Madeira, October 3, 1879—August 2nd, 1899.'

'Two years younger than I am now. What would our lives have been like had you lived, Mama? If Papa hadn't taken us away? Sunday dinners at grandma's. Overnight stays with Aunt Hulda and Uncle Ralph.'

"Family," he said aloud.

Glancing up at the graceful limestone statue, he suddenly became aware that the mourning girl's thin, flowing gown revealed her breasts, navel and pudenda. He had witnessed the horrors of war: limbs ripped from bodies, faces obliterated. Still, there was something so shocking about discovering the sexuality of an innocent young girl that he fell to his knees in anguish. He tore at his face—ripping the patch from his eye. As the sun turned the sky a pale yellow, he knelt there, prayerfully—sobbing like a child.

For a moment, he considered not returning home, starting life anew far from Prospect. He'd left town in shame, convinced it was banishment for a guiltless crime; however, on the battlefield, it felt more like a death sentence for every sin he'd ever committed. He slowly raised his head and forced himself to look at the statue. 'I have to go back. Papa and Amelia need me.'

Due to the delay in overseas mail, he had not yet been informed of Fredo's death.

FOURTEEN

After a brief layover in St. Louis, Karl took the Iron Mountain Railway train, originally established to deliver iron ore to St. Louis from the mines located between Prospect and Ironton, where it then connected with the Southern Railroad all the way to Texarkana. Prospect's depot was two blocks south of the town square. The only passenger debarking, he found the railroad yard virtually uninhabited except for a brakeman and a porter, who pulled a handcart filled with shipping crates and boxes on the loading dock. A scraggly mongrel trotted along the tracks, headed towards the city dump, less than a hundred yards away.

Memories of unhurried, placid days from childhood flooded in—catching Karl off-guard and revealing a fragility that left him feeling exposed and vulnerable. He recalled countless excursions to Wildcat creek, a quarter mile down the road. He and his buddies skipped rocks and skinny-dipped there every summer. On the ridge above the creek, they'd discovered an ancient Indian burial mound. For the first time since he left home, he thought of the cherished arrowhead collection he kept in an old Red Cloud cigar box—summoning the smell of stale tobacco and the...

CA-CLANG! His reverie was shattered by a metallic thunderclap, the violent collision of metal hitches, as one freight car locked onto another. Like a bolt of electricity, adrenalin shot through him as he dove to the ground. In a panic, he dug into his knapsack and pulled out a revolver. Unholstering the gun, he pointed it in the direction of the blast. The barrel danced about, frantically, in a futile attempt to locate the source of the concussion.

Cautiously, as if anticipating a barrage of bullets, he raised his head. A gust of wind—carrying the acrid stench of burning trash and offal from the city dump—engulfed him. To avoid inhaling what he believed to be mustard gas and burning flesh, he buried his nose in the flap of his canvas jacket. Suddenly, the heavy iron hitches clanged together again—jolting him back to the present. Lowering the gun, he spotted the brakeman and porter—cowering and staring at him with alarm.

He jumped to his feet and waved, sheepishly. "Hey...sorry. I...I...sorry," he stammered—shrugging his shoulders as if to say, 'Don't know what got into me.' He hurriedly retrieved the canvas knapsack and shoved Alex Easterly's old service revolver down inside. Hoisting the duffel bag, he headed out, the crunch of coal bottom ash and boiler slag punctuating every step.

It was Wednesday, November 28th, 1917. The temperature had reached an unseasonably mild sixty degrees. Still breathing heavily from the traumatic episode, he removed his jacket and flung it over his shoulder.

The walk to West 6th was nearly a mile. He crossed the tracks past old wooden grain bins that reeked of wet, moldy corn; a bevy of squawking crows picked at the leavings, while field mice skittered about. A block from the town square, he encountered the Granite Quarry Hotel, even shabbier than he remembered it, the brick foundation, coated with rust-colored clay dust and encroaching moss.

Cutting through the park past Fredo's statue, only the base of which remained, he contemplated stopping by the soda fountain at Prospect Pharmacy. It had been nearly three years since he'd enjoyed a fizzy phosphate or velvety ice cream cone, and he'd spent many desolate hours in the hospital at Ypres—dreaming of soft drinks with chipped ice, malted milkshakes, banana splits and nickel sundaes drenched in chocolate and strawberry sauce. Still feeling adrift, he decided those delectables could wait; anxious to get home, he sprinted across the newly bricked Main Street and headed up Park Street towards the school.

The schoolyard was bustling with young children playing hopscotch, jumping rope, shooting marbles and racing with hoop sticks. A small group encircled two boys rolling in the dirt. He spotted a pretty young teacher with fiery red hair—attempting to break up the wrestling match. He figured it must be the new first grade teacher Amelia had befriended. *It will be nice having that next door.* Catching sight of Miss Belle Armstrong charging towards the melee, he hurried on before she recognized him and ruined his homecoming surprise.

The vision of West 6th filled him with such unexpected joy,

he broke into a run. Sprinting across the side yard, he failed to notice the missing garden statues. He yanked open the screen door and let it slam behind him. Dropping his duffel bag and knapsack, he entered the kitchen as if he were entering a holy sanctuary, reverently. How many times had he longed to walk through this door, to smell dinner cooking on the stove, to sit down with his sister and Papa at the dining room table and devour a home-cooked meal? How often had he wondered if he would ever experience it again?

What remained of an apple cobbler sat, uncovered, in a pie tin on the stove. He dipped his finger into the pan and noisily sucked up the thick cinnamony syrup. *God, how I've missed Sis's food!*

Immediately, another familiar scent engulfed him—a comforting bouquet of the lavender Amelia grew in her garden. It was so redolent of all he had yearned for, it staggered him.

Unable to restrain himself any longer, he rushed towards the stairs. "Papa! Papa, it's me, Karl! I'm home!"

The reunion between Karl and Amelia was a sober one, in tone though not in reality, since he'd 'put a hurt' on a pint of whiskey. Before she could even express her joy over his having arrived home safely, he launched into an inquiry, which to her felt like an interrogation, surrounding the circumstances leading to Fredo's death.

"This is ridiculous. You've been drinking."

"Bought it in Cincinnati," he said—walking to the cupboard and snatching up the near-empty whiskey bottle. In a defiant gesture, he raised it to his lips and took a swig. "Haven't been home for over two years, little Sis, and I walk in the door to find Papa dead. *Morto!* That was a little hard, you know. Not that he and I always got along so famously, but it was a shock finding the house empty and him...gone."

"I wrote you, but the mail was impossibly slow."

"The war's a whole world away from here."

"And I didn't know exactly when you'd arrive."

"So...after all I've been though, are you going to deny me a little drink?"

"I know you've had a hard time, but you have no idea what the past three years have been like for me."

He raised the bottle towards her as if to invite her to continue. Then, he pressed it to his lips and drained it.

"The head injury he sustained turned him into an invalid. He was always out of sorts...sullen and demanding. He ran me ragged—ranting about God this and Millie that. When I got him up...no easy task, he was overcome by dizziness and could barely stand. For the past few months, I've had to dress him and help him use the chamber pot. It was horrible. Night after night, he'd cry out in agony. He experienced the most miserable headaches and he—"

"Don't tell *me* about headaches. I know all about headaches."

"...he was irritable. Couldn't sleep. So, how was I to get any rest? There were days I taught on fumes..."

"Amelia...Amelia, Amelia... I know it wasn't any picnic 'round here, but you can't imagine what war's *really* like," he said—moving closer. He reached up and straightened a stray lock of her hair. "I've missed you, little Sis. God, how I've missed you." He let his hand slide down to her shoulder. "I've seen things...such hor...horrible things. Did I tell you about my friend, Alex? Alex Easterly...?" His whiskey breath caused her to wince.

"You wrote me about him," she said—pulling away slightly. "I believe you said he died from exposure to mustard gas."

He stared at her for a few moments, but his expression was blank. "I can't...talk about this...anymore..." His head nodded forward, then jerked back as if he were falling asleep standing up. "Can't...talk," he said, his voice trailing off again. Then, as if to show he was unaffected by the alcohol, he walked stiffly out of the kitchen to the side porch—pausing momentarily before continuing out into the garden.

Amelia had seen him drunk in the past, but she'd never seen him so subdued. In some ways, she felt as if she barely knew him. It wasn't just the eye patch or his haggard appearance, though both had, at first, distressed her; there was an unsettling baseness, a crudity he now possessed. And, something else. Something missing. Something indefinable.

Since childhood, she believed it her job to find a solution to every problem before it boiled over into a bigger one. In the years following the destruction of Fredo's statue in the town square, she lived in anticipation of his alcohol-induced tirades, many of which involved his frustration in not being recognized for his artistic ability and his frequent denunciations of his son for the court fine that impoverished them. Now, the thought of having to cater to Karl's needs was...

A familiar voice returned her to the present.

"Hello...you must be Karl."

Bessie! She dashed out to the porch. A smiling Bessie was approaching him. Amelia frantically waved—trying to catch her attention.

"And you...*you* must be the new first grade teacher."

"Bessie Sweeney. So pleased to finally make your acquaintance," she said—offering him her hand.

"Not as pleased...as I am." He took her hand and held it. "Amelia said there was a pretty red-haired teacher who took...uh, Miss...uh..."

"Miss Murchinson."

"Yeah...Murchinson. You took *her* place...right?"

She gently removed her hand from his and smiled with downcast eyes.

"Oh, listen...I'm soorry," he said—slurring the word. "Am I...I'm embarrassing you, aren't I? You see...I've not been around...people for a while. I mean, not the kind of people who are... You know what I mean...I just—"

"I know how delighted Amelia is that you're home. She's talked of nothing else for weeks. You know, she's been through so much with your father...his long illness and then his..."

He failed to acknowledge her words. "What happened to the statues?"

"We all so admire what you and the other American troops have done. The sacrifice you..." Her voice trailed off again as he continued to stare past her.

Determined to save the moment, Amelia pushed through the back door. "I see you've met Karl," she said—hurrying towards them.

"Yes, I was just telling him—"

"Papa's statues are gone," he announced in a lifeless monotone.

"I know."

"All gone...every one..."

"I know. Come on back inside now." She gently took his arm and turned him back towards the house.

"You'll have to excuse us. It's been a long, hard trip and he's in need of a necessary quietus."

"He'll be so angry," he mumbled to himself. "So angry..."

"I understand completely. It was nice meeting you, Karl."

Amelia glanced back at her, apologetically.

"Mother asked me to invite you both to dinner tomorrow."

"We'll talk later," she said, as they disappeared into the house.

It took little effort to convince Karl to lie down and rest. He seemed completely enervated. She covered him with a lightweight quilt. After Fredo died, she thoroughly cleaned Karl's old room—trying to restore it to a semblance of what it was like the day he and Max took the train to St. Louis for their induction. Still, it wasn't the room that had undergone a metamorphosis; it was Karl.

"Sorry, Sis" he whispered. "I forgot...Papa's...dead."

"It's all right. Just sleep a little...*dormir*."

She waited until his breathing settled into a steady rhythm before quietly descending the stairs. Determined to slip across the backyard and apologize to Bessie for his behavior and decline the dinner invitation, she first removed his knapsack from the dining room table. Fearing it might contain another bottle of liquor, she opened the flap and reached inside.

Is that...a GUN! Removing it warily, she stared at it in disbelief. "I will not have that thing in the house!" she declared—shoving it in a drawer of the old sideboard. The discovery left her weakened. She pulled out a chair and collapsed onto it. Having anticipated his return for nearly three years, she now found herself confronting thoughts that appalled her, but ones she couldn't defend against. 'What if he'd been killed, then I wouldn't have to...? *Stop it!* 'What if...'

She looked at the rucksack and was seized by the need to search it. Inside, she discovered a bundle of letters bound with twine. Although a few were from Sarah, most were letters she'd written him over the past three years. There was also a creased graduation photo of Sarah that she'd apparently sent him.

"And, what's this?" she said aloud—removing a leather-bound book. "*Le Fantôme de l'Opéra*—by Gaston Leroux."

The inside cover contained ornate script, slightly smudged: '*Pour Mon Cher*, Erik (Karl), *Je reste votre amour*, Christine (Ninette).' Out fell a tintype, the photo of a young nurse wearing a white smock and a head covering affixed with a double Cross—a symbol she recognized from reading *Joan of Arc*—the heraldic Cross of Lorraine. On the back was a faded lipstick impression, surrounded by a crudely drawn heart.

"Well, well, you must be Ninette!"

As she replaced the photo and the letters, she discovered another envelope. "Godofredo Madeira, Rt. 3, Cincinnati, Ohio." 'A letter addressed to Papa from Aunt Clara! *Sealed...and post-marked, San Francisco, March, 1900.*' She grabbed a knife from the silverware drawer. Carefully, she inserted the blade under the seal—slicing open the flap and removing the letter, written entirely in Portuguese.

> Dear Brother,
>
> Not a day passes I don't think about you and wonder how you are. If your Millie had not written me, I would still not know your where-abouts. She seems like such a sweet girl and I would give anything to see young Karel and my niece and namesake. I must ask you, Godofredo, do you blame me? Is that why you cut yourself off from your family?
>
> Papa's last words were, 'Where's my son?' Mama talks about you all the time. You should know, my dear brother, that I have forgiven you for abandoning me. I know how frightened you were, but you can't imagine my fear.
>
> After weeks of...('tortuosa perguntas')...

'Questions of torture? No...torturous questions.'

> After weeks of torturous questions, I finally told Mama the father was Humberto Ribeiro's cousin who had visited here from Cupertino. Papa put on quite the show, acting like he was determined to find Humberto and make him confess. But Mama convinced him it would only bring more ('vergonha').

At the mention of 'shame,' Amelia paused.

> Godofredo, I constantly pray to God. I ask

him to forgive me, and maybe one day he will. I should have lied about the baby. If I had, perhaps you wouldn't have left. There was nothing you could do, my brother. Papa would have denied everything. Mama would have believed him over me. She didn't want to know the truth. I know why you had to leave Godofredo. I know. You could not protect me even though you wanted to! Please do not blame yourself. God punished me by doing what I prayed He would do. The baby died. He lived but a few days...and then, mercifully, he was taken. God rest his soul!

Papa never bothered me again, Godofredo. You should know that much. And, when he died, I never shed a tear. Not one! He took away my childhood. He took away any chance I had of living a normal life. And, for years, it has felt like he took you away from me, too. Please, do not let him continue to have this power from the grave!

I miss you every day, my dear brother. Do you still love me enough to ever want to see me again? Remember how close we were and know how much I love you still. I await your reply.

Your sister,
Clara Amelia

She sat motionless—unblinking. It was obvious Karl suffered from some sort of devastating trauma, but it couldn't be more debilitating than the concussive effect of her Aunt Clara's words. Even though she now realized Fredo's delirium and ceaseless rambling were expressions of life-long guilt from failing to rescue his sister from their father's abuse, the knowledge afforded her no relief.

Sickened, Amelia carried the letter into the kitchen, fumbled for a kitchen match, struck it on the stovetop and let its flame lap the pages before dropping the fiery letter into the ashes below.

FIFTEEN

On a snowy Saturday morning, Chester O'Malley stood on Miss Madeira's front porch—struggling to unbuckle his rubber goloshes, the metal clasps encrusted with snow. Due to the near zero temperatures, several had frozen. He removed his thin cotton gloves and dug at the clasps with his wet fingers, stiff from the cold and glowing a rosy red. The door cracked open behind him.

"There you are...come in, come in."

"Afraid I'll track in snow." His lips were numb and the words stuck together.

"You can't hurt anything."

In an attempt to remove any loose snow, he stomped his feet several times on the porch.

"Hurry, dear, you're letting in the cold. Kick off your boots on this old braided rug and come stand by the stove. I just stoked the fire."

There was a large enameled pan full of water sitting atop the old potbelly stove—vapors rising as from a fumarole. When Chester moved closer, he noticed stems of lavender floating in the steaming bath.

"Is that what smells so good? Lavender, isn't it?"

"Just trying to keep a little moisture in the air, but I do love the fragrance. I have a garden full of it every summer. Every fall I make lavender soap. Got the starts years ago from Miss Minnie."

"I was sorry to hear she's failing."

"She's not been well for some time. Go ahead...warm yourself."

He held his hands over the steamy water—rubbing them together. "Mother said she's planning to go live with her sister in Ironton. Guess she'll be selling her house."

"That's the plan. How is your mother? I haven't seen her for a while."

"She's...fine."

"You know, my brother's working for Herb Müller now. He passes by your father's shop on his way to the lumberyard. He sees Blackie every now and again, but says he almost never sees Pearl."

"Is he at work today?" he asked—hoping to change the subject. "I mean...I didn't know if he worked Saturdays, and with the weather and all..."

"Left around six this morning. Here...hand me your coat and muffler."

He unbuttoned his old wool coat. Removing it, he stuffed the hand-knitted muffler down one sleeve and handed her the coat. As she hung it on the coat tree by the foot of the stairs, she noticed a missing button. And then, the oddest thing...

At that very moment, she realized how much she'd come to love this brilliant young man, who not only enlivened her classroom but also challenged her daily. He'd recently missed two days of school, due to a bronchial infection, and his absence had noticeably altered her mood, her eagerness to teach. She had planned a special lesson, one she knew he'd appreciate. But, learning Chester was ill, she assigned a short story instead, and asked students to read it while she graded test papers. As her fingers traced the thread holes, it occurred to her that in a few short months, he would be gone.

"Is something wrong?" he asked—startling her.

"You're...uh...missing a button..."

"Pardon?"

"A button," she said—pointing.

"Oh, that. I thought, perhaps, it was a euphemism...like having a screw loose." He pointed to his head and made a comical face. "It was a joke."

"Hilarious," she finally said, with an embarrassed grin.

He smiled back, and for the first time she noticed he had but one dimple, which somehow made his smile even more endearing.

"I could sew one on for you if you'd like. Might have one that would almost match."

"Thanks, but right now I'm anxious to have you read the essay. It's in my coat pocket."

"Which...this one?"

"The other," he said. "It's okay, just reach in and get it."

She pulled out the folded papers.

"It's five pages...both sides. I wrote rather small to save paper. May be slightly more than the fifteen hundred-word limit. I lost count."

"If so, we'll have to edit it down. Later, we'll go up to the school and use Mrs. Dean's typewriter."

"It's that illegible?"

"The penmanship's fine. I just think it would look more professional typed, and I'd like to have a carbon. May I?" she asked—indicating the essay.

"That's why I'm here."

She brushed past him and took a seat at the dining room table.

"I beg you...employ your keenest critical eye."

"My only intention is to help, not criticize. Besides, I know virtually nothing about this...what do you call it...?"

"The undifferentiated aesthetic continuum," he said—pulling out a ladder-back chair and plopping down beside her. "As a form of literary criticism, the whole Western approach is relatively new, but as it relates to aestheticism, the Asians incorporated it decades ago."

"Whatever gave you the idea to apply it to one of T. S. Eliot's poems?"

"My aunt Clarisse, the one who lives in St. Louis, sent an article on Eliot that appeared in the *Post Dispatch*. It mentioned he'd read the *Bhagavad Gita* and the *Upanishads*. Dabbled in Sanskrit, too. The Eastern influence is there in his work. That's when I got the idea to apply that aesthetic to *The Love Song of Alfred J. Prufrock*, and study the continuum between the aesthetically given self and the aesthetically natural object."

"Interesting..."

"You knew Eliot grew up in St. Louis?"

"Not until you mentioned it. Honestly, I'm not that familiar with his work, but when you told me his grandfather helped found Washington University, I thought if we could get someone to publish your critical essay on one of his poems, maybe it would open the door to your receiving a scholarship there."

"Let's hope," he said, "if for no other reason than to permanently silence my father."

"Chester."

"Sorry, but nothing I do pleases him. Besides, he's a total embarrassment and getting worse. Twice last summer, we found him passed out in the park. He owes everybody in town. Rainey's won't let mother put anything on account anymore. No one will. You can't imagine what it's like living with someone who cares more for his liquor than his own family." He gestured towards the essay. "See what you think. I'll just sit idly by."

She slipped on her reading glasses and smoothed the wrinkled pages. While she read, he scanned the room. Other than the crocheted tablecloth and a few knickknacks on the sideboard— including what he recognized as the commemorative glass from the World's Fair—the room lacked any "homey touch." The one bright spot was a huge Christmas cactus—cascading from a metal washtub—on a footstool by the double window; the blood red blossoms lent vibrant color to the dreariness. Next to the ancient plant sat an old rocking chair. He noted the armrests, polished smooth like river stone from years of wear.

Inconspicuously, he studied his teacher. Her large dark eyes were her most prominent feature. They matched her silky brunette hair and her thick eyebrows. Her skin was flawless, except for a little mole on her right temple. Admittedly, her prominent nose, cheekbones and jaw-line were not overtly feminine; still, he couldn't understand why the other boys didn't consider her attractive. He guessed it was because they found her so intimidating. Personally, he loved her self-confidence, how she refused to kowtow to Johnston and Robertson—to anyone for that matter.

He looked closer. 'Is that rouge?'

She suddenly looked up—aware of his penetrating stare. He quickly looked away.

"What? I'm reading slowly, I know, but some of this is very technical."

"You mean boring," he said, relieved she'd misread his attention.

"Not in the least. I mean scholarly."

"Oh, dear…that sounds boring."

"Hush up now and let me finish."

"*Pardonnez moi, Mademoiselle. Je serai discret comme une souris!* Quiet as a mouse," he silently mouthed—pretending to zip his lips before breaking into a wide grin.

She couldn't help noticing how much more self-assured he seemed than the halting, reticent boy who first appeared in her classroom. 'This is not the same timid young man Miss Orton described…far from it.' *Fragile? Delicate?* 'Now there was a description that deserved *ignortoning*. Though she would never admit it, she was glad none of her female students seemed attracted to him; certainly, none was remotely intellectual enough to interest him or understand him.

It appeared to him that Amelia was re-reading many of the paragraphs. He assumed it was because she found them confusing. Finally, she stopped and removed her glasses.

"Tedious, wasn't it? Pedantic? You can tell me…promise I won't be offended."

She slowly refolded the essay—her eyes avoiding his.

"Well, say something. Did you hate it?"

At last, she looked up at him, quizzically. "Where did you

come from?"

His eyes narrowed.

"I mean no offense, but it's difficult to believe you're the offspring of those two people. It's like when Hephaestus split Zeus' head open with an ax and Athena sprang forth...fully formed and armored. I'm not sure how, but from somewhere, you, Chester O'Malley, have sprung fully formed and brilliant, with a voice of sheer intellect and an uncanny mastery of language. A gift from the gods...and all the armor you'll ever need."

He blushed, and for an instant, she felt the impulse to kiss his dimpled cheek.

"Does that mean you liked it?"

"The word doesn't begin to do justice."

He looked deep into her eyes. Neither looked away.

"Admired?"

"Yes, but something more...much more..."

"Does that mean...you loved it? Really loved it?"

*   *   *

When word spread that Karl Madeira was clerking at Müller's, the small talk in Luke's Barber Shop centered on Herb Müller's reasons for hiring him.

"I'm tellin' ya, since America entered the war, Herb's lost more business to Nance's Lumber over in Ironton than you can shake a stick at. Why else do you think he hired Karl?" asked Luke Phillips, Prospect's only barber.

Charlie Wirth, Clyde Grantham and Vern Jennings, one of the few remaining locals who fought in the Civil War, gathered almost daily at Luke's. Occasionally, one got a haircut. Today, Vern, still alert at age seventy-four, was getting a straight-razor shave as the others conversed.

"I ain't givin' my business to no Hun. I don't care if he hires John J. Pershing hisself!" Charlie Wirth scoffed.

"Hun? What the devil's wrong with you? We both went to

school with Herb Müller. Your sister, Winnie, almost married him," said Clyde Grantham.

"Stop it, you...two," sputtered Vern, who burst into laughter, followed by a coughing jag.

"Hold still, Vern, I darned near slit your throat," said Luke.

"If yer gonna do it, make sure ya cut an artery. I don't wanna bleed to death slow like General Albert Sidney Johnston did at the Battle of Shiloh."

"Wake up, Clyde," barked Charlie. "It don't matter how long we've known Herb. It's 1918, and need I remind you...we're still at war. All I can say is, Karl Madeira gettin' hisself all gassed up won't make a tin-penny damn bit a difference when people need lumber or seed. Folks 'round these parts ain't gonna be givin' their hard-earned cash to no German sympathizer whether they know him or not."

"German sympathizer? I swear to God, Charlie, you've done lost your mind."

"I'm surprised he'd wanna work for Herb," said Luke—squeezing a moist towel and wiping dabs of shaving soap from Vern's face, "...seein' how the Jerries took his eye and all."

"My stars...you're startin' to sound like Charlie. Are you blamin' Herb for Karl gettin' gassed?"

"Not directly."

"Good to hear," said Clyde.

"But, you gotta admit there's a connection," said Charlie.

"Whoa, boys! Look over yonder in the park," howled Luke—grabbing a cobalt blue bottle of aftershave from a long row of colorful bottles. "There goes Blackie headin' for the hotel. Look at 'im! Deep in his cups, and it ain't even noon."

"Don't know why Pearl puts up with him," said Clyde. "Fine woman. Feel sorry for her."

"D'ja see where that oddball kid of his won some damn prize?" asked Charlie."

"It was a poem printed in a book of poems...or somethin'. Heard he's some kind of genius," added Vern.

"Queerer than a three dollar bill, if you ask me."

"The poem or the kid?" asked Vern, who then elicited a tortured tobacco wheeze.

"Both, likely," said Charlie.

Luke and Vern cackled like a couple of brood hens.

"Karl's sister had a lot to do with it gettin' printed and all," said Luke. "Read somethin' 'bout it in the *Banner*."

"She's a queer one, too...always was."

"Did any of you people even read the article?" asked Clyde. "It was a pretty big deal."

"Speakin' of that," said Vern, "I 'spect Karl gettin' hired had a heap to do with Doc's letter in the *Banner*...sayin' how badly boys returnin' from war need a job. Know a little somethin' about that myself. Why, I remember when I got back from the war in '65, I had—"

"Aw, no more of them sad 'ol Civil War stories. Heard 'em all a thousand times," said Charlie.

"Vern's right in sayin' Doc's article probably influenced Herb in hirin' him, though," said Luke—shaking a puddle of cologne into his palm.

"Not that Bay Rum," Vern protested—waving him away. "Whew-ee Lord!"

"You might oughta said somethin' 'fore I went and wasted it. This here's Ogallala Bay. Costs a pretty penny," said Luke—rinsing his hands in a pan of soapy water and drying them on a towel.

"Muriel says it makes me smell like a floozy...like some of them gals at the hotel."

"Ya want cologne or not? Makes me no nevermind."

"Pardon me, *ladies*," said Charlie, "but we're havin' a serious discussion here. And if ya wanna know the truth, Doc did more harm than good writin' that sentimental bull crap to the editor."

"How'd ya mean?" asked Clyde.

"For all we know, Herb Müller may be shippin' our dollars over there to help pay to kill our boys."

"Charles Grantham Wirth! What in the Sam Hill's gotten

into you? Cousin, that's the dumbest damn thing I've ever heard you say," said Clyde in disgust. "And in the fifty years I've known you, you've said a heap of dumb things!"

SIXTEEN

"Nothing means anything until we assign it a meaning."

"Here we go," Willie whispered to Chester. "She's off and runnin'."

In one week, the seniors in Miss Madeira's English IV class were to graduate. Madeline Jones would be named Valedictorian. Thanks to Wendell Robertson's incomprehensible speech ('Pahthahgorush') and his undeniable incompetence ('thuh Cohsine ish oppuhshit the hypothuhnush') he managed to destroy Chester's love of Geometry and Trigonometry. Those sub-par math grades prevented him from achieving straight "E's," thus demoting him to class Salutatorian.

For her part, Madeline, who had sacrificed friendships for grades, would receive a small stipend from the 3rd District State Normal School—Miss Madeira's alma mater, which she would attend for only one semester before transferring to Draughon's Practical Business College in St. Louis. Chester's essay entitled, "Reality and the Undifferentiated Aesthetic Continuum: A Reflection on Eliot's *The Love Song of J. Alfred Prufrock,*" was published in the March Edition of *POETRY* magazine with the Editor's note:

> We are delighted to print, for the first time, a splendid essay by a high school student— one Chester O'Malley of Prospect, Missouri. To date, we have never published an essay unless it is

of the highest quality work from a noted academic, but an exception was made due to the learned and scholarly nature of Mr. O'Malley's excellent exploration of a fairly new and not commonly explored area of literary thought: 'the undifferentiated aesthetic continuum,' and how, in this case, it relates to Thomas Stearns Eliot's acclaimed poem, "The Love Song of J. Alfred Prufrock."

We feel we would, as a nod to Eliot's epigraph, be condemned to the eighth level of Dante's "Purgatorio" had we failed to publish this erudite and, frankly, extraordinary accomplishment by a youngster from America's heartland (and surely, no longer its literary wasteland!). We predict great things from this exceptional young man.

POETRY also extends kudos to his English teacher, Miss Amelia Madeira, who encouraged young O'Malley to submit his work.

Harriet Monroe,
Founder & Editor

It had been Amelia's idea to use the essay as a springboard for him to gain admission to Washington University. She submitted a glowing letter of recommendation, along with some of Chester's best work—including the March edition of POETRY. Though he would have to secure a part-time job to afford incidentals, everything else— his tuition, room and board and textbooks —was to be covered by scholarship.

"What gives a person's behavior meaning is determined by the observer—which may be totally in conflict with the person being observed," she explained. "What does that suggest?"

All eyes turned to Chester, who in the past few months

preferred to be called Chet.

"That there is an illusory nature to meaning," he said, confidently.

"Illusory nature," Melvan repeated—giving a puzzled shake of the head. "Ain't he a doozy?"

"Yes, exactly," she continued. "For instance, in the poem, *I Felt a Funeral in My Brain*, we assume Dickinson is writing about a descent into madness. Those observer-critics indicated she was writing about herself, her loss of connection to reality. Madeline, why do you think this observation is accurate or inaccurate, and can you cite another Dickinson poem to support your opinion?"

"Truthfully, I have difficulty with this type of in-depth poetry analysis. Perhaps you should ask Chet."

"It distresses me to think that when you are challenged, you almost always capitulate, yielding to Chester…Chet, or feign the lack of ability to reason out an answer. Believe me, I understand the cultural bias that says a woman is somehow intellectually inferior to a man, but I beg of you, do not give in to this tyranny. And, whenever or wherever you encounter this antiquated thinking…*demur!* That goes for all you young women. You can't clamor for equality and not demonstrate you're deserving of it."

"Madeline ain't…isn't the only one," said Raymond Miller. "Sometimes, I think you and Chet are talkin' in a foreign language."

Other members of the class nodded in agreement.

"When, exactly, do you think we'll ever use poetry or Shakespeare in real life?" asked Daisy.

"Yeah, I'm gonna be a farmer like daddy," said Melvan. "Doubt Emily or Uncle Walt's gonna help me plow a straight furrow."

The class roared, even Chester.

"It is my hope, students, that no matter what career path you choose…be it farmer, homemaker or scholar, you will continue to enrich your lives through poetry. Literature is the alchemy that turns the base metal of life into something golden, something precious that enriches the spirit."

No one smiled. There was no whispering, no aping or mockery, no mumbled protests or eyes rolled in disgust. It had taken months, but as a group, there was now a genuine appreciation for the economy, the clarity, the precision of the perfect word and the rhythmic power of a dynamic phrase that might reveal a simple truth or enlighten human experience.

"I think you forget how far you've come. Before this year, some of you had never read an unassigned book." She moved around to the front of her desk.

"Raymond...you told me how much you enjoyed *The Adventures of Huck Finn,* how efficacious it was in helping you understand the immorality of slavery.   And, how it led to a discussion about prejudice with your father."

"Effi...*what*?" he asked, instantly realizing he should have let it pass.

She slowly raised an eyebrow.

"I know...look it up," he said—hopping up to retrieve a dictionary.

Her glower melted into a smile.

"Daisy...remember how transformed you were by *Madame Bovary*? You declared you would never let your life be about acquiring objects."

"I felt sorry for her. I'll never let myself be trapped like that...never."

"I'm happy to hear it. So, then, it's rather ironic you would ask when literature will ever be used in real life—especially due to Emma Bovary's fondness for reading and how it shaped her existence."

She moved towards the windows—raising one to let in some fresh air.   Turning back, she spotted Melvan. "Do you remember how impressed you were by Thoreau's accounts of Walden Pond in *Life in the Woods*?"

"Yeah...I liked it pretty good. But, that was about *real* stuff, not all that made up rigmarole."

"Non-fiction will continue to inform your lives as long as

you live…just as works of fiction still impact readers' lives millennia after they were written. Such is the unparalleled force of literature."

"If you say so," said Melvan, with a shrug of his broad shoulders. "Though I did kinda like some of them weird stories…by what's his name."

"Edgar Allen Poe," said Maisy.

"Yeah, him. The one about the buried heart."

"The *Tell-Tale Heart*," said Willie.

"Uh huh…and that other one…you know, about that creepy house. I liked them pretty good."

"Speaking of Poe, Maisy…in your essay on his short story, *Leigia*, you discussed how its Romantic themes contrasted with those of the previous century. That's comparative literature…something that may have never occurred to you previously, but is an indication you are now able to compare and contrast, to analyze and synthesize in ways you were unable to do only a few short months ago."

"So, what you're saying is…you're a better teacher than Miss Orton," said Maisy, who had softened towards her of late.

"Certainly not. All I'm saying is you're a better student now because you have acquired the ability to think more comprehensibly. I take no credit…for I have no control over when someone will or will not become a better thinker."

"Well, you sure did get Chet over his shyness," said Willie. "I'm not sayin' he wasn't always a heck of a lot smarter than the rest of us, but tryin' to get him to talk in class used to be like pullin' teeth."

"Now you can't get him to shut up!" said Melvan.

The class, including Chester, laughed.

"Thanks, Melvan," he said, happy to be the butt of any joke that made him feel more accepted.

"How'd we do, Raymond?"

"Efficacious…'effective as a means, measure or remedy.'"

"Make sense?"

"Yes, M'am."

As she walked back towards her desk, she slowly scanned

their faces. Had it only been nine months since she first stood before them? *Look at the transformation.* Even those who resented her taking the place of their beloved Miss Orton, those who griped about keeping a journal, who resisted every assignment requiring them to interpret, to compare and contrast, to create—even those were changed. The changes were not only internal but also external. Visible. She felt a rush of emotion…and that emotion was love.

Just look at them. I do…I love them.

"Dear students, I want you to know it has been my distinct pleasure to be your English teacher this year. Truly, I have learned as much from you as you have from me…perhaps even more. Personally, this was a very difficult year, but it was made easier knowing I could come to school and be uplifted by your enthusiasm to learn. As my first English IV class, you will forever hold a special place…a special place…in my heart…" With those words, her voice broke.

"I never thought I'd say this, but you made me want to come to school."

"Why, thank you, Raymond."

"I was afraid I'd miss some crazy thing you might say or do."

Again, the class howled.

"I think we should give Miss Madeira a round of applause for makin' us better thinkers," trumpeted Melvan. "Come on, I ain't kiddin'!"

The class applauded. Several of the boys whistled.

She was genuinely moved, but when she saw tears streaming down Chester's face, she excused herself and hurried from the room.

SEVENTEEN

Though the 1917-18 school year officially ended Friday, Amelia spent the following Monday morning organizing textbooks and discarding papers. Lost in her work, Chester startled her.

"How long have you been standing there?"

"Not long. Do you need any help?"

"Actually, I could use some help toting these old McGuffey Readers and ancient grammar books back to the library. I've convinced Mr. Johnston to replace them with something published this century. There was a little reluctance, but I finally succeeded in persuading him."

"You're very persuasive. I imagine his argument sounded something like, 'Now, Miss Madeira, good grammar don't change from century to century.' Come on, admit it, that's close."

"Actually, I think he said, 'the business of grammar'." Normally, she would not have made any comment she considered unprofessional, but this was Chester and he was now a graduate. Over the past few months, they had grown exceptionally close.

"So, what brings you to school on this fine spring day? I should have thought by now you were more than ready to be done with Prospect High."

"I came…to see if you were here."

"How nice. If you don't mind, grab those and follow me."

He picked up a large stack of books and followed her out of the room. "I saw Karl down at Müller's and I asked about you. He said you were either at home or at school. I stopped by your house, but—"

"Is something wrong?" She paused to study his face. "More resistance from your father?"

"No, nothing."

They entered the library. "Set them down here," she said—indicating a long table just inside the door. "Right there, thanks. I'm thinking of starting a county library downtown if we can find the proper building. These old books and dozens more like them would have a home."

He had never seen his teacher in such casual attire. She wore a dark navy cotton skirt with a light blue sash and a white dotted Swiss blouse from her college days. Instead of a clasp, she'd pinned up her hair loosely and attached a bright blue ribbon.

"So...nothing's wrong?"

"No, I'm just a little bored at home, and thought I'd see what you were up to."

She stared at him with an amused expression.

"That didn't come out right...sorry. What I meant to say was...I wanted to see you." He could feel the heat at his throat and he knew he was blushing. "Is it all right? I mean, do you mind me being here?"

"Of course it's all right. Why wouldn't it be?" She started back towards the door and without breaking stride added, "As long as you're here though, you may as well help me with the rest of the books."

"Happy to oblige."

They worked in relative silence for the next few minutes. When they finished, both repaired to the library office.

"I wish I could offer you a drink, but I'm afraid Mr. Stokes turned off the water in this part of the building. Some plumbing something or other. Mr. Johnston's gone to Ironton for a district meeting. Robertson's working on his farm trying to get in some planting delayed by the spring rains."

She sat down and began restacking papers as she continued

to explain everyone's whereabouts. "Mrs. Dean would normally be busy in the office entering last minute grades in the permanent records, but I think she's taken advantage of Johnston's absence. Can't say I blame her. They pay her virtually nothing and between you and me, she runs the school."

He sat in silence, but it was obvious he wanted to say something. She waited a moment to see if he had a comment to add. When he hesitated, she continued.

"Bessie...Miss Sweeney...was planning to come with me and work in her room, but her mother asked her to run to Rainey's for some fruit jars. She's planning to make some strawberry jam as soon as the berries ripen. They have a large patch in their backyard. Her mother makes the best jams and jellies you've ever—"

"I love you..."

She was dumbstruck.

"I do...I love you, Miss Madei...Amelia."

"Don't Chester...why would you say such a thing?" She jumped up and moved to the office door—closing it behind her. She suddenly wished she hadn't. What if someone comes?

As she started to reopen it, he swung around to face her.

"Because it's true...that's why."

"Whatever makes you think that...is just a feeling of...of gratitude...for me helping you with your college applications and such. Just affection associated with kindness, that's all."

"I know what love is. I've been in love before. I know what it is and what it isn't, and I'm telling you, I love you. I wish you'd believe me." His eyes instantly brimmed with tears and his voice sounded hollow—submerged.

"Don't you see—"

"Please, let me finish," he said—wiping away a tear with the back of his hand. "Before you came here, I was the saddest person you can imagine. Lonely. Misunderstood. Etiolated. Do you know that word?"

"I...I believe it means drained of color."

"Deprived of sunshine...and that's what life was like,

except for the little ray of love my mother dared to share for fear of enraging my father. Without books, I don't know what I would have done. But, then you came and everything changed. I changed...because of you."

Blindsided by his words, she was speechless.

He rose and moved closer. "Your words...your intelligence...your need to know. The French have a word for it, *curiosité*. It means so much more than just being curious. It's a hunger for knowledge, a nagging need. Without it, life is dull...purposeless. Because of you, I suddenly realized the life I was living didn't have to be the one I would always live. It no longer seemed necessary to be less than myself just to have people accept me. I know it sounds like you gave me hope, but it's more than that. We connect, you have to admit it."

His intensity made her look away.

"We share all kinds of interests, commonalities others disdain. Don't you see, Amelia...I think you're beautiful." He reached and took her hand in his.

"Oh, no more...please..." She pulled away. "I don't know what to say, and it's so stuffy in here I can hardly breathe."

He moved to the window and raised it. "May we sit? This is awkward enough," he said.

She tried to appear composed though she felt her heart palpitating. "Take my chair," she said—pointing to the one behind her desk. "I'll sit here."

When she was seated, he sat, leaned forward with his elbows on her desk and peered straight into her eyes. "I'm not asking whether or not you have any feelings for me because I know you do."

"You have to understand—"

"Please let me say what I need to say, what I've needed to say for some time now."

She lowered her head and nodded, 'Go on.'

"I'm not like other people. When I was younger, I thought I was, but then I learned I wasn't, and I had plenty of help in that department. I've always been attracted to people who are kind-hearted...like Willie. Or, intelligent. Though until I met you, I didn't know many of those, except some I encountered in books." He smiled at the absurdity of his own words.

"What I'm trying to say, and this isn't easy...is that the gender of a person isn't the issue. Not with me. That kind of thing doesn't matter. It's about connection. People have always tried to make me feel ashamed of who I am, but for some reason my understanding isn't affected by others lack of understanding."

"I know what you're saying," she answered without hesitation.

"I know you do."

For a moment, she wished she could tell him about her feelings for Sarah. And, some part of her wanted to share her feelings for him as well, but she knew that was impossible. Impossible! She suddenly became aware of the uncomfortable silence. He seemed to be waiting for her to be present again.

"When you were in school here your senior year...I always wanted to know you, but I was just a skinny little freshman and I knew there was no way. But you're what now...twenty-one, twenty-two? And, I'm eighteen and a half. That's only a couple of years difference."

"That's not the problem."

"My mother was barely sixteen when she married my father, and they had nothing in common. We connect. You know it's true. Why is it so impossible to think I would find you attractive? Or, is it me? Are you not attracted to me...because it sure feels like you are?"

"Before you say any— "

"Whenever we're together, I—"

"Chester...Chet! Before you say anymore, you should know this conversation is totally inappropriate. If Johnston were to walk in and hear any of this, I'd be terminated immediately."

"Well, thank God he's in Ironton, though I'd love to see that constipated look on his face."

"Seriously…this is…this is—"

"Uncomfortable, I know, but I've wanted to have this conversation for months." He ran his fingers through his hair and shifted in his chair.

"Admittedly, I don't know how any of this would work. Thanks to you, I'm going away to university in September, and I'll be gone for most of the next four years…except for an occasional trip home. I know you have your job, but there are plenty of teaching jobs in St. Louis. I'm not saying you have to move there right away. I don't even know what I'm saying, but—"

"What you're saying is…this is an impossible situation."

"Improbable, yes, but not impossible. If I were twenty-one and you twenty-four, who would object?"

"But you're not. You're my student, Chester…my student."

"Your former student."

"All right, yes, my former student…but you're only eighteen. Granted, in some ways you're very mature for your age, and you're the smartest person I've ever known, but the reality is—"

"Tell me you don't care for me, and I'll leave now and never bother you again."

"I don't want you to say that kind of thing ever. I'll always care what happens to you. I've loved having you as a student…and I'm very fond of you. You're brilliant and your future is limitless. I will always want to know how you are and what you're doing. I will always be proud of your accomplishments…wherever they take you."

"Tell me now you don't love me!"

"Please don't shout. Mr. Stokes is still in the building."

"Think I care if Mr. Stokes or anyone else hears? I have never loved anyone as much as I love you."

"Stop this right now!" she said—covering her ears.

"Just say it…do you love me or not?

"I love your mind…yes."

"That's not what I'm asking. Say it! PLEASE, just say it!"

"NO!"

"No, you won't say it…or no, you don't love me?"

"No…I can't love you, Chester…I ca-a-n't…" She covered her face and began quietly sobbing. She struggled to regain control so she could speak. "Don't you…understand? I love you…but I can't love you!" She slowly raised her head. The door was open and he was gone.

What just happened…? No, no, no! Oh, Chester! Chester!

Amelia sat for a moment, stunned, when she suddenly detected the 'whisk, whisk' of Mr. Stokes' broom in the distance. She froze—her stomach knotted. She quickly dried her tears. The sweeping sound grew louder; she saw him emerge from Miss Clark's eighth grade room at the end of the hall—sweeping paper and dirt towards a larger pile in the middle of the hallway. Cautiously, she moved towards the door. That's when he spotted her.

"Still at it, Miss Madeira?" he called, his voice echoing down the empty hallway.

"Yes…but I'm about finished for this morning. You?"

"Always plenty to do."

She closed the library door behind her and started down the hall towards her classroom. A diffused blue light spilled into the darkened corridor from the open classroom doors—casting an eerie glow. She felt like she might be sick to her stomach. This would require all her Thespian skills; she steeled herself. Approaching him, she gestured, "Just need to get a few things from my room…then I think I'll call it a day."

"D'ja see the O'Malley boy? He was lookin' for ya."

"Uh…Chester? Yes… He was good enough to help carry some of those heavy old textbooks into the library for me."

"Nice young man. Smart, too."

"He certainly is."

"Heard he's off to college."

"Washington University."

"Well, ain't that somethin' now?" he said in amazement. "Guess you'll miss havin' a special one like that around."

She offered a slight nod, careful not to reveal any emotion.

"Asked me if I could use any help this summer. Said he needed to make some money before headin' off to college. 'Spect he'll need plenty livin' in the big city. Told him I could always be usin' help, but doubted Johnston would go for it...him bein'...ya know, kinda close with a penny and all."

"Yes, well...I'd better be going. Don't work too hard, Mr. Stokes."

"Try not to. Have a nice summer vacation, Miss Madeira. Ya earned it. Kids these days...ain't they somethin'? I swear, people don't know what teachers put up with. If they did, yall'd get a nice big raise instead of complaints about workin' only nine months outta the year."

"Yes, if people only knew..."

PART TWO

There is a pain—so utter—
It swallows substance up—
Then covers the Abyss with Trance—
So Memory can step
Around—across—opon it—
As One within a Swoon—
Goes safely—where an open eye—
Would drop him—Bone by Bone—
~Emily Dickinson

ONE

I had a little bird,
Its name was Enza,
I opened the window,
And in-flew-enza.

In November of 1918, Ronald Jones, Jr., the 20-year-old brother of Madeline Jones, died from bacterial pneumonia; having served two years in the U.S. Army, Ronnie had just returned home from overseas duty. At first, Doc Simpson misdiagnosed his illness as cholera, due to watery diarrhea and occasional vomiting. When he developed a persistent nosebleed, Doc became deeply concerned; fortunately, he quarantined Ronnie, or he might have infected even more people.

It was three days before Madeline, attending the 3rd District Normal School in Cape Girardeau, learned that Ronnie, her mother and father and one of her two younger sisters were victims of the world's largest pandemic—the Spanish flu—which, over the next 14 months, would claim between 50 and 100 million victims worldwide. Madeline's sisters—including Esther, then in sixth grade—went to school in spite of Doc Simpson's warning that Ronnie's initial cholera diagnosis might, in fact, be something as serious as dengue fever. Since Esther and her younger sister, Virginia, showed no immediate signs, they convinced their mother to let them go—which proved fatal to Esther, five of her classmates and her teacher, Goldie

Maddox. By lunchtime, Esther had developed a low-grade fever but said nothing; it wasn't until her nose began to bleed that Miss Maddox was aware of her illness, though she failed to comprehend its seriousness.

It was one o'clock before Doc discovered the Jones girls were at school. He immediately called Johnston's secretary, Mrs. Dean, who alerted the superintendent.

"W.O., there's somethin' goin' around. May be a flu bug, but I've never seen anything like it."

"What is it?"

"Damned if I know...but Ronnie Jones just died and his lungs were gushin' blood. Ronald and Mary are showin' signs. Now, don't start a panic, but you better be sendin' the girls home right away."

Within three days of exposure to the virus, Miss Maddox awoke with a high fever, blanketed with dozens of bloody petechiae and gasping for air. Hysterical, she telephoned her sister, Marie Wallace, who rushed to her aid. When Mrs. Wallace arrived, she found Goldie hemorrhaging from her ears. Before the doctor could be summoned, she suffocated—her lungs, half-filled sacs of foamy blood. Ironically, the date was November 11th, 1918. Armistice Day, the end of the Great War. In all, eighty-nine of Prospect's nearly 1500 residents died over the next three months—including Doc Simpson.

Two weeks later, Sarah Jamison arrived at the train depot in Prospect—met there by Karl Madeira, who had borrowed Herb Müller's delivery truck. In anticipation of being hired to replace Miss Maddox, she brought along most of her clothing and personal possessions in a steamer trunk, which, with some difficulty, Karl loaded onto the flatbed truck.

"It's so nice of you to meet me. I'm not sure what I would have done without your assistance."

Sarah Jamison's blonde hair was swept back away from her face, where it ended in a cascade of curls—protruding through an opening in the back of her flowered bonnet. In high-button shoes, she was nearly as tall as Karl, a solid six-footer.

"I've been looking forward to your arrival ever since Amelia said you were taking Miss Maddox's place."

"How kind of you, but I don't actually have the job. Not yet anyway. Bringing all this," she said—indicating the trunk, "...is a bit presumptuous." She made every effort to look directly into his eyes; she found his eye-patch intriguing. "However, if I'm hired, I expect I'll begin immediately."

"I think you can count on it."

She took his hand as he helped her step up into the truck cab. "How's Amelia? You know we've seen each other just once since we graduated. It's only through letters we've managed to stay in touch."

"She's...fine...just fine," he said—joining her in the cab.

"I must say I was a little worried there for a while. She seemed distraught over your father's death...and then, this past summer I detected an odd tone in her letters. Almost as if she were holding something back."

"I've moved my things downstairs to Papa's old room so you two will be able to share the upstairs. Wanted to repaper it for you, but Amelia said it wouldn't be proper for you to stay there permanently...because of me. Don't see why not, but you know how people talk."

"I know all about that," she said—remembering the horrible things people said about her father's accident. "When Amelia called, she indicated a neighbor was willing to rent a room. The connection was so bad I could barely understand her."

"The Sweeneys."

"Of course...Bessie and her mother. Amelia's written so much about them and how helpful they've been."

"Yes."

"So, I'll be right next door. Won't that be nice? We can all walk to school together. The girls, I mean."

Amelia was ecstatic. In anticipation of Sarah's arrival, she had been in a constant state of preparation. The house was brighter and more cheerful than it had ever been. To help welcome Sarah, she had invited Bessie and her mother to Thanksgiving dinner. With so much to be thankful for, she was determined to put on a royal spread. That meant a large pot of chicken and noodles, a turkey stuffed with cornbread dressing, giblet gravy, candied sweet potatoes, pickled yellow wax beans, a rhubarb conserve, which, along with the beans, she and Bessie had canned the previous summer, and apple and pumpkin pies. Bessie, a superb baker, was supplying hot yeast rolls and her mother's famous strawberry jam.

Amelia had just retrieved the pies from the oven when she heard the truck door slam. She's here!   She couldn't remember the last time she'd felt so happy. Removing her apron, she hurried to the side porch.

Karl was in the process of helping Sarah down from the truck when her heel caught in the hem of her handkerchief-bottomed dress; she lunged forward, almost falling. Fortunately, he caught her and lowered her to the ground. Embarrassed, she straightened her bonnet with one hand and pressed the other against her breast. She said something to him and they both laughed.   It was then she noticed Amelia.

"You go ahead. She's dying to see you. I'll fetch your trunk."

"It's so heavy. I should help you."

"I'll make it."

Unable to contain herself any longer, Amelia pushed open the screen door and rushed towards her. They met in the middle of the side yard and fell into each other's arms.

"Oh, how I've missed you." She bussed Sarah's cheek and whispered in her ear, "Desperately."

"And I, you," she said—pulling away slightly. "We should help Karl don't you think? My trunk's dreadfully heavy. I brought practically everything I own."

"I'm sure he can manage without us. Do come in. You must be parched. I'll put on water for tea."

"Would you have any coffee? I'm afraid I've developed the

habit. Life on the farm starts early."

"You're in luck. Karl drinks it. I'll make a fresh pot."

The reunion was exalted with storytelling and punctuated with laughter. Amelia recalled some of the more preposterous things her students had said the past year.

"I now have a perfect example of a spoonerism thanks to a freshman boy who pointed out the McDowell twins as 'those sin twisters!' And, as for pure nonsense, another student suggested that if we hadn't won the American Revolutionary War we might now be speaking English."

"You should keep a list," said Sarah. "By the time you retire, you'll have enough for a book."

"Tell her what that Rucker kid said," chuckled Karl, "Or, on second thought, maybe you shouldn't."

"What...? Go on, tell me."

"If you insist. We were lining up the seniors for graduation practice last year and one of the boys, Melvan Rucker, a big old farm boy, not the brightest but a jovial sort, asked if the band was going to play "Pomp and Circumcision."

"Oh, dear!" exclaimed Sarah—both hands flying to cover her mouth. She glanced at Karl, then quickly averted her eyes.

"You're blushing," said Amelia.

"Forgive me, I'm not used to such frank talk. Since I moved back to the farm, I feel like I've regressed into the life of a convent nun."

"Old Professor Martin would approve."

"Isn't that the truth?" she said—gathering herself. "The more I think about it...I'm not certain I'm up to the precocity of today's youth."

"Tomfoolery's more like it," said Karl.

"Another time, when I asked the best way to improve school, several boys shouted in chorus, 'Burn it down!'" As the words escaped her lips, she looked apologetically at her brother as if to say, 'Sorry. How thoughtless of me.'

That brought an end to the frivolity. The conversation

quickly gravitated towards more serious matters: the flu pandemic and the necessity of Sarah's mother having to put her farm up for sale.

"My younger brother, Rex, hated farming. He got married last June, and he and his wife moved to Little Rock. That was bad enough, but when Joey got killed last July, less than a month before he was due to come home, Mom and I knew we couldn't keep the farm. With me gone, she's decided to move to Little Rock. It's too soon to tell, but I don't think she'll ever get over losing Joey. Having him buried in France doesn't help."

Karl shot to his feet. "Listen, I'm gonna run down to Rainey's and see if I can get Big Joe to come up and help me haul the trunk up to Sarah's room. He gets off work at six."

"I think the three of us can do it, don't you?" asked Sarah.

"I just need a little air," he said. "I'll be back shortly."

"Tell Big Joe he can stay for supper," Amelia shouted after him. She looked apologetically at Sarah, shrugged and sighed.

"I'm so sorry...I shouldn't have mentioned about Joey dying."

"I'm afraid he isn't able to talk about the war at all. He still has terrible nightmares. Between him and Papa, I can't remember the last time I had a full night's rest."

"He's such a sweet boy. I do hope he'll be all right."

The first few months were pure bliss. Though she still missed Chester dreadfully, knowing Sarah was next door at the Sweeney's, that she'd be seeing her every day, elevated her spirits. Not wanting to detract from her time with Sarah, she masked her melancholy as best she could. It wasn't until Sarah mentioned Chester, that she allowed herself to speak his name. Sarah had come up to the library after school to see if Amelia wanted to walk to town; she found her shelving books. After several minutes of general conversation, from out of nowhere she inquired: "Whatever happened to that student you had your first year? You wrote me about him several times."

"Which one would that be?"

"You know, that strange brilliant boy. The one who won a scholarship to Washington U."

"You mean, Chester? Chester O'Malley. There was nothing strange about him. Why do you ask?"

"Karl says you were absolutely crazy about him…talked about him all the time."

"That's ridiculous. I may have shared some of his work with Karl, once or twice, but that's all. Whatever gave him such a preposterous idea?"

"You needn't get upset. I'm sure he meant nothing by it."

"He was a special student. You would've had to have had him in class to know what I'm talking about. Light-years beyond the others. A born writer…with a vast knowledge. I'd be fooling myself if I thought there'd ever be another like him."   Thinking her explanation had put an end it to, she continued shelving books.

"Do you hear from him at all?"

"Why would I? I imagine he's totally consumed with his studies. His mother says he doesn't even have time to come home for a holiday. Why the inquisition?"

"Karl says the boy owes you a debt for all you did for him."

"Karl says? Do you two talk about me?"

"He just meant you went out of your way to help the poor boy."

"That's what teachers do. They owe it to their students to help direct them to their futures, and, believe me, the last thing you can expect is a 'thank you.' You have sixth graders now, but wait a few years when your first class graduates high school. You'll see. Once they're gone…they're gone. And if you don't mind, I'd prefer you didn't explain my brother to me."

For weeks, Amelia had been brooding over their apparent infatuation with each other. When the three of them were together, she felt like she was intruding or nearly invisible. Recently, Karl had taken Sarah for long rides in the country.

"Apparently, you're not the least bit concerned about her

reputation," she told him when he returned from one of their lengthy jaunts.

"What now? Another attempt to keep us apart?"

"Keeping you apart is not what worries me. Making sure she doesn't lose her position is my only concern. Single women do not gallivant around the countryside with an eligible bachelor. And, schoolteachers do not appear in public with potential beaus. What're you thinking? What's she thinking?"

"We're just friends. I know women teachers can't marry? I've been around old maid school teachers my whole life."

"Old maid school teachers are not all old maids by choice. Teaching is my life's work, and if I want to keep teaching, society says I'm not permitted to marry. Nor can Sarah."

"Like a couple of nuns, huh?"

"What choice do we have?"

"Well, Sarah's not sure she wants to continue teaching. Says she'd rather have children of her own than be a surrogate mother."

"Those are her words? Surrogate mother? Is that what she thinks I am?"

"That's what you were to that O'Malley boy. Or, was it somethin' more?"

"Helping Chester escape his drunken father and his victimized mother was my sole intention. That, and giving him the chance to realize his full potential. Wherever did you get such an outrageous idea?"

"From his father."

"Blackie? What did he say? When?"

"He stopped me one morning on my way to work. 'Say, Karl,' he says, 'that sister of yours is puttin' some pretty strange ideas into my boy's head.'"

"I'll bet he did! Strange ideas like 'get as far away from that abusive drunk-of-a-father as you can.' Not only does he beat his wife, he knocked Chester around, too. Criminal, that's what it is."

"He said you two spent an awful lot of time together. Time that had nothing to do with school."

"For God's sake, Karl. You know my only intention was to help him get a scholarship and get away from this small-minded town. Nothing more."

"I'm not just talkin' about your intentions, Sis. Accordin' to Blackie, the boy's mother found some things he'd had written about you. Things that went way beyond the student-teacher thing."

"Thing? I am not listening to this another minute. Believing the lies of a drunk over your own sister says as much about you as it does about him. Besides, we were talking about you ruining Sarah's reputation, and I think I know a thing or two about your lack of concern when it comes to...to a woman's...chastity."

"Meaning?"

"Her virtue...the sanctity of her body." She glared at him— as if to dare him to deny her accusation.

He furrowed his brow in attempt to understand. Then, his head dropped and he sighed, "Will you never let that die?"

"Why should I? It's haunted me for years."

"We were children...just innocent children. Both of us."

"Children, yes...innocent, no. If it had happened once, perhaps, but there comes a point where innocence is lost and there are no excuses."

"Well, think what you want," he said, "but as far as Sarah's concerned, the more you pursue her, the more she turns to me."

Knowing how he felt about Sarah was one thing; however, when it became obvious her affections were turning towards Karl, Amelia panicked. Once, in desperation, she went to the Sweeney's and pretended to retrieve something from Sarah's room. Instead, she placed one of her camisoles in the bottom of her lingerie drawer. Nearly a week later, Sarah discovered it. Confused and somewhat alarmed, she carried it to the Madeira's back door, where she confronted Amelia, who was sweeping the porch.

"Is this yours?"

She stopped sweeping and came to the screen door. She looked at the camisole and, with an air of astonishment, announced, "I've wondered where that disappeared to..."

"I found it...just now...in my dresser drawer."

"Hmm. However did it come to be there do you suppose?"

"I can't imagine."

"Perhaps you accidentally removed it from the clothesline."

"I would have noticed when I folded and put it away."

"Apparently not. No worry, though," she said—opening the screen door and taking it from her. "I have others."

Sarah said nothing, but stood, immobile.

"Something else...?"

"Could you...would you check to see if you have one of mine?"

"I'll look...but I seriously doubt I'll find anything."

Eventually, Sarah confided in Bessie her growing sense of dread regarding her relationship with Amelia. "In college, we were serendipitous. That is until the final weeks before graduation when she began to cling to me as if she could prevent our inevitable separation. It put a terrible strain on our friendship. She made me promise to write 'every day'...as if that were possible. Like her, I had enormous responsibilities at home. Mother needed me. And when my brother was killed in France, she needed me even more. Had I gotten a teaching job right out of college, I would have had to decline it. I came to dread her letters...knowing she expected me to respond in kind. Sometimes, I question her grasp on reality." She waited for Bessie to concur, but, as always, she withheld any response.

"When I first received her call about Miss Maddox's death and the chance to fill in, I almost turned it down. Now, of course, I'm glad I didn't. Not because of her...and please, promise to never repeat any of this...but because of Karl."

Though Bessie had grown fond of her in the few months they had known each other, she felt a betrayal towards Amelia anytime she permitted Sarah to unburden herself. Still, she said nothing. Nor did she have the courage to tell her of her own misgivings about Karl, based on several encounters when he'd been drinking. Instead, when details or complaints became too uncomfortable to hear, she made excuses. 'Sarah, if you don't mind, I need to leave early for school. Would you please tell Amelia for me?' 'This Friday, I won't be able to do tea. Mother needs me to go to Rainey's...to the pharmacy...to...'

Amelia had no idea why Bessie seemed to be removing herself from their daily rituals. And, as for Sarah, she obsessed about their disintegrating relationship until she could no longer maintain her composure. The confrontation occurred one day after school.

"Please wait!" she shouted as she hurried to catch up with Sarah, who had just reached the Sweeney's front steps. "You can't even wait to walk home with me now?"

"I'm sorry. I thought I told you. Karl and I have plans to—"

"I need to know what's going on..."

"...?"

"...with you and Karl. If I didn't know better, I'd think you were actually getting serious."

"Amelia—"

"You hardly spend time with me anymore. I thought you came up here to be with me."

"I came up here to take a job...and I hoped it would give us a chance to continue our friendship."

"Oh, is that what we have now? A friendship? What's happened to you? At Cape, we were as close as two people could be. We loved one another. You told me you loved me more than you'd ever loved anyone. You said so!"

"You might want to lower your voice. Here comes Miss Adams. "Sarah acknowledged her with a wave.

Miss Sylvia Adams—carrying an armload of papers and books—yelled from across the street, "Have a nice weekend you two."

"You do the same," Sarah answered.

Amelia glanced towards her—acknowledging her with a slight tilt of the head.

"So...suddenly, we're just friends. Is that what you're

saying?"

"Whisper, please. The woman's a terrible gossip."

"*My friend must be a Bird—because it flies! Mortal, my friend must be because it dies! Barbs has it, like a Bee! Ah, curious friend! Thou Puzzlest me!*"

"Amelia, please..."

"You traipse all over the countryside with my brother and you're suddenly worried about what people think?"

"I won't have this conversation if you're going to be so...so—"

"What? Say it!"

"Childish!" With that, she quickly disappeared into the house.

Amelia stood for a few moments—staring blankly at the door. To show how hurt she was, she copied a quatrain from another Dickinson poem and left it in Sarah's school mailbox:

> *She dealt her pretty words like Blades—*
> *How glittering they shone—*
> *And every One unbared a Nerve*
> *Or wantoned with a Bone—*

Karl and Sarah were engaged mid-summer. She informed Supt. Johnston she would not be returning in the fall; six months on the job had shown her teaching was not her calling. Besides, Karl had occupied nearly every spare moment since she arrived in Prospect, and his persistence had overwhelmed her sense of independence, or so it seemed to Amelia.

All these things: Chester's absence, Bessie's guilty withdrawal, and Sarah's abandonment threatened to unhinge her. If there were any consolation to the marriage, it would be in getting Karl out of the house—even if that meant knowing he had destroyed her dream of having Sarah all to herself.

Her only solace was her job. She vowed to give it her full attention.

TWO

Chester's first year at Washington University in St. Louis was exceptional, his entrance exams so impressive he had been accepted into special Honor's courses in English, French and history. To earn spending money, he was assigned student employment in the English department. His immediate supervisor, Miss Edwina Mercer, a perfectionist, demanded promptness and accuracy from all of her student workers. Because he typed sixty error-free words per minute on the new "noiseless" typewriter, Chester quickly became her favorite student employee. If a professor needed something typed for a class or for publication, she assigned Chester, who earned the maximum 25-cents an hour. As students were permitted to work only fifteen hours per week, he learned to survive on $15 a month. Because of that, he came to dread holidays; he needed the money. Apart from that, the necessity of work gave him an excuse to avoid returning home to Prospect.

In early October of his second year, Miss Mercer surprised him with a bundle of letters. "Apparently, you haven't been checking your mail. Your dormitory couriered these over."

Immediately, he caught the scent of lavender. The letter on top carried the return address: Miss A. Madeira, 906 W. 6th St., Prospect, Missouri. It was sealed with red wax.

"The fragrance suggests it's from a young woman. What secret have you been keeping from me, young man?"

Chester felt a sharp stab in his heart; he visibly winced

before masking the expression with a phony smile. "No secret," he said. "It's from an old high school acquaintance."

He placed the letters on top of his French Conversation textbook and went about his business. When Miss Mercer was summoned to take dictation from the department chairman, he hurriedly removed Amelia's letter from the bundle. It was the first he'd received from her and the first communication of any kind between them since he'd revealed his feelings.

He braced himself.

Miss Amelia Madeira
Prospect, Missouri
October 10th, 1919

My Dear Chester (Chet),

Another new school year has begun. It seems only yesterday I walked into my room and stood before your class for the first time. Remember how angry the McDowell and Shepard twins were to find their dear Miss Orton had "flown the coop?" The reality is that it's been nearly seventeen months since we last talked...an eternity.

I saw your mother in Rainey's yesterday and she told me you were on the High honor roll both semesters last year, as if I would be surprised, (delighted but not surprised). She also said you were working in the university English department and it did not permit any free time for frivolous things like a visit back home.

I don't wish to alarm you, but I detected several bruises on your mother's neck and cheek. I could tell she had made an effort to cover them with powder. My brother passes by your father's shop every day on his way to work. Only last week, he found Blackie passed out. Karl says it was from alcohol. It's none of my business, but I thought you should know.

I could tell you Pearl misses you—which she does, but that would only be my way of trying to manipulate you into feeling just a wee bit guilty. So, let me just admit I have missed you terribly. You spoiled me, Chester, making me eager to reach school each day, anxious to see what insightful essay you'd written or hear your personal interpretation of one of Dickinson or Whitman's poems.

It's sad to think my first class may be the highlight of my teaching career. In comparison, last year's senior class was a disappointment, primarily because of the expectation I had that it might measure up to yours. Fortunately, this year's class shows more promise. Still...

No doubt you heard about Willie Stansbury's accident with his beloved Paint. Willie and his horse were hand-in-glove (please excuse the apt cliché). My brother talked to Willie's father when he came into Müller's to purchase some lumber awhile back. Apparently, a blue racer spooked Paint—causing him to rear up and throw Willie. Prospect's new doctor, Albert Carlson, said he's lucky to be alive, but due to spinal cord damage, he'll be permanently paralyzed. He had recently become engaged to one of the Shepard twins—Sandra, I believe. How tragic! I've been meaning to visit him, but I've yet to make it out to their farm.

I know how close you two were. His father asked that if I ever talked to you, to please let you know it would really raise Willie's spirits to hear from you.

I certainly did not mean for this letter to be so morbid. Forgive me. And, please forgive me if I hurt you. It was not my intention. You are very special to me, and nothing will ever take away the joy I feel or the pride I take in having been your teacher. I hope, in time, it will be possible for you to communicate with me again. I so miss our conversations.

Wishing you continued success.

With utmost affection,
Miss Madeira
P.S. I close with some of Emily's words...

Could I buy back those tender days—
With coins of Rectitude—
Or cleanse my Heart—of dark despair—
With Life's own Solitude—

For a moment, Chester sat, immobilized. He recalled other poems she had written solely for him. Words meant to console. 'Does she really think I don't recognize they're not Dickinson's but her own? And what of the news? What were those words meant to produce? Guilt? What consolation was to be found in knowing my father beats my mother? What solace was being offered by her 'utmost affection?' He would never give her the satisfaction of knowing he still thought of her a hundred times a day.

He tucked the letter away in his French book just as Miss Mercer returned. He quickly typed an exam and some lecture notes.

"You do such fine work, but I'm afraid that's all I have for you today," she said, when he turned in the finished papers.

"Didn't I overhear Professor Butler mention he had a course

outline that needed typing?"

"He's back in his office. You might go ask him. And, please deliver this to Dr. Jayneway on your way."

He took the lengthy treatise and hurried down the darkened hallway past doors with frosted glass panes; one was open. Old Professor Jayneway, a Greek and Latin scholar, sat hunched over a magnifying glass—reading from an ancient text. He glanced up when he heard Chester footsteps.

"Ah, there you are. Did you finish typing my monograph?" His thinning hair was pure white and his skin, nearly translucent. Blue veins rippled at his temples, and his papery lips were moist and pink.

"Just now," Chester said—handing him the folder.

"Thank you, young man. Most appreciative, as always"

"I enjoyed reading your paean to happiness, sir. I think you make a strong case for a connection to Plato's Republic."

"What about my argument concerning happiness being an inalienable right? Does it hold water?"

"Well, since evil beings can be just as happy as good ones, I believe the pursuit of happiness becomes an interesting moral question when it comes to inalienable rights."

"Very good, my boy. Hope you'll sign up for my Honor's seminar next spring."

"Looking forward to it, sir. Well, I best be on my way. Professor Butler has some typing for me."

"Tell Butler I need to speak to him before he heads out...would you please?"

"Certainly."

"And tell him not to forget. He always forgets."

"I'll tell him, sir."

A series of dust-covered filing cabinets obscured the entrance to the last office on the left. Chester knocked lightly on the door.

"What?" boomed a deep baritone.

"It's Chester."

"Door's open...*entrez*."

Harris Butler, thirty-two, was an associate professor of English. Sporting an unruly beard and tousled black hair, his rumpled appearance featured a tweed jacket badly in need of pressing. His office, redolent of an exotic spice, stale cologne and mildew, was a fortress of periodicals, monographs and books that threatened to swallow him. He appeared to be grading papers.

"I'm a little swamped right now. These essays are hideously bad and require more time to grade than they did to write. I'm not prepared for my graduate seminar and I have a department meeting at four."

Chester knew Butler was always running late and prone to blaming everyone but himself. "Sorry to bother, but you mentioned an outline that needed typing."

"Oh, the outline! God, I forgot...thanks for reminding me." He tore through a pile of papers—finding nothing. He frantically opened every desk drawer—shoving things about. "I know I brought the damn thing in..."

"Is this it?" asked Chester—pulling a lined sheet of tablet from a large textbook perched on the corner of a filing cabinet.

Butler pushed back his chair and stood. He slowly slid the paper from Chester's fingers, then leaned forward and kissed him on the mouth. Chester pulled back—glancing out the second-story window.

"How many times have I told you...no one can see in?"

"I'm just trying to be careful."

"What would I do without my sweet, cautious boy?" He looked at Chester, smiled and shook his head. "Better run along before Betsey Trotwood misses you."

"Why do you call her that? She's not my guardian. Have you even read David Copperfield?"

"I teach it."

"Not the same as actually reading it," he said, as he turned to leave.

"Forgetting something?" Butler asked—holding out the

tablet sheet.

He reached for the paper, but Butler held it for a moment before releasing it. "I love when you talk mean to me," he said— grabbing hold of his wrist.

"I wish I did," said Chester, as he freed himself from Butler's grasp.

"Oh, by the by, I talked to Dr. Sylvester about your research paper, and he thought it was 'ingenious' and asked why I was interested. Said I'd had you in Comparative Lit last spring and found you to be exceptional. That seemed to satisfy his curiosity." He pulled him closer. "I wanted to tell him I've had you in other ways, too, and just how exceptional you are...not only in ways literary." He leaned forward to kiss him again, just as Chester turned to leave— missing him by inches.

"Honestly, Harris, it's not even noon. You should chew some Sen-Sen before one of your students or a colleague detects the alcohol."

"Worried I'm turning into daddy?"

Chester stared at him, blankly. "Dr. Jayneway asked that you stop by before your class...and not to forget. I'll be in the library until supper."

"Wait...have we anything to eat?"

"The soup I made last night. I think there's still enough for both of us."

"Good. After supper, perhaps I can think of something for us to do...so we won't be bored."

"I'm sure you can."

"Is something wrong? You haven't been yourself recently. More parental angst? Another rejection letter?"

"I think Miss Mercer may suspect I'm no longer living in the dorm."

"Is that all? Sure nothing else is bothering you? Remember the school motto, *per veritatem vis*...through truth, strength."

Chester offered a weak smile.

"No. Nothing."

THREE

She stood in the dark by her bedroom window, the panes glazed with frost. The crystals, as ephemeral and intricate as the geometry of snowflakes, sparkled with refracted moonlight. She placed her hand against the glass—leaving it for a few seconds. Knowing the handprint aperture would quickly steam over, she anxiously peered across the icy street to Miss Minnie's old house. The upstairs bedroom window flickered with candlelight, the kind of bedevilment that would plague her deep into the night.

'He's touching her. They're making love.' That thought might have engendered joy in others, but for Amelia it was torturous. She had never felt so isolated. During the day, she was surrounded by students. But at night, she was left alone with her own thoughts, which, of late, had become a siren song. 'What had Emily called it?' *One's own self encounter in lonesome place.*

Having married almost one year to the day of her arrival in Prospect, Karl and Sarah had purchased Miss Minnie's old home. "We'll be nearby...in case you need anything." Though at first she was relieved Sarah would be living so close, she now rued her good fortune—having her across the street in plain view but 'separated by a sea of agony.'

Amelia became so obsessed *(obsessão)* with thoughts of the two of them together, at times, she feared a loss of sanity. It was one thing to be envious of Karl for taking away her beloved, but even more upsetting was the resentment she now felt towards Sarah. She berated herself for turning a jaundiced eye on them both. Yet, she seemed to have no power over what was clearly covetousness.

Sometimes in the evenings, she would sit for hours in complete darkness—rocking back and forth in Fredo's old chair—unable to silence the disturbing voices that endlessly imagined their life together. Or, she would lie awake for hours, plagued by thoughts of: the welcome-home kiss, the embrace, the trivia of the workday, the shared meal, the companionship, the union of flesh...

From the moment they announced their engagement, Amelia's demeanor shifted, her mien noticeably affected. Students inquired about her well-being. 'Are you all right, Miss Madeira? Is something wrong?' Colleagues were concerned about her health. 'You look tired, dear. Are you ill?' Others warned, 'You're working too hard...better slow down.' Bessie, who never ventured into the area of the personal, offered, 'If you need to talk, you know I'm always here for you.' In all cases, she denied everything, and if pressed, she would become downright indignant. In the weeks leading up to the wedding, her behavior grew increasingly strange.

While Karl continued to work at Müller's, prior to the wedding, Sarah busied herself in their future home—'making it livable.' Amelia volunteered to help scrub the woodwork. What began as casual conversation, eventually led to a startling accusation.

"Do you remember our vow?"

"Vow?" repeated Sarah.

"To never marry...to always be together?"

"If I recall correctly, we were out to prove we didn't need men in our lives. I remember how adamant we both were. Ah, college girls...so naïve," she said. "Hand me that scrub brush, would you, please?"

"Well?"

"Well, what?" Sarah asked—still chuckling to herself.

"*Votum, votus, vovere.* What happened to that vow?"

"You can't be serious." She glanced at Amelia, whose jaw was rigid and whose eyes narrowed into an accusatory squint.

"You *are* serious. We were only eighteen for heaven's

sake," she said with forced laughter—hoping to relieve the tension.

"What difference could that possibly make? I was completely capable of pledging my devotion at that age, and I'm certainly capable of keeping my word now."

"Dear one, we're going to be sisters-in-law. Sisters. We'll be in each other's lives for decades. I'm marrying your brother. What more could you ask?"

"More than you can possibly imagine. As for my brother, there are things about Karl I could tell you...such things. And, I don't just mean his drinking."

"I have no idea what things you're referring to, but I do know siblings often experience contentiousness. I certainly suffered disagreements with mine. Rex, especially. It's a natural part of sibling strife. You should know that I love him very much...as I do you."

"Apparently, you love him considerably more than you do me...if, in fact, you ever did."

Sarah started to protest, but then looked empathetically at her friend. "You are so intuitive when it comes to other people's needs, but when it comes to your own...to matters of the heart, you're still that little girl...searching for her mother."

"So much insight to into my problems. For once, let's talk about your fears."

"Mine?"

"You love me. I know you do. But you're afraid...admit it." She was unyielding.

At first, Sarah appeared ready to deny it, but then, as if Amelia had crushed her reserve, she sighed. "Okay, yes...I do love you. And honestly, it terrifies me." She steadied herself. "That day at the river..."

"Not a day goes by I don't think of it," said Amelia. "And, the kiss? Tell me you didn't experience the same rush of emotion."

"Don't you see, nothing can ever come of it? No matter what we wanted or thought we did, this could never be more than friendship."

"So your vow meant nothing? Perhaps I should warn Karl you're incapable of keeping one." She stared at Sarah a moment, then tossed her cleaning rag into a pail of dirty soap water and headed for the door.

"Please don't leave this way!"

Amelia paused but remained facing away, in an effort to hide her tears.

"You are my very dearest friend in the whole world," Sarah said, tenderly. "I hate that I've hurt you. Surely you know there was never any way the two of us could be together. Not in these little towns. Imagine the talk. You've heard it before, the 'queer sisters,' whispered with disgust about two women with no proof of anything, with no provocation. Nothing but small-town, small-minded speculation."

Amelia turned to face her. "I'll go away with you...to St. Louis...Chicago... Anywhere you want. I just... want...to be...with you..."

Sarah moved closer. She removed her bandana and began to dry Amelia's tears. "And what do you think your students or your friends at the Presbyterian Church would say if they knew how you feel? Who you are?" She cupped Amelia's cheek with her hand. "Don't you suffer at all knowing the kind of love you propose is condemned?"

"My beliefs are simple. I accept a God of love...a love that knows no boundaries or conditions. I'm not interested in other's interpretations...or their personal fears." She removed Sarah's hand.

"Well, then...you're living in a world that doesn't exist and probably never will. As it is, I'm not strong enough to fight it."

"I won't listen to this. I don't even know who you are anymore. I guess I never did."

"Please let me finish. Suppose I had been able to stay with you here in Prospect. What would have become of Karl? He's gotten so much better in the last few months. He rarely drinks, but he still has moments when the war inhabits him like a phantom. He needs me. He needs you. You're his family." She took Amelia's hands in hers.

"You're such an amazing teacher. I could never hope to reach students the way you do…to lift them up and encourage them to be their best selves. But, I can be a good wife to your brother…to encourage him and lift him up…help him heal from the terrible shock of that damnable war. I lost a brother to that war, and I'm not going to lose a husband. He's all that's left of your family. Let me do this for him. Let me have this…for me. In time, you'll see it's for the best."

"Time will heal regret?"

She brushed back a strand of hair from Amelia's forehead. "Yes, I believe it will."

"Memories will fade?"

Again, she nodded.

In a broken, child-like voice unfamiliar to Sarah, she softly sobbed, "I will never forget…all the precious things…Karl has taken from me. Never…"

Amelia was 'too ill' to attend their wedding at the First Baptist Church. She awoke—clammy and feverish. Immediately, Karl ran next door to inform Bessie that "Plan B" was in effect. Fearing the onset of the flu, Sarah asked her to assume the maid-of-honor duties in the event Amelia was too sick to fulfill them.

Though disappointed, Sarah was also relieved.

*   *   *

In the spring of his third year at Washington University, Chester was snubbed by the faculty committee who convened to select the next editor of the college literary magazine, *The Intrepid*. No reason was given, but the rumors swirling around campus like malevolent dust devils—concerning his "relationship" with Prof. Harris Butler—were obviously to blame.

Prior to this slight, he had been hailed by the university's English department for his brilliant novella, *Janus*, which he had written under the pseudonym, S. A. Moon. Not only had it won the department's prestigious student writing competition, several chapters had been serialized in the *North American Review*. Even more remarkable, an editor from Charles Scribner's Sons had shown genuine interest; however, the deal was scotched when Chester refused to make several minor changes.

For nearly a year, he threatened to move back to the dorm and break off their relationship, but anytime he broached the subject, Butler became contrite and somewhat pitiable. Recently, Chester suspected him of being infatuated with a new student, Stefan Montgomery, whose name he had worked a few too many times into recent conversations. He frequently observed Montgomery leaving Butler's office. Finally, he confronted Butler, who denied the charge—saying his interest in Stefan was 'purely academic.'

"He's a very talented poet. You should read some of his work. I think even you'd be impressed."

"How exactly does his poetry figure into the equation?"

"Are you suggesting I should have no interest in poetry?"

"I'm *saaaying*...I don't understand why a student who's not taking any course work from you would need to visit your office three or four times a week."

"He doesn't visit he—"

"*Especially* when you keep very strict office hours and limit appointments to your real students, who actually have a need to conference with you and who are unable to schedule you when you aren't engaged with an attractive young man who wants you to read his latest sonnet."

"That's not true."

"Which part? The fact that you're spending an inordinate amount of time with *Stefan*...or that you rarely conference with your actual students? Lest you forget, I've been one of those students. And, unless you've changed your *modus operandi*, he's receiving a lot more than academic advice. Lucky for you, no one can see into the second story window."

"Look, Chester, I'm not going to get into word games with

you. I admit you're more clever than me."

"Cleverer than *I*."

"Jesus! That Madeira completely ruined you for casual conversation!"

"We're talking about you now, and, for once Harris...try to tell the truth. *Per veritatem vis*! You're infatuated with another pretty boy, and this has nothing to do with poetry. Admit it."

"Why don't you meet him and see for yourself. He's a great kid. Funny...smart, I think you'd like him."

"Suggesting a *ménage à trois*?"

"When you needed out of that dormitory with all those plebeians, I offered to let you live in my apartment...rent free. Granted, you cook and keep the place looking nice, but it costs me twice as much for food. So, in the long run, I'm not really saving anything."

Chester stared at him in disbelief.

"Stefan's family is well-to-do. His father sends him $15 a week...pen money. He hates the dorm as much as you did, and he's willing to pay $20 a month for the extra room we never use. That's why he stopped by my office...to talk about renting a room."

Chester started to protest, but instead walked directly into their bedroom. He pulled a suitcase from under the bed, slammed it down on the mattress. Then, he went to the closet and began ripping clothes from the wooden hangers—furiously stuffing them into the suitcase.

"Please don't do that!" pleaded Butler, his normally modulated baritone elevating in pitch.

Ignoring him, Chester yanked out the bottom dresser drawer and dumped the entire contents into his suitcase.

"Oh, that's just excellent. Where do you think you're going to go at ten o'clock at night?"

He continued to pack in silence.

"Well, say something." When no response came, Butler panicked. "Don't leave...I'm sorry. We can figure this out."

"There's nothing to figure out."

"I won't let you go. This is *crazy*," he said, his voice breaking. "I…love you."

"Please, spare me the tears, the dramatics and any mention of love. This is nothing more than a convenient arrangement for you. That's all it's ever been."

"How can you say that? I care for you…I really do," he said—wrapping his arms around Chester and holding him tight.

"Take your hands off me. Seriously, Harris…let go…now!"

He dropped the bear hug and moved to the foot of the bed. "All right, you win. If you don't want Stefan to move in, I'll tell him."

"Tell him whatever you like. You're great at making things up."

"What's that supposed to mean?"

"It means that you, Harris Butler, are from Skokie, Illinois…*not* Cambridge, Massachusetts. I collect the mail for Miss Mercer. Did you think I wouldn't notice the return address from your mother? Oh, by the way, she called the English Department office last week…looking for you. We talked for a few moments. Seemed very nice. I asked how your sister was doing, the one who's deathly ill. The one you went home to Cambridge to visit over spring break. 'Sister?' she said. 'Why Buddy doesn't have a sister. Buddy's an only child.' *Buddy.* Buddy Butler from Skokie, Illinois. Now, that's someone I might have liked."

He began buckling the straps on the suitcase. "Oh, and I called the registrar's office. My friend, Sylvia, works there. Asked her to look up Stefan Montgomery. And, what do you know…it seems that *Stephen* is also from Cambridge. *Quelle coïncidence.*"

"I can't believe you've been spying on me. You really disappoint me."

Chester struggled to fasten the last strap. Giving up in disgust, he dragged the suitcase off the bed and headed for the door.

"So…you're really going?"

"I believe it's called a moment of clarity." He sat the suitcase down and retrieved his old jacket from the coat tree by the front door. He slipped it on and began furiously buttoning it. When he came to a missing button, his mind flashed to Amelia. He smiled—ironically.

For a moment, Butler looked hopeful.

"For your information, Professor Butler, it's *pin* money…not pen money. Katheryn Howard…the fifth Mrs. Henry the eighth, coined it. It refers to the extra money she set aside to pay for the luxury of acquiring straight pins from France. Sadly, her frugality didn't pay off. Ol' Henry had her beheaded. Not because of the pin money, mind you…but because she was unfaithful."

"I love that you know that."

Chester stared at him but said nothing. He walked to fireplace and grabbed several books from the mantle. "I believe these are mine. If you find anything else that belongs to me, books…or anything, please drop it off at the English office."

"Oh, come on…this is ridiculous. I really do care for you."

Chester opened the door and descended the front steps.

Suddenly, Butler's expression altered. "Wait a minute!"

Chester stopped.

"Please…can you *please* not say anything to anyone in the English department about Skokie. It's a harmless little lie. You know how snobby some of those bastards are. I'm under a great deal of pressure to get something published. It's not as easy as you think. Do you know what kind of ribbing I took from Jayneway and the others when parts of your novella got serialized in the *North American Review*? If Scribner's had published *Janus*, I'd never have been able to live it down."

Chester sighed.

"Come back in. There's no place you can go tonight."

"Goodbye…Buddy."

"Okay, fine…*leave!* If you get tired of wandering the streets, you might find a spare bed at Dr. Sylvester's. He has a big crush on you in case you hadn't noticed. I'm sure his wife won't mind. Or, maybe you can run back home to that lesbian you're so in love with!"

When Chester arrived for work the next day, Miss Mercer 'regretfully' informed him that his job had been terminated. When he asked why, she said she wasn't at liberty to discuss it. Stricken, he hurried to the stairwell, where he stood for a minute—trying to catch his breath.

"I'm so sorry," whispered Miss Mercer, who followed after him. "I hate to lose you, dear. You've been a wonderful help, and I think you're a really sweet boy. But, Dr. Piedmont said I have no choice in the matter. I know it was Professor Butler who did this. He rushed in here early this morning demanding to see Dr. Piedmont, who came out a short time later, telling me I had to let you go."

"I don't blame you…"

"I'll be more than happy to write you a letter of recommendation. I don't care about all that gossip. Never believed some of the things people were saying."

"That's the thing about gossip, Miss Mercer, there's usually just enough truth to give it wings."

"I'll miss you, Chester."

She watched him descend the steps. As he exited the building, she added, "And I'll pray for you."

FOUR

In 1921, the summer before his final year at Washington University, Chester returned to Prospect for a brief visit. It was his first and only trip home in three years. Amelia was unaware of the visitation until she ran into Sandra Stansbury in Jones' Dry Goods on a Saturday morning. The former Sandra Shepard had recently married Willie, and they were living with his parents on the old Stansbury farm.

"Sandra?"

"Oh, Miss Madeira."

"I thought that was you. How are you, dear? I was so happy to hear that you and Willie got married. Did you receive my card?"

"Yes…and thank you. You needn't have given us anything, but the money was very much appreciated."

"Oh, it was nothing," she said, modestly. "How's Willie?"

"He does pretty well…considering. Between his mother and me, we try to keep his spirits up. It's hard, but you know Willie."

"Yes…"

There was a momentary silence.

"Guess you heard Chester came to see him?"

"Chester was in town?" She tried to mask her disappointment. "No, I hadn't heard. How is he?"

"Changed quite a bit…you know, filled out. Really a handsome young man. Never really thought of him that way before, but he looks great and Willie just loves him."

"I knew they were close."

"Talks about him all the time...about the good ol' days. His visit meant a lot."

"When was that? Recently?"

"Just yesterday. He was only home two days. Heard him say he got into a fight with his father. Tried to talk his mother into getting away. Said he wished he could move her to St. Louis. She has a sister there, I believe. You know how Mr. O'Malley is. Willie says he gets drunk and hits her sometimes."

"Tell me, what else did he say?"

"Not a lot. Couldn't stay long...had to get back into town to catch the train. You know, him... always was a real sensitive boy. Tried to act like nothing was wrong with Willie, but I could tell he was shocked to see him...the way he is."

"Yes..."

"'Course, he asked about you. Told him I hadn't seen you in ages."

"He *did*...ask about me?"

"Surprised he didn't stop by to see you. Certain he planned to. Or, maybe he did and you were out."

*   *   *

Seeing Willie incapacitated—atrophied legs, emaciated and grim countenance—was shocking. The lively boy Chester remembered was vacant and devitalized when he first arrived, but it didn't take long before his eyes shone with enough energy to give him hope that Willie might survive—if not intact, at least as a remnant of his former self.

The Stansburys were so happy to see Willie rally they left the boys alone to talk. He wanted to hear all about college life, and Chester told him about the novella he had written and his work in the English department, but when Willie asked if he'd met anyone special, Chester shrugged and said, 'No.'

"Can't be that there ain't a carload of pretty girls around.

You too shy to ask?"

"I don't have time to socialize." He wondered what Willie would have thought of Harris Butler.

"Know you're busy, but you could drop me a line every now and again."

"I will...and I'm going to try get back here at Christmas time. I'll be out for a visit. By then, if you keep working, you'll have regained some strength. Promise me you will. I can't bear to see you give up. That's not you, Willie. If you won't do it for yourself or Sandra...do it for me."

"Think I wouldn't if I could? Heck, most of the time it don't feel like I'm even here. Not here in my body anyways. It's like I'm sittin' outside lookin' at someone that used to be me. Watchin' him dry up and slowly disappear."

"I know it's hard."

"That don't touch it," he said—tearing up.

Chester reached forward and gently squeezed his arm. "I love you, Willie...you know I do. I hate to run, but I've got to get back. Train leaves at 3:20."

"Whatcha gonna do about your mama?"

"It may come to blows, but I'm taking her back with me."

"Wasn't gonna say nothin' but..." He lowered his eyes.

"What? You can tell me anything...you know that."

"...about your daddy..."

"What...just say it?"

"The day of my accident, couple of shoes were givin' Paint fits, so I rode in to have Blackie level off his hooves. Coulda done it myself, I guess, but I wanted to ask if he'd heard anything outta you. Ten o'clock in the morning, and he was already drunker 'n skunk. Shoulda turned around right then and headed on home, but thought a bad nail might split and prick the quick on the way back, so I asked him to check 'em. While he was trimmin' the ragged pieces off one of the soles, his drawin' knife slipped and the point pierced right through the frog. Paint went nuts...reared up and knocked him down."

"'Control your goddamn horse!' he shouted. No, apology…no *nothin'*. Acted like it was Paint's fault he got stabbed. I left without payin' a cent. Paint was plenty riled up after that."

"Are you saying that's what caused him to—"

"The racer spooked him, but if he hadn't already been skittish, he woulda *never* throwed me…not Paint."

Shaken by that startling accusation, Chester declined Mr. Stansbury's offer of a ride and instead walked the four miles back into Prospect. Many times in the past, he'd traveled down this same dirt road with his arms wrapped tightly around Willie as they trotted home on Paint. The leaves of the sumac blazed a burnished red. As boys, they'd taken the sumac berries and concocted a tart drink known as "Indian tea." There were myriad medicinal uses for sumac; though no ancient remedy would bring back movement to his lifeless limbs, Chester wished he could boil or mash the berries into some elixir that would relieve Willie's debilitating depression…and his own.

Knowing what he faced when he returned home, he was struggling with his own feelings of desperation. He was at a loss as to what to do with his mother and how to rescue her from the alcohol-induced abuse that threatened her on a daily basis. Her sister, Clarisse, had offered to take her in. Earlier that morning, Chester had nearly convinced her to return to St. Louis with him on the late afternoon train—only to have that idea quashed by Blackie.

The ensuing argument was a replay of every confrontation they'd had since he first stood up to his father his senior year in high school; however, this one became physical when Blackie hurled Pearl's suitcase across their bedroom and pushed her down on the bed.

"Come home for the first time in over a year and think you're all grown up and can tell me what's what, do ya?"

"I'm not afraid of you."

"I'll show you afraid," said Blackie—starting towards him, his fists doubled.

"If you touch him, you'll never see me again!" shouted

Pearl.

Blackie pulled up short. His face registered a look unfamiliar to them both. "That's about right," he said. "From the beginning...it's always been you two against me. You two...and your *words*."

"That's not true," she said.

"Speakin' French and spoutin' poetry. Cuttin' me out...like I'm too stupid to be part of it..." His shoulders slumped and his eyes teared.

This was an emotion Chester had never seen.

"You used to love playin in the shop," he said to Chester. "Bein' there with me..."

"Dad...I'm...I—"

Blackie's hand silenced him; his eyes narrowed. "*One more word* about your mother goin' anywhere and I'll teach you both a lesson you'll never learn from books!"

Chester could see the look of resignation in his mother's eyes—eyes that warned him not to speak, not to incite Blackie's anger. In frustration, he headed towards his room.

"Where'd ya think yer goin'? We ain't finished with this!"

He followed after Chester, who disappeared up the stairs.

"Let him be, Frank," said Pearl—hurrying down the hallway. "He's promised to go visit Willie."

"Runnin' off to see his little buddy is he? Poor little Willie?"

"Have you no feelings for anyone!" Chester yelled from the top of the stairs.

Blackie shook his head and laughed.

"He'll never walk again and you find that funny?"

"I coulda told Ben Shepherd's girl she was marryin' a cripple long before he ever had an accident."

Chester descended the stairs. "Willie's my best friend and I'm not going to let you—"

"*Friend*? Is that what they call it nowadays?" He glared at him with disgust. "You boys make me sick...you always did," he said—heading back towards his bedroom.

"Pearl...get in here and pick up them clothes. You ain't goin' nowhere."

The brisk walk helped clear away some of Chester's confusion. He was determined no verbal or physical threat was going to prevent him from rescuing his mother. As he approached the house, he sensed something awry. Opening the back door, he observed a kitchen chair—smashed and lying in pieces in the downstairs hallway; his parent's bedroom door was hanging from one hinge.

"Mother?" He started down the hall. No answer. "*Mother...?*" he called again as he approached the bedroom.

He stepped over the chair legs, past the splintered door, and that's when he spotted her twisted and bloodied body by the foot of the bed—the pointed end of a raising hammer piercing her skull. The top dresser drawer had been flung against the far wall, but an open suitcase, half full of neatly packed clothes, sat on the bed undisturbed.

His first impulse was to collapse on her corpse. Instead, he stood there, motionless—staring at her lifeless body. 'How small she looks...how fragile.' In the silence, he could hear her singing an old French nursery rhyme:

> *Ah! Vous dirai-je Maman, ce qui cause mon tourment!*
> *Papa veut que je raison-ne, comme une grande personne.*
> *Moi, je dis que les bon bons, valent mieux que la raison.*

'Ah! I will say this to you Mama, this is the cause of my torment! Papa wants that I reason, like a grown-up person. Me, I say that the sweets are worth more than reason.'

Suddenly, he felt his chest heave. Something inside him shifted; his vision blurred a violent red. He headed straight for the shop. Entering the doorway, he stopped abruptly. Blackie lay on the dirt floor, unconscious and reeking of cheap whiskey. His overalls glistened crimson like a blood-spattered canvas. For a moment, Chester thought he would wretch.

Glancing around the shop, his eyes settled on the forge—still glowing an incandescent red-orange. As if reenacting a well-rehearsed scene, he went to the workbench and grabbed some old metal tongs. Slipping on tattered work gloves, he lifted a small crucible from the edge of the forge, grabbed a handful of lead sinkers from a rusty coffee can and tossed them into the graphite cup. Using the tongs, Chester carried the crucible back to the forge and held it over the refulgent coals. As he waited for the lead to liquefy, his mind was adrift

What is that which has one voice and goes on four legs in the morning, two legs at noon and three in the evening? 'Simple!' "Crawling babe, eager youth…and aged man with cane," he said aloud—as if answering a question posed by a spectre. 'If only life's riddles were as solvable as that of the Sphinx,' he thought.

When the crucible was half-filled with viscous liquid lead, he went searching. "There you are," he said—snatching a two-inch bolt from the worktable. Returning to Blackie, he placed the crucible on the earthen floor, removed the gloves and with his bare fingers, pried open his father's mouth—wedging the bolt between his palate and lolling tongue. The stench of rotgut whiskey and congealed blood sickened him.

"So…was this foretold, father? Am I responsible for this ill-fated end because I sought the answers to life's riddles in books? If so, you were right to hate my obsession for reading, my love of words."

Blackie moaned. He appeared to be regaining consciousness. Chester didn't panic, but his mind was conflicted. Taking justice into his own hands meant Blackie would be spared hanging; yet, revenging his mother's murder using a method employed by the Romans and the Spanish Inquisition, a method he discovered through his omnivorous reading, seemed apropos—considering how often his father had criticized him for 'wastin' time in them goddamn books.'

Nothing means anything until we assign it a meaning.

"Thank you, Buddha…and Amelia. Just the philosophical impetus I need."

Lifting the crucible, he held it above Blackie's gaping mouth. For a moment he hesitated, then he flashed on his mother's bloodied body.

She never did anything but try to love you...you selfish bastard! "We *both* tried to love you!" he wailed—tipping the crucible and pouring the hot molten lead straight into his father's mouth.

With the first rush of steam, Blackie's eyes sprung open wide. Chester recoiled. The choncroid and striated muscles in his father's neck rippled from the intense heat, laryngeal mucosa crackled and sputtered like hog fat in a frying pan, and steam escaped from his ears, nostrils and mouth—the mouth, from which such bile once spewed, now frozen in a rictus of malignity. Blackie's eyes became gelatinous—melting into amber glycerin. The thermal explosion in his lungs brought instantaneous death. The fetor of burning flesh gagged him. Before leaving the shop, Chester placed the crucible in his father's bloody, gloved hands.

Two days after learning of Chester's visit from Sandra, Amelia sat in the glider swing, reading, when she noticed Bessie hurrying her way, her expression, grief-stricken.

"What is it…what's wrong? Is it your mother?"

"Oh, my heaven's Amelia…it's terrible…just terrible. No one's called you?"

"What's happened?"

"I can't believe it…" She closed her eyes and shook her head.

"What's wrong…? Say *something*."

"I…I hate to be the one to tell you, but Chester O'Malley's…" Her voice choked and she began to sob.

"Has something happened to Chester?" Amelia gasped. "*What?* Tell me!"

"It isn't Chester. It's his mother...*and* his father. Blackie O'Malley killed Pearl! Beat her to death with a hammer. They found him this morning in his shop...dead. A suicide."

Amelia covered her face and moaned, "No, no, NO!" For a few moments, she sat—frozen, her skin horripilated. "*Poor* Chester. This will absolutely destroy him."

The incident occurred on a Friday. It took until the following Monday afternoon before anyone discovered the bodies, and it was Wednesday before authorities were able to locate Chester—"too distraught" to return from St. Louis for the double funeral.

When he heard the news, Willie Stansbury rallied—briefly. He told the county sheriff Chester admitted he was afraid Blackie might make good on recent threats to kill Mrs. O'Malley if she were to leave him. A call to her sister in St. Louis confirmed Pearl feared for her safety. Based on similar testimony and eyewitness accounts of Blackie's abuse and frequent blackout episodes, the county coroner declared the deaths a murder-suicide. Chester's visit to Prospect was widely discussed, but no one suspected him, though everyone agreed his visit most likely fueled the fatal argument.

The regulars in Luke's Barbershop spent days speculating about the tragedy. "How drunk would ya have to be to do somethin' like that?" asked Luke. "Plum wet-brained, I 'spect."

"That's near as bad as when Shorty Howard's wife drowned her twin baby girls in Wildcat Creek," said Vern Jennings, who was still on the mend from a recent heart attack. "Y'all probably too young to remember that, but it was a big scandal 'round these parts. She thought Shorty done got killed in the second battle of Newtonia over near Joplin, but when she heard he survived and was headin' home, she kinda lost it. Turns out Shorty's youngest brother—"

"It don't follow," said Charlie Wirth—ignoring Vern. "Blackie was a mean drunk, but he wudn't crazy."

"You don't think buryin' a hammer in your wife's head is just a little nuts?" ask Clyde Grantham.

"Oh, I don't know... Whenever Gladys starts in about her

mother comin' to live with us, I've had worse thoughts."

"That's right, Charlie, make a joke..."

"The point is," said Luke, "...thinkin' it ain't doin' it."

"I wonder how that poor kid of theirs will ever get over somethin' like this?"

For once, being thought 'a little too artistic' had its advantages. The case was closed. The O'Malley house and business were padlocked. It wasn't until a year and a half later that Chester left St. Louis and returned to Prospect—for good. Not that goodness had anything to do with it.

FIVE

Still reeling from the nightmarish events of his trip home, Chester had been invited to stay with his aunt but declined. For the past eighteen months, he had resided in Tower Hall, built on the Washington University campus as housing for the 1904 World's Fair. Having acquired additional credits each of the past two summers, he was entering his final full year of study.

Following the graduation of his former roommates, he was assigned a new room with Jimmy Buckelew, an underclassman, and Morris Moody, a third-year divinity major from Downers Grove, Illinois. Before transferring, Moody had attended evangelical Wheaton College, and beneath his conservative exterior smoldered the religiosity that would eventually bolster his career as an evangelist.

Plagued by insomnia, Chester struggled to maintain his equilibrium. It had been a difficult decision to remain in school, but the Rhodes Trust had recently informed him he was being considered for a scholarship to pursue a Master's Degree in English Literature from Oxford University. He hoped a new environment would enable him to leave the ever-present images of that tragic day behind, and he couldn't wait to escape the provincial, bigoted Midwest.

During the fall semester, Chester petitioned the Student Government for permission to establish The Wilde Society, named in honor of Oscar Wilde. The request was roundly defeated. Undaunted, he circulated a petition. At first, he had difficulty convincing any students to sign it for fear of reprisal from the university; even though he eventually obtained the necessary twenty-five signatures, his proposal was once again denied because Washington University, a private school with no support from the state of Missouri, was 'under no obligation to address any perceived inequality or injustice.'

His campaign brought him into direct confrontation with Morris Moody, who initiated an on-campus "revival"—protesting the establishment of an organization that would glorify the Irish author of 'soul-damning, nation-destroying' filth.' On several occasions, Moody attempted to engage him in a dialogue concerning the 'wicked transgression of homosexual sin.' To his chagrin, Chester's stock reply was, 'Methinks thou dost protest a little too much.'

The atmosphere in their dorm room grew inhospitable—glacial. Thanks to Moody, the same chilly reception permeated the entire dormitory. Thus, Chester spent every spare minute in the campus library. The Dean of the College of Liberal Arts, Dr. Cyrus Showalter, summoned him on several occasions, each time imploring him to drop the idea of The Wilde Society.

"Mr. O'Malley, you may be a brilliant scholar, but son, this idea of yours proves you're lacking common sense. May I ask you why in heaven's name you're doing this, knowing how people feel? It's a risky idea to say the least."

"'An idea that is not dangerous is unworthy of being called an idea at all.' Oscar Wilde."

"Between you and me, the man was a literary genius," said Dean Showalter, "but to the average person, merely a pederast and the epitome of debauchery. Homosexuality is against the law in every state of the union, and an organization named for a man convicted of crimes against nature is unthinkable. Not my opinion, but enough said. St. Louis may have impressed the world two decades ago with its progressive World's Fair, but it's as intolerant as a Baptist minister pretends to be about prostitution when he's not sampling its wares. If I were you, I'd finish my degree and move on to bigger and better things."

"Give in to the bigots?"

"Chester, there isn't a religion in the world that doesn't condemn homosexuals to hell's fire. Son, you don't stand a chance against the Morris Moodys of the world. They've got God on their side."

"Not any God I'm interested in."

"Don't you care what people say about you?"

"There is only one thing in the world worse than being talked about...and that is—"

"Not being talked about...*The Picture of Dorian Gray*. To a man who put so much emphasis on style, it's a notable epigram. But, surely you don't believe that?"

"Apparently what I believe, Dean Showalter, is of little consequence to anyone."

In time, he relinquished the idea of The Wilde Society, but not before he had antagonized much of the student body—most of which viewed him with antipathy. The disdain he experienced from fellow students and faculty alike made him determined to complete his degree and get far away from the buckle of the Bible Belt; however, one semester shy of graduation, an incident in Tower Hall brought a swift and jarring end to that dream when Morris Moody accused him of making sexual advances. Summoned to appear before Dean Showalter, he attempted to explain.

"I'd been up writing until 1:30 a.m. Jimmy, my other roommate, had already left for his 7:30 class. I awakened to find Morris sitting on the edge of my bed—his hand lightly gripping my erect penis. 'What do you think you're doing?' I asked him. 'Nothing,' he said. 'Would you kindly remove your hand and get off my bed?' He looked at me and replied, 'Are you sure that's what you want?' 'That's definitely what I want,' I said. I didn't over-react. I didn't threaten. I just reached over and removed his hand. Then, he randomly began quoting scripture."

"Scripture?"

"Proverbs 25:16. 'Do you like honey? asked the Lord God. Don't eat too much...it will make you sick.' Luke 21:34. 'Be careful or your hearts will be weighted down with dissipation, drunkenness and the anxieties of life. And that day will close on you unexpectedly like a trap.' 'I know you, Chester,' he said. 'Recognized you the minute you appeared. You are a tempter of the Devil, an adversary…the son of the morning star.'"

"Before I could reply, he leaned forward and tried to kiss me, but when I turned away, he bolted for the door, flung it open wide and began shouting, 'QUEER, QUEER, QUEER!' The crowd that gathered was immediately whipped into a frenzy by his preposterous storytelling. Truthfully, I was mesmerized by it myself. He could give Billy Sunday a run for his money. I'm grateful he didn't encourage them to stone me…because he had them believing they were totally justified."

Chester's explanation was in complete opposition to the one Moody fabricated. In it, Chester was the aggressor and he the unwilling victim. The dean of the Divinity School vouched for Moody, who had recently become engaged and planned to be married in the university chapel. Once again, Chester appeared before Dean Showalter, who informed him of the charges.

"You can't be serious. I have an impeccable academic record. I'm twenty hours shy of graduation. Morris Moody's a liar, a homophobe and a hypocrite…but, you're taking his word over mine?"

Due to the previous rumors surrounding his sexuality, corroboration of allegations from Harris Butler by the chairman of the English Department, and finally his recent attempt at establishing the ill-fated Wilde Society, Dean Showalter said he had no choice but dismissal.

Crestfallen, Chester walked back to Tower Hall. Upon entering his dorm room, he discovered Moody sitting at his writing desk, preoccupied with his biblical studies. He said nothing to Morris, who continued reading. Instead, he opened the top dresser drawer and removed his shaving kit. He walked out of the room, down the hall into the second floor bathroom. Setting the kit on the porcelain sink, he looked into the mirror and studied his sad, hazel eyes, which appeared to belong to a much older version of himself.

Outside, he heard approaching footsteps. "Enough!" he said aloud. Reaching into the shaving kit, he removed a straight razor and, without hesitation, slit his left wrist. A long diagonal gash. He found the blade's bite nearly imperceptible, the gush of blood—mesmerizing, dizzying.

"*What are you doing*?" came a shout from the doorway.

Quickly, he switched the razor to his bloody left hand. As the blade slashed his other wrist, he suddenly collapsed—his head striking the edge of the sink.

When he regained consciousness, he awoke to the blur of hospital dreariness—gray-green, cracked plaster walls. The nauseating miasma of ether, disinfectant and death permeated the air. Barely able to raise his head, he glanced down and saw his wrists bandaged and his arms restrained by thick leather straps.

From the next room, he heard a howl—a ululation of unfettered agony. Had he the strength, he would have answered in kind.

Following an extended stay at Barnes Hospital, not far from the university campus on Kingshighway, he was released. Had his primary care physician not been a member of the medical faculty of Washington University, he might have been transferred to the City Sanitorium—the normal procedure for suicidal patients. When the physician, Dr. Hiram Solomon, read the report furnished by the university, he determined Chester's condition would only worsen in a mental ward—insisting he remain at Barnes under constant surveillance.

"Sounds like you and that roommate were at odds," said Dr. Solomon. "Conflicting philosophies, one might say."

With a slight lift of his head, Chester acknowledged the sarcasm in the physician's statement. "I'm assuming...he was the one who—"

"Saved you? Ironic, isn't it? Thought you might like to know he's been admonished for preaching on campus and warned further evangelizing will result in his expulsion."

"Morris Moody isn't the disease," said Chester, still groggy from the mild sedative. "He's only...a symptom."

"And what disease might that be?"

"Sexual repression...homophobia."

Solomon left the room briefly. When he returned, Chester seemed more alert.

"You mentioned homophobia before. So, you are homosexual then? I only ask for clarification...no other reason."

"Actually, I think sexuality is rather...fluid. Although I've had only one same sex partner, I've been attracted to another male in the past...a high school friend. Likewise, I've been sexually attracted to a woman...a teacher, actually. Sex, for me, is just an expression of my genuine feelings for someone. It isn't something I would compartmentalize or assign one of those emotionally charged labels to."

"That's a very forward-looking explanation, I must say," said Dr. Solomon, whose thick glasses magnified his green eyes to comic dimension. "But you do realize psychiatry finds anything beyond heterosexuality a form of mental illness. I tell you this, not because I agree with that interpretation, but because there are those in residency here who would recommend you be incarcerated at City Sanitorium."

"Psychiatry is where medicine was less than a century ago. Blood-letting, purgation...all that superstitious cant. If psychiatry can't find a satisfactory cure, it looks for a drug to numb the pain...or worse yet, tries to lacerate it. Whatever happened to *primum non nocere*...do no harm? Now, it's *melius anceps remedium quam nullum* and damn the consequences!"

"That's pretty cynical. It *is* better to do something than nothing."

"Cynical? No, doctor, that's reality in the 20th century. Here's a little nihilism for you. At this point, I could care less where I'm incarcerated. Everything I've ever wanted...everyone I've ever loved...is lost to me. *La vie est la merde!*"

"My boy, it's never easy for one with individualistic ideals...one whose life choices do not run parallel to the mainstream."

"Ideals? Life choices? I wonder what Kierkegaard would think about carving up one's wrists with a razor?"

Dr. Solomon ignored the comment. "May I ask...*why* the suicide attempt? Why the need to create a Wilde Society? If you don't mind my saying, not very bright for such a bright boy."

For a moment, Chester felt compelled to tell him the truth. Here was his chance to unburden himself of the ever-present guilt for murdering his father—even if it meant imprisonment or death. Dr. Solomon seemed like the kind of man who might even be sympathetic towards a crime of passion, a justifiable homicide, retribution for years of physical and emotional torment. From out of nowhere, he suddenly recalled the Dickinson poem Amelia first used to challenge his class: *A Secret told – Ceases to be a Secret-then – A Secret – kept – That-can appall but One...*

Dr. Solomon could see that Chester was lost in reverie. "I shouldn't have asked you that," he said. "Forgive me for being so blunt."

"Unlike a razor blade..."

Dr. Solomon chuckled. "Though purely from a psychological standpoint, I would like to understand your motivation for these clearly self-destructive acts."

Recalling the final words of Amelia's eulogy for her father, he wanted to offer, "Guilt demands punishment?" but instead answered, "Temporary insanity...or, perhaps, permanent insanity. You tell me, doctor."

Dr. Solomon could sense his growing agitation. "You should know I do not believe you would benefit from any treatment you could receive in a mental hospital. Rest now...and we'll talk again when you're feeling better."

"I've given up on ever feeling better," he said with a tone of complete resignation.

SIX

Power lines helped usher in the 20th century to rural America—two decades after the fact. The completion of a new coal-fired power plant in 1920 made electricity available to all residents within the Prospect city limits. With the backing of Herb Müller, Karl received a start-up loan from the Bank of Prospect and opened Madeira Lighting and Appliance. Since his return from the war and his brief stopover in Cincinnati, he'd anticipated how much electricity would impact life in small towns. The answer proved to be beyond his wildest expectation.

Madeira Lighting and Appliance began in a building adjacent to O'Malley's Metalworks. At first, Karl stocked the store with moderately priced lighting fixtures and small appliances: percolators, toasters and the wildly popular electric iron. Women who had labored for years with heavy flatirons heated on stovetops were anxious to own this modern wonder, followed in short order by the newly manufactured vacuum cleaner. After years of dragging heavy rugs outdoors for the semi-annual "beating," homemakers were ecstatic about the idea of vacuuming rugs weekly; however, the early models often proved less effective than sweepers, routinely developing mechanical problems. Aware of this, he added a repair shop and hired his old high school teammate, Bobby Allenby, who traveled to St. Louis to learn the repair trade.

Within eighteen months, Madeira Lighting and Appliance had repaid its initial loans and Karl expanded the business to locations in Ironton and Potosi, the latter quickly becoming his most profitable store. Following those successes, he and Sarah, pregnant with their first child, moved to Potosi in 1922.

"Please, don't be sad. Potosi's not that far away," Sarah reassured Amelia. "And, a baby in the family...just think. If it's a boy, we're calling him Fred. If it's a girl, Millicent, for your mother. We're so happy, and you'll be Auntie Ammie."

That summer, Amelia spent most of every day in her garden. Gardening had been a hobby since Miss Minnie first introduced her to that "labor of love." For nearly two decades, she had carefully cultivated a wide variety of perennials given to her by the old woman. If there were any peace to be had, she found it working the soil, pruning shrubs and planting new annuals. She even enjoyed the drudgery of weeding. Once the threat of frost vanished, usually by mid-April, she spent her weekends prepping the soil, mulching and planting. When school ended in early May, gardening became her avocation.

This year, the garden would be her sanctum and her saving grace. With Karl and Sarah's recent move to Potosi, Amelia's anxiety emerged as a chronic presence—gardening providing a temporary balm. However, the tranquility was short-lived when city workers moved into the neighborhood and began digging trenches for a citywide water and sewer system. Before he left town, Karl paid the $75 fee to have the lines run to 906 W. 6th. At first, she thrilled to think she would have running water and an indoor toilet, but when she experienced the upheaval caused by the excavation, the clamor and the intrusion, Amelia blamed him for 'the further molestation of my peace of mind.'

In the intervening years since their marriage, the bitterness she felt towards her brother and sister-in-law had slowly mollified. Sarah made every effort to include her in all their holiday plans. Sunday dinners rotated between the two households. Eventually, she came to realize this was as close to the dream of having Sarah in her life as she would ever have. Therefore, she buried her feelings and accepted, as best she could, how her life had become the perfect example of situational irony, though one she could never use in the classroom.

Early on, Bessie served as her sounding board, but after months of listening to Amelia relive every slight and dredge up every incident—consistently painting herself the victim of other's callousness—she finally spoke her mind. "Don't you see how you create situations where you can be hurt? I know it seems like someone is always injuring you…but Amelia, the pain you feel is based on the unmet expectations you place on others. It's difficult, but you must learn to expect nothing."

"You simply don't understand what it's like to lose someone…someone irreplaceable. The pain is unbearable…ever-present and inescapable!"

"Mother always says pain is part of life, but suffering is a choice—choosing to go back and relive painful things over and over again. You simply must learn to let the past go. Let it go, dear, and move on."

Following that conversation, she did not speak to Bessie again for several weeks. She remained convinced people simply did not understand the depth of her sensitivity, her feelings, her despair. There was one who did, but…

To Amelia, one plant in her garden best symbolized those feelings—*Dicentra spectabilis*—the Bleeding Heart. Miss Minnie had given her several starts years ago. Now, they were spread around every partially shaded area in her garden; the delicate, feathery leaves and the abundant pillowy teardrops of pink, heart-shaped blossoms were pure poetry to her: *There is a flower that Bees prefer—And Butterflies—desire—* Dickinson had written those lines as an ode to purple clover, but she preferred to assign them to the Bleeding Heart, which she felt encompassed all the beauty, fragility and sadness borne of the human dilemma. Intellectually, she found the idea overly sentimental, perhaps even trite and bathetic, but that's how she felt.

Whenever she saw a Bleeding Heart, she inevitably thought of Chester. The cascade of hearts on a delicate green stem embodied all the pain she associated with their relationship. She regretted how she'd handled the encounter in the library office, how she'd failed to report Blackie's abuse. She felt responsible for much of his turmoil and despair—her contribution to his life '*closing twice before its close.*' Regret...so much regret.

Once the blooming cycle of the Bleeding Hearts passed, she cut the stems back before they could turn brown and wither; she couldn't bear to see them slowly die. And, each spring when they again pushed through the soil, she told herself that someday, Chester, too, would reemerge and blossom.

It remained her fondest hope.

*   *   *

In April, 1928, Sarah's mother died of cancer of the blood. Under normal circumstances, Amelia might have accompanied them to Valley Ridge, but Sarah convinced Karl that Millie, not yet six, was too young to be exposed to the drama surrounding a funeral and there was still a fear that cancer might be contagious. She asked "Auntie Ammie" to care for her niece in their absence. Nothing made her happier than spending time with Millicent Jamison Madeira. She loved reading to young Millie; she found herself experiencing a joyousness she'd missed in her own childhood.

"Daddy says you were the smartest little girl that ever was," said Millie, as she sat on her auntie's lap—holding a picture book Amelia had ordered from a Montgomery Ward catalog.

"He told you that?"

"Uh huh...and he said you should teach me to make homemade noodles 'cause mommy can't make 'em good as you."

"When you're a little older. I was six when someone taught me," she said—remembering Miss Minnie, who had recently passed away at age eighty-five. "And, I'll show you how to start a flower garden, too."

"Auntie Ammie...do you think I'm smart?"

"Oh, yes, dear heart...very. And, beautiful, too...like your mommy."

The day before her parent's scheduled return, Millie awoke early—complaining of a headache and running a low-grade fever. "I want my mommy and daddy," she cried, again and again.

Panicked, Amelia contacted Dr. Carlson. An examination revealed nothing; however, by the next morning, a small rash peppered the child's forehead and she summoned him again.

"She's burning up and the rash is spreading."

"Sounds like measles. Doc Blevins over in Potosi says they've had a bit of an outbreak. There's not much I can do. The fever usually lasts three or four days. Listen, Fern Lewis is having contractions every five minutes. Gotta get over there. As soon as the baby comes, I'll drop by." It was three o'clock in the afternoon before he arrived. The rash had spread to her arms and chest; her fever spiked at 103.

"Got 'em all right. Has she been coughing much? The virus is highly contagious."

"She's been coughing off and on since last night."

"Ever had 'em?"

"I've been exposed many times over the years. Remember the outbreak we experienced three or four years ago? Half the freshman class came down with them. Fortunately, I was spared."

When Karl and Sarah arrived later that evening, they were horrified to see their "baby" covered with the red blotches.

"Did you call Doc Carlson?" Karl asked. "The girl's on fire."

"Of course I did. He's been here twice."

"Well, what did he say?"

"Said Potosi experienced a recent outbreak. She must have been exposed to someone there."

"I mean, what did he say we should *do*?"—panic powering every word.

"Karl, please," said Sarah.

"How long's she had this fever?"

"It started last night. The doctor says it should break in three or four days."

"Three or four days? Come on, Sarah…pack up her things," he commanded. "We're taking her home. Doc Blevins will know what to do."

"Do you think that's a good idea? Maybe she should stay here until her fever breaks."

"I think Amelia's right. She's too sick. Why don't you go on home and I'll stay here with Millie. When her temperature stabilizes, we'll move her then."

"I'm not taking any chances." He picked up his daughter and headed for the car.

"At least let me give her a goodbye hug."

Ignoring the request, he continued on.

"Karl…! Sarah, you know I did everything I could."

"Of course you did, dear."

"I love Millie as if she were my own."

"I know. He knows it, too. He's just upset. I'll call you as soon as we learn something."

They hurriedly embraced, and Sarah ran to the car. Distraught, Amelia wandered out into the yard and watched until their taillights disappeared around the corner, past the school.

Millie's fever broke on the fourth day; the rash lasted a total of five. All signs of the measles completely vanished, to everyone's relief. However, nearly two months later, within hours of complaining of a sore throat, she developed a high fever and suffered the first of multiple convulsions. Dr. Blevins said her brain was swelling; he feared she'd developed encephalitis associated with her previous measles infection. Following a final convulsion, the child lapsed into a coma from which she never recovered. Forty-eight hours later, young Millicent Madeira was dead.

Dr. Blevins wasn't entirely convinced the encephalitis was a result of the measles infection or the meningococcal virus. From everything he'd read on the subject, the incubation period between a case of measles and a rare encephalitic reaction was usually closer to two weeks; this had taken four times that long. When he consulted with an old colleague at St. Louis Children's Hospital, his suspicion was confirmed.

"Do you know if the child's father served in World War One?"

"He did, yes...lost sight in an eye from exposure to mustard gas. Why?"

"He may be a syphilis carrier. A lot of those boys came home with it."

"But that was ten years ago."

"If he has tertiary syphilis, he may not show any signs for decades. But the combination of the girl's measles and any dormancy from a hereditary standpoint may have provoked the encephalitis. Did you examine her throat?"

"Found significant swelling."

"Anything like a spongy mass?"

"I did notice a little pouch that had ulcerated."

"Probably a gummy tumor...a gumma. Has the mother shown any signs?"

"None I know of. What should I do?"

"Well, this is a prickly situation, but maybe you should talk to the father."

"That won't be easy," said Blevins. "He's a bit of a hothead as it is, and really taking the child's death hard. Havin' to ask him if he was exposed to syphilis seems like it would be a pretty cruel thing to do at this point. From the beginning, he's been looking for someone to blame. Think it might drive him over the edge if he thought he was the culprit."

"It's your call."

"He has a sister over in Prospect...a teacher. Maybe I'll contact her and see what she knows about it."

SEVEN

On the 4th of July weekend in 1928, the Class of 1918 held its tenth year reunion by the bandstand in City Park. Of the twelve graduates, only nine were present. Among those attending were: Maisy (McDowell) Jennings, her husband, Leonard, and their twin daughters, aged seven; Willie and Sandra (Shepard) Stansbury; Mr. and Mrs. Melvan Rucker and their four sons, aged eight, five, three and eleven months; Madeline (Jones) Barnard; Miss Daisy McDowell and Miss Kendra Shepard (Sandra's twin); Mr. and Mrs. Raymond Miller and their nine year old daughter, Raylene, and 6 year old son, Larry; and Miss Amelia Madeira.

Tony Reeves and Horace (Lefty) Bishop, both of whom joined the army before the start of their senior year, were also in attendance along with their wives and children—just as they had been for the 5th year reunion. Still missing was Chester O'Malley.

All of the class's former teachers had been invited. Several, unable to attend because of ill-health or 'the heat,' sent letters to be read; others, indifferent from years of perfunctory invitations, failed to respond—primarily because they felt slighted compared to the fawning attention and flowery adulation usually heaped on Miss Madeira. In addition to Miss Goldie Maddox, long dead from the Spanish flu, two other teachers, Miss Minnie Lajoy and Miss Florence Orton, had died since the 5th year reunion in 1923.

At the request of Raymond Miller, Amelia prepared a large cast-iron pot—brimming with her famous chicken and noodles.

Having no means to keep the dish warm, she arranged for Raymond to pick her up and bring her to the park.

The women, most of whom brought picnic baskets stuffed with fried chicken, potato salad, baked beans, green beans, corn on the cob, deviled eggs, fresh sliced tomatoes and cucumbers and a variety of desserts, fussed around the picnic tables. The men, whose only contribution was a cumulous cloud of cigarette smoke, hung out in the shade of a large elm tree, in an effort to avoid direct sunlight. The children played on and around the bandstand; two of the oldest were in charge of making sure the younger ones did not tumble down the steps or wander into the dank, smelly restrooms below.

By 11:30 a.m., the mercury on the temperature gage at Feldman's Filling Station, located on the southeast corner of the square, registered eighty-four degrees—headed for an oppressive ninety-three. J.T. Feldman, who purchased the old wood and tin shed formerly housing O'Malley's Metalworks a few years after the murder-suicide, had demolished it and replaced it with Prospect's only gas station within the city limits.

In addition to gasoline and fuel oil, Feldman's sold large blocks of ice and had recently installed a cooler full of carbonated soft drinks—including Coca Cola, Barq's Root Beer, Red Crème Soda and Sunkist Lemonade. A new concrete sidewalk in front of the station had been inlaid with hundreds of colorful, cork-lined bottle caps—the design pressed into the cement like candied-fruit in *panetón*.

Dispatched to purchase ice, Melvan Rucker was reporting on this 'work of art' as he chipped away with an ice pick. "Willie, I tell ya, 'ol J. T.'s some kinda artiste! With them little bottle caps, he's turned that damned sidewalk into a buncha...you know. Oh, hell, what's them things made outta little pieces of glass called?"

Willie remained, expressionless.

"You know what I'm talkin' about, Raymond. Tony, Lefty...?"

"I can honestly say I never understood half of what you were tryin' to say and nothin's changed," said Raymond—adding a big wink. Lefty and Tony howled.

"Miss Madeira!" Melvan bellowed, "'Member when you told us about that Roman sidewalk them archeologimacallems found over in England? The *great* somethin' or other?"

"The Great Pavement...at Woodchester."

"That's it! What's that art made with them little pieces of colored glass called?"

"Do you mean mosaics?" offered Daisy McDowell.

"MOSAICS...that's it...mosaics! See, Miss Madeira...told ya I was payin' attention!"

Similar mundane conversations were humming at various tables. Some began with 'Do you remember when we...' Others revolved around the rigors of raising children. Although most were prosaic, one was not.

"How's Willie doing?" Miss Madeira asked Sandra, as the two of them spread a tablecloth on one of the picnic tables farthest from the cigarette smoke. Willie's father had driven him and Sandra into Prospect; Melvan and Lefty carried him from the automobile to a folding chair set up under a shade tree. Though he had limited use of both arms, he remained paralyzed from the waist down.

"See for yourself," she said. "Thin as a rail. Can't remember the last time I saw him smile."

"I know it must be difficult."

"That don't begin to describe it. You know, we only dated three times before we got engaged. Then, Willie had the accident. For several months after, he tried to break it off, but I told him we were in this together. Maybe I thought he'd walk again...or, maybe I thought we'd have some kind of normal life...but, I was wrong."

"I know you don't mean that."

"Oh, but I do. Unless you've loved someone...planned a life together...only to have it end before it even had a chance to begin, you can't know what I feel. Not sure how much more I can take, and I hope no one brings up '*poor* Chester O'Malley' at this reunion like they did the last one."

"Why, Sandra, I'm surprised to hear you talk this way."

"I've lived with Chester's ghost hovering over my marriage from the beginning and believe me—"

"Hello there, you two," said Madeline, who'd come up behind them. "Looks like you're having a serious conversation."

"Sandra was just catching me up," said Amelia, relieved she'd interrupted them.

"I was going to inquire if either of you had seen Chester lately. I asked Willie, but he seems...distracted. I wonder if he's gotten any better. The last I heard he—"

"Excuse me," said Sandra—her eyes connecting with Amelia's. "I need to check on Willie." She walked away, but instead of heading towards him, she joined her sister, who shared a table with Daisy McDowell.

"I'm sorry. Did I say something to offend her?"

"I think she's just exhausted from taking care of Willie. It can't be easy."

"No, I suppose not," said Madeline—glancing towards him.

Raymond and Melvan were cracking up at their own jokes as Willie sat, stone-faced.

"He's getting worse, isn't he?"

"Your husband couldn't come this year?" asked Amelia, who continued to set the table; Madeline pitched in.

"No...well actually, he hates these things. Won't even go to his own class reunions."

"They can be a little difficult if you don't know anyone. Hand me the salt and pepper, would you please?"

She reached into the small basket, pulled out the glass shakers and handed them to Amelia. "It's hard coming back here. Some people still blame my family for spreading the Spanish flu. Years ago, I received several hate-filled letters."

"I know how cruel people can be."

"Truthfully, I only came to see you...and I hoped to see Chester. Other than a trip out to High Ridge to visit all the graves, there's really nothing left for me here. If Betty Gentry hadn't invited me to stay at her home, I probably wouldn't have come this year either."

"Are you still working at that big radio station in St. Louis?"

"KMOX. Yes, but I'm looking for something better. I'm basically a glorified secretary, at the top of the bottom of the pay scale. My business degree from Draughon's was secretarial. I should have gotten one in accounting, but I wasn't very confident in my own abilities back then."

"I always told you that you could be anything you wanted. You were valedictorian."

"Way too much was made of that," she said with a sigh. "Grades mean little in the real world. Besides, I knew kids always called me "brown-noser" behind my back, and I guess I really was. I had to study all the time…while Chester, with that photographic memory of his, never did. I read because books were assigned. He devoured books because he loved words and ideas. It was if he absorbed every little bit of knowledge he ever came into contact with, while I learned it just long enough to pass a test. I wanted my family to be proud of me…to make all E's, and I did…except for the S+ you gave me first quarter of senior English. Remember?"

"I only wanted you to take learning more seriously…to become a better thinker. Oh yes, I do remember how upset you were."

"Thought my life was over when I got that report card. I actually hated you for a long time. Took me awhile to realize it was the best thing that could have happened. When I went off to Cape, I became a different type of student, but then the epidemic just destroyed everything."

"Don't know how you survived it…truly I don't."

"Well, I think I more or less sleepwalked my way through it. I honestly don't recollect most of it."

"That's how many of us get through tragedies."

"Wish now I'd stayed at Cape, but I needed to get a job to help support Virginia and myself, so I moved to St. Louis, transferred to business school and worked part-time."

"You did what you had to do."

"Thought things always had to be just so...*perfect*, you know? But death is messy, really messy. I questioned whether I'd survive, or if I even wanted to. In truth, I did it more for Virginia than me...and I did it completely out of fear. I never really had very much confidence in my own intelligence. Always pretended I did, of course, but you saw through it, and certainly Chester did. When I compared myself to him, I realized I was just average."

"Well, I wouldn't—"

"How is he? Do you ever see him? Heard he's completely let himself go."

"Afraid so."

"What happened? I don't mean about the tragedy with his parents. It had to be something more."

"You can't know how many times I've asked myself that question. Some incident in college, perhaps?"

"Funny you should say that, because once, shortly after I transferred to Draughon's, I took the trolley to Washington U. and tracked him down. He was living off-campus with one of his former English professors. I thought that was really odd."

"...?"

"I met him...the professor...and there was something about him I didn't like. Felt like he was just using Chester...kind of draining him of the vitality, the passion he always had in your class."

"It's the first I've heard of it."

"Miss Madeira, I think I can tell you this..." She lowered her voice. "I got the feeling they were...you know..."

"Madeline..."

"Come now, you have to admit everyone always thought he was that way."

"That was just talk...pure provincialism. But, even if it were true, what difference could it possibly make. Chester was Chester...and that's why we loved him." She suddenly realized she'd revealed more of her feelings than she intended.

"Is he still living over there in that old house?" she asked—

glancing toward Feldman's.

"Yes. He sold the shop but kept the house."

"I'm tempted to walk over there right now. I'm not leaving town until I see him. What does he do? Does he have a job?"

"Spends almost every day in the county library...reading. And, he appears to be writing something."

"Oh, then you've seen him. Have you talked to him?"

"No...the librarian keeps me informed. He knows I'm in school, and the librarian, Phyllis Jenson...do you remember Johnny Jenson? Well, he met Phyllis in college at Cape. Anyway, Phyllis says Chester watches the clock like a student eager for the final bell. When school's out, he heads straight home. He knows I often stop by the library after school. He purposely tries to avoid me. I think he's too embarrassed or something."

"Why don't you just go over to his house?"

"I did *once*...not long after he returned. I know he was in there, but he wouldn't answer the door."

"I can't believe he won't see you. You were his biggest inspiration. He truly loved you. That was obvious to everyone. Why, the night before graduation, he and Willie came by to see what I was doing. It was the first time the three of us ever had a really serious conversation. You know how kids are. We talked about some of the funny things we remembered. About how Melvan stuck pencils up his nose and made Daisy McDowell laugh so hard she wet her pants. How she was so embarrassed she left the room in tears. Then, Maisy started bawling and ran after her. They never could react as individuals. Like the Hydra you told us about. If you cut off one head, two grew back."

"What a thing to say."

"Well, it's true...admit it," she said, finally coaxing a smile from Amelia. "We all joked about how Mr. Johnston tried to stop Willie from riding Paint to school and how frustrated he'd get whenever they'd come trotting into the school yard. We joked about ol' coach Robertson...how he fell asleep in algebra and expelled so much gas that half the class left the room and he didn't even know it."

"Oh, my…"

"And we talked about graduation and leaving Prospect…what we were going to do with our lives. But mostly, we talked about you and what a difference you'd made in the way we saw the world. You'll never know the influence you've had on your students."

"That's always nice to hear."

"Especially, Chester. Senior year, it was like watching this little bud suddenly blossom into an unbelievably beautiful rose. You were the gardener, his soil and water and his sunshine. I don't think Chester would have ever been Chester without you."

Although Amelia welcomed the praise, she could not ignore the disconnect between Madeline's words and reality. 'Chester would never have been Chester without me? Then that makes me responsible for the Chester he's become!'

At that very moment, she noticed Sandra handing a cup of ice water to Willie, who barely acknowledged her presence. Her eyes blurred with tears. She suddenly found herself squinting from the bright sunlight. The oppressive humidity closed in around her, and she felt dizzy.

"Maybe we shouldn't talk about him anymore. I know it makes some people really uncomfortable. Sandra, for one."

"I'm sorry, but that's ridiculous. That's just because he and Willie were so close. She had to marry him to find out what I already knew. Willie would never love anyone more than he loved Chester, and I admit I used to be jealous because I was in love with him for years."

"Please—"

"I'm not going to pretend he's dead just because it makes some people uncomfortable. You'll be glad to know I stopped caring what others think a long time ago. Especially the Sandra Shepards and the Daisy McDowells of the world."

"Well then, Madeline," said Miss Madeira, "perhaps you'll do it for me…"

EIGHT

In Prospect, there was no immediate reaction to Black Thursday. News of the initial stock market crash of 1929 didn't reach the majority of Prospect's residents until the following Wednesday, when the *Prospect Banner* made mention of the stock plunge.

Like many small-town banks in the Midwest, the Bank of Prospect had been hit hard in recent years with an inordinate number of farm foreclosures. Because the drought of 1930 produced insufficient crops, coupled with the implementation of high tariffs on crop exports, farmers were defaulting on loans in record numbers. In addition, a number of businesses failed because consumers no longer had available cash. Still, it wasn't until the fall of 1931—nearly two years after the infamous crash—that the Bank of Prospect closed its doors to prevent a run on the bank.

In good faith, Karl had accepted dozens of "I.O.U.s"—some for hundreds of dollars. Unable to collect, Madeira Lighting & Appliance defaulted on expansion loans held by both the Bank of Prospect and Farmers and Merchants Bank of Potosi. As a result, he was forced to shutter first the store in Prospect, then the one in Ironton. Merchandise from both stores was impounded and auctioned off. The only thing keeping the Potosi store from facing foreclosure was the fact that ownership had been transferred out of Karl's name the previous year.

Following Millie's death, Karl plummeted into a deep depression. At first, he blamed Sarah. 'If only' they had taken her with them to Valley Ridge for the funeral, they might have been able to immediately respond to her illness. Over his objection, she had insisted she was too young and they best leave her with Amelia; therefore, he held her responsible. Then, he shifted the blame to Amelia for any numbers of reasons, none of which made sense. An invitation for the weekly Sunday dinner was withdrawn 'until Karl feels a little better.'

Month after month, he continued to grieve, it became a ritual. He refused to let Sarah touch anything in Millie's room: clothes, toys—even forbidding her to make the child's bed. He spent hour after hour, day after day, sequestered in her room, often refusing to come out even to eat. He was physically unable to go to work, partly due to his depressive state, partly due to his near-constant inebriation. When on the rare occasion he did leave, he'd padlock the door to prevent Sarah from entering.

Finally, after more than a year of his erratic behavior, Bobby Allenby, who originated the repair-arm of the business, convinced Karl to let him buy into the Potosi store. When Karl's credit came under fire, he agreed to shift the title of ownership to Bobby.

Unable to console him or convince him to seek help, Sarah finally turned to her sister-in-law. "When will it end? It's been nearly three years. It's not just the drinking...it's his mental condition, his refusal to let Millie go. He keeps the door padlocked. I'm not permitted to come in. He's sits in her room and actually talks to her. I hear him. He says things that...that make me want to scream."

"What kind of things?"

"I know it's mostly because of the alcohol, but some of the things he says make me think that... Oh, I *can't*...I can't say it." Always thin, Sarah had lost so much weight she looked gaunt. Her normally healthy coloring had turned pallid and her eyes—the eyes Amelia had loved from the moment she first peered into them—were dull and lifeless.

"Those things you insinuated...years ago. I can't help but

wonder if—"

"*No*, Sarah. Karl would never. Don't ever think that."

"He doesn't want anything to do with me. Nothing. I understand how dead inside we both feel, but we have to do something to get out of this dreadful place. I tried to talk to him about having another child and he looked at me with such contempt. I don't know how much more I can endure."

This wasn't the first time she'd discussed their problems, but she'd never before revealed such intimate details. Amelia decided it was time to bring up the possibility that Karl may have been indirectly responsible for Millie's death.

"Only a week or so after she died, Dr. Blevins called me."

"Why would he?"

"Because he wanted to know if Karl had been exposed…to syphilis, while stationed in France."

"But, that's ridiculous. That was years ago. He's never shown any signs. What made him think such a thing?"

"He'd talked to a specialist at St. Louis Children's Hospital who treated rare cases like Millie's. He said something called tertiary syphilis might not show up for years, but when a child is exposed to measles, combined with a delayed reaction to dormant syphilis, it could result in the swelling of the brain. If it's the type he says, Karl wouldn't even know he was a carrier."

"But he swore the only two places he saw in France were the battlefield and the hospital. Either he was lying…or…I don't know. I just don't know anymore."

Amelia had never seen her so distraught. Even when Millie died, she had managed to maintain a certain composure—at least in public.

Sarah bit into her lower lip, her anguish now suffused with alarm. She watched as Amelia rose from the table, went to the sideboard, retrieved an old tin box and set it down before them. "What's this?"

Amelia pried open the lid, removed a photograph and handed it to her. "Her name was Ninette. She gave Karl a copy of

The Phantom of the Opera when he was in the hospital. The day he returned from the war, I got home from school to find him drunk and in a rage. He hadn't received my letter telling him Papa was dead, and he insinuated maybe he wouldn't have died had I taken better care of him. Most of it was the liquor talking, but after I finally got him into bed, I found this as I was unpacking his things."

"Who is she?"

"Obviously, some French nurse...probably cared for him while he was hospitalized. After finding this, I reread some of his old letters and detected several references to how 'helpful' and 'comforting' some of the nurses were. I don't know, but if he really does have syphilis, he may have gotten it from one of them. That could explain a lot of his irrational behavior...and it could explain why Millie died."

"But that means I've been exposed, too! Why would you wait so long to tell me? *Why?*"

"Oh, my dear...I've wanted to say something so many times, but I didn't know how to do it without destroying everything. Can you ever forgive me?"

"What the hell are you trying to do?" he shouted into the receiver. Incensed by Sarah's accusations, he immediately phoned Amelia. "Hoping you can finally have her all to yourself?"

"Karl, please...this is a party line. I won't have this conversation on the telephone." The line went dead.

"Damn her! She hung up on me!"

Sarah tried to calm him, but he picked up a flower vase and smashed it—before departing in a fury. She watched him jump in his truck and speed away. Alarmed, she placed a call to Amelia, who, thinking it was Karl, ignored the ring.

Half an hour later, Amelia heard tires screeching to a stop in front of the house. Before she could even get to the window, he bolted through the back door. "What are you doing here? Have you lost your mind?"

"Don't *ever* hang up on me again, do you hear?" His face

radiated a flush of anger, and his eyes were glazed from too much alcohol.

"Then please don't ever call me up, screaming into the phone like a crazy man. Besides, you're drunk. I've told you many times—"

"Don't talk to me like you're my teacher. This is still my house as much as it is yours…more even. I paid for the plumbing and I've paid taxes on it ever since I got back from the war. So, I'll come here any goddamn time I want!"

"Please, stop shouting. Bessie will hear you."

"*Seu cabrão!* Before we got married, she told Sarah I made passes at her."

"She would never say something like that. I told Sarah myself."

"*Why* would you do that? It almost wrecked everything?"

"You've never needed any help wrecking things… remember? You started early and you haven't stopped since. M*y life had stood-a loaded gun—in corners-till a day…*"

"None of that poetry shit!"

"*…the owner passed-identified… and carried me away!*"

"What does any of that mean?"

"Do I need to spell it out?"

He stared at her in disbelief. "I loved you, little Sis. All we ever had was each other. The old man was never really there for us…after mama died. Had his carving…and his women."

"What women? What are you raving about now?"

"The whores…down at the Granite Quarry Hotel. Where'd you think all the money went?"

"That's nonsense."

"And that *Annan* woman. Remember when she came here…all the way from St. Louis?"

"Miss Anna? The one who took us to the fair?"

"Her name was Enid…Enid Annan…the wife of Papa's boss. I was only eight or nine, but I knew what was going on. I could tell by the way they acted. Why do you think we moved here? Papa got fired for screwing the boss's wife. He told me so once when he was fallin' down drunk."

"I don't want to hear any of this!" she cried—retreating from the kitchen into the dining room.

"No, you never want to know anything about *real* life," he said—following behind her. "You live in a fantasy world with your poems...and that crap you write in your journals."

"You want *reality*...try this. Know why Papa left San Leandro? Know why he never went back? Because his *father*...our grandfather, got Aunt Clara pregnant...and Papa felt guilty because he knew about it and couldn't stop it. That enough reality for you?"

"Who told you that?"

"The letter you brought back from Cincinnati, the one you thought you lost? It was all in there...the sins of the father. And it's in my journals...the only way I have of coping with all this insanity."

"Where are those damn things?"

She looked at him with alarm.

"You better *never* show those to anyone! I mean it! If you ever told Sarah about...you know...any of that—"

"She knows," Amelia said—staring at him in disgust. "You bet she knows."

"WHAT HAVE YOU DONE?" He lunged at her—clutching her arms and forcing her down on the dining table. "I'll kill you...I swear it!" he said—spittle flying from his mouth.

"*Stop it!*" screamed Sarah from the doorway. Anticipating the worst, she followed him in the family car. "Are you crazy? Let Amelia go!" She started for him.

"How did you...? Get out of here!" he shouted—shoving her backwards.

"Take your hands off me!" demanded Amelia—pulling away.

"Can't believe you followed m-e-e-e," he slurred as he staggered towards Sarah.

"I can't live like this anymore...not like this. Not with the drinking. Not with all the crazy mumbling in Millie's room..."

"Don't you dare say her name!" he threatened—doubling up his fist.

"MILLIE, MILLIE, MILLIE!"

As if he'd been shot, he staggered backwards—crashing into the table before losing his balance and falling to his knees. He grabbed hold of the edge of a chair and slowly pulled himself to his feet.

"Eu vou matar-te!" he sobbed. "I swear...I'll kill you *both!"* He lunged towards Sarah, but before he could strike her, his face contorted in agony. He clutched his head with both hands, spun around and staggered past Amelia towards the dining room windows. His momentum carried him into the old conductor's stool—knocking the giant Christmas cactus to the floor.

"Ohhh!" he moaned—collapsing into Fredo's old rocker. His fingers tore at his scalp and he began rocking violently, back and forth.

"What is it?"

"Those shooting pains he gets."

"Should I call the doctor?"

"Answer her, Karl. Do you want Amelia to call Doc Carlson?"

The rocking stopped. Slowly, his hands slid away from his face and he glared at them with a look of pure enmity. He struggled to his feet and stumbled towards them. Before she could react, he lunged again for Sarah, but tripped and fell against the sideboard—knocking over a hurricane lamp that shattered on the floor.

"Now see what you've done!" Amelia shouted—rushing to the sideboard and catching her cherished World's Fair glass just as it rolled off the shelf.

For a moment Karl remained slumped over the credenza. Then, he seized the handle; yanking open the drawer, he began frantically rummaging through it—wildly tossing the contents on the floor.

"Stop this! What are you *doing?"*

"Where is it? I know you kept it. What have you done with

it?"

"I don't know what you're talking about…"

He studied her a moment, then his lips curled into a malevolent smile. "You don't, huh?" Pushing past her, he made his way to Fredo's old bedroom.

"Have you completely lost your mind? It's not here anymore! I got rid of it years ago!"

"What's he talking about? What's he looking for…?"

Before she could answer, they heard a cry from the bedroom.

"Amelia…?"

When Sarah saw her eyes widen, she quickly turned. Karl stood in the doorway—holding the old revolver. Unfastening the leather snap, he slid the gun from the holster. Amelia pulled Sarah close.

"Got rid of it, huh?" he said with a sneer. "Always knew Alex's gun would come in handy one day."

"Karl!" Sarah gasped. She started towards him, but Amelia held her back.

"Please put the gun down before someone gets hurt," said Amelia—in a calm, measured voice.

"This isn't you, Karl. This isn't you," cried Sarah.

"No? Then *who* am I? Do either one of you have any idea who I am…or what I've been through? You *can't* begin to know. I've seen things…such horrible things. Things…I can't shake… I come back from hell to find Papa…dead. And just when life started to get a little better… Millie…my precious little Mi-i-llie…" His voice broke and his face contorted in agony.

"Oh, Karl…honey, don't…"

"A man can only take so much. How much more do I gotta lose? You know everything, Sis. Tell me, how much more?"

He stared at the gun, then slowly raised it—shoving the barrel into his gaping mouth.

BANG! BANG! BANG!

There was a loud rapping on the screen door. Startled, Karl

lowered the gun. For an instant, Amelia feared it might be Bessie.

"What's going on in there, folks...? It's me, Big Joe. Everything okay in there, Miss Madeira? Neighbor said there was some yellin' going on." The screen door swung open—the wire coil squeaking like a rusty bedspring. "I'm comin' in now..." He held the door to keep it from slamming behind him. His white butcher's apron and shirtsleeves were smeared with blood.

Karl turned to face him.

"Whoa...whatcha got there?"

"This ain't no business of yours Big Joe...so kindly get the hell out!"

"Karl, ol' buddy...you need to calm down. Better give me that gun before somebody gets hurt."

"*Somebodies*, you mean. Some*bodies* around here...deserve to get hurt," he said—his eyes narrowing. "Because *some*bodies have made my life a living hell..."

There was no official police report. Joe Shanks, who moonlighted as city police chief, told the county sheriff there was no need. Without further incident, he had managed to talk Karl down. The rumors that surfaced after Karl was disarmed, taken into custody and eventually transported to the State Psychiatric Hospital in Farmingdale were circulated by Beatrice Witherspoon, the local Bell Telephone operator and the town's pipeline for recycled drama. It was Beatrice who rang up Bessie.

"Better go check on Miss Madeira. That crazy brother of hers just called and was making all sorts of threats and accusations. Mabel Jennings tried to get on the party line for a good ten minutes...so we both happened to overhear. It was *terrible* the things he said to her. That poor woman is a saint for putting up with a crazy father and a lunatic brother."

Bessie was determined to stay out of it, but a half-hour later—hearing his truck screeching to a halt and the truck door slamming, and watching Karl stagger, menacingly across the yard—she called Rainey's and summoned Joe. When he was finally escorted away by the sheriff, Bessie wanted to rush to Amelia's side; however, knowing Sarah was still there, she refrained.

Part of Amelia hoped Sarah might now, in the midst of this turmoil, turn to her. Instead, she returned to Potosi, packed up some personal belongings and drove to her brother's in Little Rock. Before she left, she pried the padlock from Millie's bedroom door. Entering for the first time in years, she put away the toys and books still scattered about, and made her daughter's bed.

*   *   *

Journal Entry: 13 January, 1932

Dear Emily,

Just finished reading your heart-wrenching poem, *Could it be Madness—this?* As you well know, the victim's "madness" results from secrecy. To prevent it you had your poetry; I have you. Yesterday, Mary Logan stayed after class. She had previously left a note stating her 'need to talk.'

So often in the past, girls have left such notes—indicating an urgency to discuss 'female matters.' I assumed that was Mary's intention; however, her need was *une cri désespéré du coeur.* Her heartbreaking story of abuse by her father, Rev. Tobias Logan, chilled me deeply.

I fear I proved no great relief to young Mary, other than a show of tears, which I now admit were not only for her, but also for myself (possibly even more for myself). I told Mary I was morally obligated to bring her story to the authorities. She begged me not to for fear her family would be disgraced.

I explained that any disgrace was her father's alone, and her well-being was the most important issue.   And like you, dear Emily, I assured her that eventually she'd "know how to forget." Would that I could have found a sympathetic sounding board for my own story of violation and shame!

When Karl was sent to Farmingdale after threatening both Sarah and me, I admit now before God and that innocent child who lives within, I was relieved both physically and spiritually! Yes, relieved, not vindicated. My shame surrounding those years of "*violação*" was a confusion of guilt and pain, and, though I am loath to admit—pleasure. Guilt and shame are eternally intertwined with anything resembling pleasure. Therefore, any hatred I have felt towards Karl has, to this point, been equally directed towards myself. NO LONGER!

Little Girl Within: I pledge to protect you, to hold you blameless, to forgive you and to love you always!

So, thank you for *Could it be Madness— this?* I know too well your suffering and pain. Our kinship emanates from what we have endured...now and for always.

Your Spiritual Sister,
Amelia

NINE

Throughout much of the "dirty thirties," Amelia led an effort to feed students most affected by the Great Depression. The drought that plagued Oklahoma and Kansas also devastated the Missouri basin as far east as the Mississippi, with yearly rainfall of less than twenty inches. As a result, livestock production was diminished due to poor pastureland and limited wheat, oats, and corn crops; wilting gardens yielded scant produce. To offset the lack of meat, rabbit and pigeon hutches flourished. Still, many families were destitute and near starvation.

Surrounded by students in rag-tag clothing and cardboard-lined shoes was one thing, but she could not bear the emaciated faces she encountered on a daily basis. She appealed for help to Bobby Allenby, who, with Karl committed to the Psychiatric Hospital at Farmingdale, continued to manage Madeira Lighting & Appliance in Potosi. In answer to her request, he donated a refrigerator and two used electric stoves to the Prospect school and rewired a basement storage room. It was there she sat up a small kitchen.

From 1932 until 1938, she routinely prepared large pots of chicken and noodles, rabbit stew, and meatless meatloaf made with barley and rice. Many of the teachers, those who canned each summer, supplied jars of green beans, corn and tomatoes. Bessie often lent a hand; homemade breads and rolls were her specialty, and she maintained a sourdough "mother" in a large stoneware crock.

When word spread that Miss Madeira was feeding the

needy, the Prospect Businessmen's Association bought a freezer for the school "kitchen." Occasionally, a local farmer butchered a hog or slaughtered a sheep and donated it to school. Amelia learned to use every part of the animal—including the offal.

At first, the new superintendent, Vestal Coffey, objected. "The aroma of fresh-baked bread and stews isn't very conducive to keeping students' minds on schoolwork, Miss Madeira."

"Neither is hunger, Mr. Coffey."

Thinking he could put an end to the practice, he naïvely brought up the matter at a school board meeting. "This is a school, gentleman, not a cafeteria. I've tried to explain, but Miss Madeira is under the impression she can do as she pleases."

Raymond Miller, who was serving his second term on the board, was first to respond. "Since you're new, Mr. Coffey, you may not understand her position at this school."

"I understand she is well thought of as an English teacher, if that's what you mean," he said. "Are you suggesting she's something more?"

"What I'm tellin' you is that Amelia Madeira is the finest teacher in the whole dang state of Missouri. True, she can scare the bejeebers out of a kid. I should know. I was in her very first senior English class. I've seen students come unglued tryin' to explain why they used such and such a word."

Several board members chuckled and nodded in agreement.

"Miller's right," said Seth Davis. "Why, she used to make me quake in my boots...literally. I lived in total fear she'd call on me."

"And she would if she saw fear in your eyes. But here's the thing," continued Raymond. "I know for a fact she's given hundreds of dollars of her modest salary over the years to students headin' off to college, or secretly bought clothing for kids who had little or nothin' to wear. Most of her former pupils could come forward and tell you how she changed their lives for the better."

"Admirable," said Supt. Coffey, "but I don't see how that addresses the issue of cooking food at school. This practice, well meaning or not, has nothing to do with education, and frankly, it detracts from it."

"Then you best redefine what education means," said Raymond. "Because teachin' students to help others, to give one's time, money and abilities to serve the community is what education needs to be doin'."

"Surely you don't mean to say any of that is more important than academics?"

"You won't find anyone more capable of teachin' grammar or literature. She has a way of incorporatin' history, art, music and philosophy into every poem, story and novel she assigns. As I've said, she can be a stickler...but the success of her former students proves the efficaciousness of her methods. Right there's a fifty cent word I picked up from none other than Miss Madeira."

Coffey started to protest but was again cut short.

"When kids from Prospect go on to Cape or Mizzou, they're often singled out," said Davis. "'You must be one of Madeira's Kids,' the professor'll say. That's because of the skills they picked up right here in Prospect High School."

"When it comes to the written word, they absolutely shine," said Raymond. "Once you've been exposed to her methods, you can make better sense of things...includin' your own life. Wouldn't you agree, gentlemen?"

"He's right."

"No doubt about it."

"My Elizabeth was always a fair to middlin' student, but she says Miss Madeira helped change the way she looks at everything," said Gill Trotter. "There's no stoppin' that girl now. She's plannin' to go on to law school."

"That's all well and good, but I still—"

"What we're tryin' to say is...and gentleman, correct me if I'm wrong, but if Miss Madeira wants to turn the gymnasium into a damn barbeque pit, she has our complete support."

"Here, here!" said the others.

*   *   *

Prospect, Missouri
17 June, 1936

Dearest Sarah,

I must confess I was surprised to learn of your marriage to Robert Moore. Though you previously mentioned him in passing, I wasn't aware your relationship had progressed to that stage. Let me offer my sincere congratulations. You certainly deserve Happiness after all you've been through. And, along with that, let me acknowledge how relieved I am you tested negative. I can only imagine how frightened you must have been to undergo the test and how relieved you must be now. I share in your relief and good fortune.

Speaking of that, dear one, you asked after Karl's condition. I see him only three or four times a year, but he seems to be relatively well, though I wouldn't go so far as to agree that he's "cured"—as he always insists. I'm not convinced the medications he receives are really helpful; they seem to keep him in a rather desensitized state…benumbed. Knowing how violent and agitated he can become without them, I guess it's for the best.

School is the same—every year another crop of young, eager faces! Occasionally, one with promise will emerge. Do you remember the Conrad family? Both children, Alberta and her brother, Wesley, were exceptional students. Alberta has gone off to Vassar. Wesley is in his third year at the University of Chicago. I have high hopes Alberta will develop into a promising poetess like another Vassar alum, Edna St. Vincent Millay. (I heard Millay recite "Renascence" and "First Fig" last summer while I was doing graduate work in Champaign. Stunning! What a fascinating woman!). Wesley is studying architecture and has already achieved recognition for his brilliant designs. The venerable Frank Lloyd Wright invited him to apprentice last summer at his compound near Spring Green, Wisconsin. Of course, those students are the rare exception.

There will never be another like Chester O'Malley. I'll never understand what turned him into a hermit and a misfit. He continues to do nothing but sit in the library and read. Children taunt him. They call him, "Boob," as if he were a mental defective. It truly breaks my heart.

Speaking of the library, we recently received a small grant from the WPA to expand the facility. Roosevelt may not be popular in the rest of the "Show Me" state, but esteem for him is on the rise here in Prospect.

Well, dear, all best wishes for your and Robert's happiness. Thank you for the invitation to come visit in Little Rock. Be careful...I might just take you up on it. I still love you as always, but perhaps I've learned to do that without needing you as I once did. Is that resignation or old age do you think? Or, is that what love is...the is-ness without the need?

Teaching has a way of distilling time. Somehow, practically overnight, I've gone from ingénue and soubrette to character actress, consigned to the role of Mutter Courage or Hestia, virgin goddess of the hearth. (Is that snickering I hear?). I'm not certain what thirty-seven is supposed to feel like, but there are mornings when I have a little trouble getting out of bed. Some of that has to do with rising at 3:30 a.m. so I can start cooking at school by five. Though it makes for a very long day, the grateful faces of those hungry children make it most worthwhile, and as Bessie says, 'Cooking for someone is the truest act of love.' Old Miss Minnie always insisted, "Love makes the food taste better.' Apparently, Love is the answer!

Do write when you have a chance, dear. I still cherish your lavender-scented missives.

With deepest Affection,
Amelia

*   *   *

On a blustery winter's day in 1940, school was dismissed early. School closings were a rarity; however, in addition to the fourteen inches of snow Prospect received earlier in the week, more than four inches of new powder blanketed the ground by mid-morning. Gusty winds precipitated large drifts, and by noon, with temperatures plummeting, Supt. Coffey made the decision to close for fear the few students who had managed to get to school would be stranded.

Amelia took the opportunity to leave early to go to the county library to pick up a reserved copy of Thornton Wilder's, *Our Town*, which she'd chosen to direct for the upcoming senior play. When she arrived, she paused in the vestibule to remove her rubber boots. Having been exposed to the biting wind, her face glowed bright pink, and she was breathing heavily. As she hung up her coat and muffler, the librarian, Phyllis Jenson, hurried her way.

"This is a surprise. I didn't expect you until after school," she said, almost in a whisper.

"Vestal cancelled school early. It's terrible out and getting worse." She removed her scarf and smoothed her hair. "He was afraid some students might get stranded. Hope they all make it home." As she turned to face Phyllis, she spotted a figure sitting at the far table near the stacks—his back to her. Amelia gestured towards him. "Chester?"

'Yes,' she nodded.

Startled, her eyes fluttered and a sharp chest pain momentarily caused her to grimace; she steadied herself against the wall. Taking a deep breath, she held it a few seconds—then slowly exhaled.

"Are you all right? Asked Phyllis.

"For some reason it never occurred to me he'd be here."

Other than the few times she'd caught a fleeting glimpse of him as he hurriedly exited Rainey's, or as he surreptitiously crossed through the park on his way home, she hadn't seen him or talked to him in more than twenty years. Today was an anomaly, and it posed a difficult dilemma.

She whispered, "Anyone else here?"

"No."

She indicated she was going to talk to him. Stepping lightly, so as not to alert him, she slowly approached. When she was no more than a few feet away, he suddenly turned. His face blanched and for a moment he froze.

"Wha...wha...what are *you* doing here?" he finally stammered—his eyes darting towards the large wall clock. "You're not supposed to be...here!" He slammed the book shut and jumped to his feet.

"Chester... I don't know what to say. I only wanted—"

"Can't talk to you now," he said—frantically grabbing his wool coat and a stack of papers. "Can't!" He rushed past her.

"But...I just...I only...I only wanted to talk..."

Phyllis Jenson reached out, as if to stop him. "It's Miss Madeira, Chester. *Your* Miss Madeira. She only wants to—"

"I trusted you!" he wailed, as he hurried on past. "Thought

you understood. Thought you were my friend!"

In a panic, he shoved open the front door and the wind whipped it from his hands. Bouncing violently on its hinges, it crashed back against the doorframe, then blew open again. A huge gust tore several loose pages from his hands, and he chased after them.

Amelia hurried to the door and, with effort, pulled it to her. Snow was swirling; the frigid air swept it along in waves. Gripping the door, she peered through a crack. Chester had already crossed the alley behind the library and was heading towards Rainey's. Before he could reach the sidewalk on the other side of the street, a group of boys on their way home from school spotted him and began pelting him with snowballs. She recognized two of them, and yelled at them to, 'Stop!'

Coat in hand, Chester continued down the sidewalk until he suddenly slipped—his feet flying up over his head as he fell backwards.

"Atta boy, retard!" yelled one of the boys.

He endeavored to stand, but skidded and fell again, as another volley of snowballs bombarded him.

"Oh, Chester…"

"What's happening? What's wrong?" Phyllis asked, as she reached the doorway.

With a voice like shattered glass, Amelia cried, "Will we *ever* know?"

TEN

The schoolboys continued hurling snowballs, like projectiles from a catapult. One, rock-hard, caught him squarely in the back of the head—knocking him to the ground.

"Hey, Boob…nice catch!" Their catcalls spurred him on.

By the time he arrived home, he had worked himself into a state of heightened anxiety. Winded and disoriented, he headed straight upstairs. He sat on his rumpled bed—rocking rhythmically, back and forth. Over and over, he relived the adrenaline-filled ambush by his former teacher and the person he considered his only true friend. Again and again, he pondered how such a thing could have happened. In the past, he often found himself obsessing for hours over the most benign scenarios.

But *this…this…!* 'Was Phyllis part of the conspiracy?' *Not her! Not Phyllis!* 'Although…perhaps Amelia persuaded her to… No, *not* Phyllis…'

Finally, he convinced himself of what he saw as the only plausible explanation: 'the inevitable convergence of the "sun" and the "moon". Must be Fate's way of saying inevitability has more power than avoidability?'

That's it! Wait… Avoidability? Is that even a word?

He tried repeating it aloud. *A…voi…da…bil…i…ty?* Each syllable produced a puff of steam. Shivering uncontrollably, he suddenly became aware of his icy breath and the bone-chilling cold. Only then did he notice his teeth chattering—violently. The house was as glacial as Rainey's new walk-in meat locker; Joe Shanks had recently let him venture inside, where sides of beef and pork hung from hooks and blocks of ice were stacked floor to ceiling. With no feeling in his hands or feet, Chester struggled to slip on his coat and gloves as he stumbled downstairs to the kitchen.

He couldn't remember if he'd lit a fire that morning before heading to the library. 'No,' there'd been no fire; a mound of cold dead ash clogged the grate. '*Hungry... Did I eat...?*' He stood for a moment—trying to recall anything that happened prior to the ambush.

Opening the icebox door, he was greeted by a lone heel of bread and a pickle jar half-filled with chartreuse liquid. A piece of cheese, marbled with mold, stared back at him from the crisper drawer. Again, his mind wandered.

Why did I run? "Because I was tricked!" he said aloud. *Ensnared! But WHY?* He pondered the question a moment longer— before admitting to himself that if he were going to confront Amelia Madeira, it had to be on his own terms. *When I'm ready...not before.* Suddenly conscious he was standing in front of an open refrigerator, he shut the door.

He began circling the kitchen table as he weighed his options. If only he could be certain she'd headed back home, he'd risk another snowball attack and walk to Street's Drugstore for a hamburger...or maybe splurge for one of Parker Street's breaded tenderloins with the sweet, homemade pickles and mustard. He paused. *Better not.* He decided to delay the trip another hour or two. He turned and circled, counter-clockwise.

'She never stays at the library more than forty-five minutes,' he reassured himself. He also knew the only time she ventured into the Drugstore was when she stopped by for a cup of coffee and a brief conversation with Alberta Street on her early morning weekday bank run for the school, or an occasional Saturday morning—that ritual lasting, "Twenty minutes, tops!"—and as predictable as the intrusiveness of his own fear. *Even if she goes to Rainey's for groceries, she'll be gone by four.* He stopped circling. "I'll wait!"

He wandered down the darkened hallway toward his

parent's old bedroom. At the end of the hall, the front door was blocked by a bed frame, a metal headboard and stacks of boxes—containing his mother's clothes and a few of her personal possessions. For the past eighteen years, the bedroom had served as his writing room. The only furniture he'd kept was the chest of drawers, now stuffed with dozens of journals, literary magazines and loose manuscripts.

A simple writing desk occupied the middle of the room. It sat directly under a bare light bulb that hung from a braided cord. On the pull-chain, he'd tied a red shoestring so he could turn the light off and on without having to rise. A decade earlier, he hired Bobby Allenby to wire the house—insisting he needed electricity only in the kitchen and "the study."

The floor was covered with cheap green linoleum, warped and cracked due to extreme fluctuations in the temperature. Where Chester's chair scooted back and forth, worn grooves pierced the black linoleum backing—exposing the original pine floor. Sometimes weeks went by without him remembering the old linoleum still harbored remnants of his mother's blood. Though several ladies from St. Stephens had come to clean after Pearl's body was removed to Forrest's Funeral Home, on his first night back, he discovered the rust-like spatters of blood on the faded flower wallpaper and dried rivulets, like blackened nail polish, in the cracks of the worn pine floor.

No doubt, returning home to the scene of such horrific memories and trading a life of freedom and intellect for a life of isolation contributed to his rapid decline. For the first few months upon his return, he seriously entertained thoughts of suicide. Had it not been for his writing, his only means of processing the imponderable events that would now and forever shape his psychological demeanor, he might have eventually taken his own life. In fact, only a few weeks after coming home, he nearly succeeded.

Deadened by depression, he had been bedridden for more than a week. Disgusted by the futility of his own existence, he copied a suicide note—*'And so I leave this world, where the heart must either break or turn to lead,'* leaving it in a copy of *Maximes et Pensées* on his writing desk—along with a sealed envelope addressed to "Amelia Madeira." His intention was to simply starve himself to death as an act of self-purification, and he might have, except for what he eventually believed to be a kind of perverse, divine intervention.

Having not eaten for days, he was approaching a state of delirium when an insistent knocking on the kitchen door awakened him. At first, he thought he was dreaming.

There it is again! 'No one ever comes to the house!' He was certain the "invader" would eventually leave, but the knocking continued, intermittently, for several minutes until he heard the door push open.

"*Chester…?* It's me…Miss Madeira." Her voice resounded throughout the house.

A bolt of terror pierced his heart.

"It's Amelia. I know you're in here. I just want to talk to you, that's all…to make sure you're okay…"

He heard her footsteps passing by the stairs and echoing in the downstairs hallway—stopping at the doorway to his study.

My writing! 'What if she sees the note and her letter?' Then, he heard her footsteps returning, coming closer—approaching the stairway to his room. With great effort, he sat up in bed. *What to do…?*

"I'm coming up…"

He tried to speak, to stop her, but before he could utter a word, another voice called from outside.

"Amelia! What are you *doing?* Come out of there!"

Chester recognized the voice.

"I'm only…something's wrong…" She went to the kitchen door and opened it. "Something's terribly wrong. I can feel it! Something's happened to him. He's not answering. Come in and help me…please!"

"No…and I want you to come out of there now," insisted

Karl. "I'll get Joe Shanks to come over and check on him. Hurry before someone sees you. Come on!"

"But, I…"

He heard the door close behind her.

Not five minutes later, Big Joe rapped on the kitchen door. Peering in the window, he saw Chester slumped in a chair at the table. It had taken all his strength to drag himself to the kitchen.

Joe cracked open the door. "Y'all right? Chester? *Chester…?*"

"Why…wouldn't…I be…" he finally mumbled—barely able to lift his head. His mouth was so dry that his chalky lips, swollen and cracked, stuck together.

"Ya don't look too good, pardner," said Joe—closing the door behind him. "Ya sick?"

"I've been…a little…under the weather, but I'm—"

"I'm getting Doc."

"No, Joe…don't…pl-ea-se…"

"People are worried about you. Some fine people care about ya…and they're worried, that's all…"

"That's good…to know," he mumbled—straining to hold his head erect. "I just…need…to rest…a little…"

"Let me help ya back to bed."

"No…not ness…ary…ne…cessary…"

"Listen now…I'm just up the street. Ya need anything… Ya hearin' me?"

"Okay, then…"

When Joe returned with Doc Carlson, they found Chester in a heap on the kitchen floor, dehydrated and suffering from malnutrition. With difficulty, Joe hauled him up the narrow stairs to his bedroom. Every day for two weeks, Carlson called on him—insisting he eat, drink plenty of liquids and bathe.

"If you don't start takin' better care of yourself, I'm gonna have to put you in the hospital."

"By hospital…do you possibly mean Farmingdale?"

"You're livin' in here like a person who's…who's—"

"Lost touch with reality?"

"You don't keep food in the house, and you've let yourself go. Don't bathe or shave. Coulda died if Joe hadn't called me."

"And I suppose that would have been a great tragedy?"

"Yes, that *is* the reality."

"Well, then your understanding of reality and mine are antithetical."

"Meanin'?"

"In opposition...*conflicting*. You don't seem to understand that death is a natural part of life. Doc, I see you and people in your profession, though well-intentioned, as someone who fears death and is dedicated to disrupting nature's own orderly system."

"That's what you think, is it?"

"As Confucius said, 'everything has its beauty but not everyone sees it.' That goes for death, too...*especially* death. Believe me, there are worse things than dying."

"So, you intend to kill yourself. Is that what you're tellin' me? Because if that's what you're sayin', you leave me no choice."

"*Choice* is really all we have."

"I'm not here to have a philosophical discussion. Are you gonna start takin' better care of yourself, or do I have to get someone to take care of you?"

"Actually...I prefer the latter. *But...*"

"What?"

"...I've several stories in the next room...the endings to which, are, shall we say, lacking sublimity. Perhaps I'll stick around awhile and see if I can wrestle them into submission. Finish the job. Is that answer sufficient to keep me out of a straight jacket and the loony bin?"

"I'll check back on you tomorrow."

"I look forward to it with great anticipation, Doc. You're becoming my best and only friend."

The years that followed marked a gradual disintegration of Chester's psyche, his self-imposed isolation gradually becoming a prison sentence.   Though writing relieved some of his mental anguish, his ability to cope with people and social situations slowly deteriorated.

Why did I run?

The question repeated itself like the ticking of the hall clock. The truth was he longed to talk to Amelia. Years ago, he'd taken her a copy of his novel, *Janus*—leaving it in her mailbox before tiptoeing away into the night. He'd fully expected her to seek him out or, at the very least, write him. But when he heard nothing, he assumed she was angry, or perhaps she hadn't realized he was the author.

He had adopted the pseudonym, S. A. Moon, in college. "S" for Sun "A"nd Moon, the two faces of *Janus*, the Roman God of beginnings and endings. Not even Harris Butler had uncovered its origin, though he taught a course in Roman and Greek Literature.

'This was my chance to talk with her again...and I ran!' He promised himself the next time he saw her, he'd confront his fears.

Et partagez mon coeur! 'I *will*...next time, I'll share my heart!'

ELEVEN

In 1942, a year into the World War II, Miss Madeira established the Delphi Book Club. It began as a way of focusing on something other than the fighting overseas, the anxiety accompanying the fate of Prospect's young men—serving in various war theaters throughout Europe and the Pacific—and the ever-present fear of what the future might hold.

Due to her reputation as a strict grammarian and a brilliant but sometimes caustic pedagogue, the group remained small. To attain temporary membership, an applicant had to be recommended by 'a member in good standing.' To gain full membership, the initiate was required to present a written and verbal analysis of a pre-selected work, adjudged worthy of admittance by Miss Madeira alone.

The Delphi Book Club met monthly. To be chosen to present a new work of fiction was both an honor and a dreaded task. When assigned a book report, Delphi members worked diligently to revise, peer-edit and generally support each other's efforts. It wasn't as if she graded the reports, but fear one might be singled out for faulty thinking, hasty generalization or the dreaded cliché, contributed to members' angst.

In the fall of 1943, she chose Franz Werfel's bestselling novel, *The Song of Bernadette*—the story of a French peasant girl, who, in 1858, believes she has encountered the Virgin Mary. Following instructions of the Immaculate One, Bernadette digs into the earth until a fountain issues forth—becoming the miraculous healing waters of Lourdes. Beatified, Bernadette slowly fades away from the physical world, dying at age thirty-five, and eventually becoming Saint Bernadette to grateful believers worldwide.

Alberta Conrad Street was the Delphi Club's most ardent member. Alberta and her husband, Parker "Doc" Street, owned and operated Street's Drugstore, which they opened in 1936 after purchasing the old Prospect Pharmacy. With Miss Madeira's encouragement, Alberta had briefly attended Vassar before returning to Prospect, where she met and married Parker Street. A more unlikely pairing would be hard to imagine. Parker, who grew up on a farm near Delbridge, would have been content to raise Yorkshire hogs on the farm he now owned, halfway between Graniteville and Caledonia.

Alberta had more refined tastes. She played classical piano and had been a voracious reader ever since Miss Madeira inspired her as a high school freshman. It was Alberta who proposed that Miss Madeira (and it was always Miss Madeira, never Amelia) create a book club to advance local culture and to support the goals of the Iron County Library, which she had founded and nurtured for nearly two decades.

Following the October meeting, where Alberta presented her report on *Bernadette*, she remained behind at Miss Madeira's request. "I know...you don't have to tell me what an appalling job I did. And, I practiced, too." Her nervous smile was more of a cringe.

"The report itself was insightful, beautifully written and quite interesting," said Amelia. "You captured the essence of Bernadette, how a young girl who's truly suffered can reach a beatific station, the saintly countenance of a tortured soul."

"However?"

"I can't understand why you get so flustered. I've known you since you were a child. In high school, you were shy, but you slowly gained confidence in yourself and were able to articulate your thoughts to the whole class. When you were accepted at Vassar, I was certain you would blossom even further. But then you dropped out and returned home after only two years. I don't believe I ever asked you why."

"One day I just looked around at some of the young women, and suddenly they seemed so...bohemian, affected and rather silly. I decided I wanted a normal life."

"By normal, do you perhaps mean less challenging? If you don't mind my saying so, working in a drugstore seems a waste of your talent and your mental capacity." Amelia could see that the words strung. "I'm sorry. I didn't mean to be so harsh."

"Miss Madeira...this is rather difficult for me to say because you know how much I admire and respect you, but not everyone can live up to your high expectations."

"All I've ever asked of my students is that they try to live authentic lives...that they discover and pursue their passion. Is that asking so much?"

"I think you underestimate your influence. I can't speak for everyone, but knowing how much you expected of me, it became a sort of burden. At times, it occurred to me I'd chosen Vassar more for you than for myself, an inherited fantasy. In some way, you convinced me that by going there I would become the next Millay."

"Oh, Alberta, that was never my intention...I—"

"I lived in constant fear I would disappoint you, and now it seems I have."

"Certainly not...no, don't ever think that. If you're happy, then you've achieved more than most."

"I'm happy...some of the time. I'm not sure a permanent state of happiness is possible. Look at what happened to Chester O'Malley."

At the mention of his name, Amelia stiffened.

"Is there anyone who ever had more potential? All I ever heard growing up was how *brilliant* Chester O'Malley was, but look how that turned out. Do you ever wonder if perhaps all that expectation was just a little too much?"

Amelia physically recoiled from the jolt of her accusation.

"He used to come into the store, sit in a back booth and talk to himself. All his mumbling disturbed customers. Parker had to ask him to leave more than once. He finally just stopped coming in. A year or so ago, someone who knew of him back in college stopped in and told about him being involved in some sort of scandal. It was rumored he'd tried to kill himself and was hospitalized in a mental ward."

"That's enough!" The force of her command startled Alberta. "I'm sorry, but I cannot have you speculate on what happened to Chester." She grabbed her coat and hurriedly put it on. "It's late...I need to be getting home. If you'll pardon me, I'll leave you to turn out the lights and lock up."

"I...I didn't mean to upset you," she said—following her to the door. "It was thoughtless of me..."

Amelia turned and faced her. "Some people...are too gentle...too *gentle*...to live among wolves," she said—the words catching in her throat. "And Chester...Chester is one of those people."

"Yes, I suppose you're right."

"Too gentle," she repeated—her voice trailing off to a whisper, "...to live among wolves..."

*   *   *

Following the school year in 1946—during which she served her first year as both teacher and principal—Amelia spent six weeks of her summer vacation in a workshop for Secondary School Administrators at the University of Missouri—Columbia. While there, she completed work on a second Master's degree.

In her absence, a new janitor was hired to replace Percy Stokes, who was retiring after thirty years. "The Stoker," as he was affectionately known by the faculty and students, had been the school's only janitor since the building opened in 1916—having outlasted five different superintendents and half a dozen principals. Suffering from rheumatism and high blood pressure, his health had been in decline for several years.

Though school was no longer in session, the new Superintendent, Charles Meeker, arranged for several teachers to gather for a "going away party." Among those attending was Miss Bessie Sweeney. When Meeker announced Percy's replacement, she immediately thought of Amelia.

'Should I call her? Write her? Or, just let her spend part of the summer adrift in educational workshops?' Finally, she decided to say nothing in hopes that, by the time Amelia returned to Prospect, Mr. Stokes' replacement would have already quit – or, more likely, have been fired.

What she didn't anticipate was that Amelia had arranged for the *Prospect Banner* to be forwarded to her while she was in Columbia. When she received the June 26th edition, she was aghast when she read the headline, "*Chester O'Malley To Replace Percy Stokes.*"

Some found it smugly satisfying to think that "the boy genius" had finally joined the ranks of the employed as a mere janitor. Some, who thought him lost and unsalvageable, were happy to believe he might be breaking out of the funk that had engulfed him for more than a quarter century. Still others worried about having "one of them" around their young children. Sadly, there were two generations who now knew him only as "Boob" O'Malley, 'that retarded guy who sits in the library all day.'

Phyllis Jenson had encouraged him to apply for the janitorial job. Knowing how often Miss Madeira inquired after him: 'Did Chester come in today?' 'Does he seem well?' 'What's he reading?' 'Do you have any idea what he's writing these days?'— Phyllis believed she would be pleased. She was dead wrong.

Amelia had nearly a month to prepare what she would say to him. Above all, she was determined to remain professional and, if possible, detached. However, when she finally encountered him in the basement hallway near the furnace room, the words she'd carefully rehearsed quickly fogged over—evaporating like warm breath on a cold mirror.

"*Oh*…there you are," he said with a smile she'd reimagined

countless times. "I…I wondered how long it would be…before we ran into each other."

Six years had passed since their brief encounter in the county library. Now, aged forty-five, Chester resembled a man a decade older—unlike Amelia, whose hair contained only a few random gray strands. Though fine lines creased her brow and dark shadows had appeared under her eyes in recent years, she still looked much younger than her forty-eight years.

She attempted to steel herself against a torrent of emotion, but the very sound of his voice shattered her reserve. She turned to leave.

"Amelia…Miss Madeira, please wait!" He came up behind her, gently took her arm and led her into the furnace room—closing the heavy door behind them.

She began to weep openly. "I can't…do…this," she sobbed. "I…can't even…have…this conversation."

He moved toward her and held out his arms. At first, she stood motionless; then haltingly, she moved into his embrace—her head resting on his shoulder. No words passed between them. For several minutes, they stood in silence. She could hear his beating heart. Everything took on a surreal quality.

'Is this really happening?' Transfixed, she was afraid to speak, afraid to open her eyes.

He spoke first. "I can't tell you how often I've imagined being able to hold you like this… I'm so sorry," he whispered. "So *very* sorry…"

'*Sorry?*' The spell was broken. She lifted her head and looked into his eyes. "Twenty-eight years, Chester. A lifetime."

"I wanted to come to you…to explain…but I just couldn't. I've agonized over this for years…for years. *Parting is all we know of heaven, and all we need of hell.*"

"You're quoting Dickinson to me…to *me?*"

"You have no idea how many times I've walked up to your front door…stood on your porch…unable to knock…wanting to…to—"

"To what?" She pulled away. "To show the least amount of common decency?"

"Amelia, I—"

"You have managed to avoid me and this conversation for decades. Why now, after all this time?" She removed a handkerchief from her sleeve and wiped her eyes and nose. "Did you think because I wouldn't acquiesce to your admission of love that I'd stopped caring for you? You sprung that on me out of nowhere. Then, just disappeared. Do you have any idea how devastating that was? How I constantly wondered how you were...tried to imagine what you were doing, thinking...feeling?"

"I wasn't sure you still cared..."

"*Cared...?* There was never a past tense in my caring. I can assure you that heartache doesn't begin to describe what you put me through... "

"But I thought, perhaps—"

"Knowing how close we were...how could you have ever reached that conclusion? Couldn't you see that what you were asking then was impossible?"

"I know... I acted like a child."

"You were a child...that was the point. A brilliant young man, but still someone too young to understand why I couldn't give you the answer you wanted to hear. *Denial is the only fact perceived by the denied.*"

"That's all in the past now. I understand why you had to say no...back then. How it would have prevented you from teaching. It was selfish not to realize what that meant. But, now those barriers no longer exist. There's nothing to prevent us from being together."

Amelia peered deep into his eyes. What she once saw there was now a half-light, a brilliance dimmed by tragedy and obscured by years of neglect and abuse, both inflicted and self-imposed. He seemed drained of vitality—not the vitality of youth but of spirit—like the boys who returned from the horrors of war.

"What happened, Chester? What happened to you?"

"Things...while I was in college. A series of really

debilitating things." He pulled his shirtsleeves down to cover his wrists. "I…I was hospitalized after my parents—"

"Oh…I'm sorry. I had no idea..."

"Like Philoctetes, my wound, though psychic, was an abhorrence to everyone—including myself. My only connection to anything has been my writing…words. And, ironically, I don't have words to explain it. I felt like a tree that had its roots wrenched from the ground. I lost my grip on everything. Developed an aversion to people. It's like I've been in some kind of haze, one that clutched me and held me prisoner. It's only recently I've been able to…to escape its grasp."

"But how? What brought about this change?"

"Doc Carlson arranged for some treatments."

"Treatments?"

"At Farmingdale? Electro-shock therapy. At first, I balked. But, because I'd stopped caring, I finally agreed—thinking it might wipe away all my bad memories. Unfortunately, that didn't happen, but it's helped in other ways. It enabled me to shake off the fog that engulfed me for so long. Though, I wouldn't say it helped my writing… But, now I'm not so anxious around people. Do you understand?"

"I understand we've both had terrible things happen. Still, none of that matters now." She took a deep breath, wiped her eyes and smoothed her suit coat.

"So, you're not angry with me?"

She stared at him a few moments, then smiled and shook her head, wearily. "No, I'm not angry. But, I must ask you…do you need this job? I mean, do you *really* need this job, financially? Because if you don't, I—"

"Actually, I do…but that's not the only reason I took it. Amelia, I've wanted to tell you there's not been a single day I've haven't thought about you, thought about how much I've missed you. How much I still—"

She gestured for him to stop. Her face was ashen.

"Please, don't say another word. And, never call me Amelia

again…not in public, not even in private. I'm Miss Madeira, now and always."

"I didn't mean to be disrespectful. I just want you to know I *still*… I never stopped."

"Whatever our feelings about the past…I'm willing to overlook all that."

He looked crestfallen.

"The novella you wrote in college, the one you left ages ago in my mailbox…?"

"*Janus.* I always wondered if you—*"

"Yes, *Janus*…the sun and moon. We are *not* the two halves of that person, Chester. We never were."

"Oh, but you're wrong. We both showed one face to the world…while the other, the real one…we revealed only to each other."

Amelia felt faint. She pushed past him—pausing at the door.

"You must realize, Mister O'Malley…for that's what I shall call you henceforth, that here in this school…*my* school, I'm your immediate supervisor not your former teacher, your confidante or friend. And, I'm not someone who can be approached like this ever again. Do you understand? Please say you understand."

"But Amel…Miss Madeira…I—"

"If you truly need this job…tell me you understand."

TWELVE

School years coalesced like the rings of Saturn—whirling past in a predictable blur—composed of an endless stream of faces. Occasionally, Amelia encountered a student who challenged her, but from the very beginning, the appellation, "Miss Madeira," commanded respect and engendered fear—giving her an enormous advantage. It was a power she acknowledged only to herself. A word of encouragement from her became the tipping-point for many students' future achievements; a telling word or look of disapproval provoked introspection and demanded action.

"Miss Madeira" was a role she enjoyed, but at times it required more energy than she kept in reserve. Still, she found the impetus to keep going. For years, she maintained such an exhaustive schedule of educational and civic activities, the average person would have capitulated. Perhaps that's why the mythos surrounding her took on such legendary proportion.

Bessie Sweeney, on the other hand, was just "good ol' Miss Bessie." Without fanfare, she helped launch generations of students who would later become "Madeira's Kids." Beginning in the war years, she began a summer reading program for a select group of first grade graduates, who were invited to her home to read aloud from A.A. Milne or Beatrix Potter. The highlight of each session was a generous helping of fresh-baked sugar cookies and a juice glass brimming with cold milk. Unlike Amelia, she emanated a motherly aura. Young children felt safe in her presence, and those selected to spend summer mornings reading at her home were made to feel special, singled out. Quite often it was those very same children who would later excel in Miss Madeira's English classes, and who went on to distinguished careers in education, business, the arts and civic accomplishment.

As the two walked home together one beautiful spring day, Bessie mentioned how she was looking forward to her next summer reading class. "This is a wonderful group. Some of the brightest children I've ever had. Really inquisitive."

"I don't know how you do it. If I had to give up my summers to spend more time with students, I couldn't face them again in the fall."

"It's only two hours…a few mornings a week. They're so darling and so eager to learn."

"You're a better person than I."

"Amelia, I've never said this to you, but you should know…I think you're the most amazing teacher, and I hold you in the highest regard."

"Well, thank you, dear. And, I you."

"I have to say I haven't always approved of some of your methods, but I think I understand why you've maintained that stern façade."

"Is that how it appears…stern?"

"Oh, yes, dear. It has a name you know. "The Madeira Menace," which I've always found laughable.

"The *Madeira Menace*…?"

"You earned that moniker the first years you taught…and the reputation's followed you ever since. You've changed so much since those early years, but students' perceptions are often formed by others…their parents, for instance. Unlike them, I've seen you at your most vulnerable. I only wish you could have let your students see it, too."

"Vulnerability exposes one to hurt, and believe me, I've not been immune."

"Mother always said that keeping an open heart was the

way to avoid being hurt. That hurt comes when we close it off. That's not meant as a criticism...far from it. Perhaps if I'd had to deal with teenagers, I might have done the same. But, this I do know...no one cares more for her students, no one demands more of them than you. And, no teacher I've ever known has asked more of herself or given more of herself.

"How kind of you to say so, but, believe me, I've not been all that self-sacrificing."

"Nonsense. Do you think I don't know what you gave up so you could continue to teach?"

Amelia looked at her as if to say, 'You couldn't possibly be talking about...'

"Chester. I'd had to have been blind to not notice how much you suffered."

"It was that obvious?"

"Not to everyone. But mother and I worried about you for the longest time after he went away. And, then, when he returned...well..."

"I had no idea."

They walked on in silence until they reached Bessie's front step, where the conversation usually ended. Today was the exception.

"Before I came here from Ironton, I was engaged."

"*Engaged?* Bessie! You...? But you *never*...why didn't you ever tell me?"

"I was too embarrassed...and hurt. He jilted me...left town without a word. Never heard from him again. Cried myself to sleep every night for a year. Without mother, who knows?"

"Oh, how terrible for you."

"Best thing that never happened."

Amelia looked surprised.

"I wouldn't trade one day of teaching for the life I might have had with him, though I didn't know it at the time. Those first months here were so difficult. Teaching saved me. It really did."

"My, my...the things we don't know about each other...and

the things we think we do."

"Speaking of that, don't you find sometimes you teach the very thing you need to learn? Like patience...or forgiveness...or love? So many times I've heard myself say something to a student, something I needed to hear at that very moment."

"Yes, but it's more likely I'll say something they need to hear and then I'll realize I'm not actually present when I say it...like it just comes through me from some, I don't know, some cosmic source. I find whatever needs to get said happens best when I get completely out of the way. What's more, I'm convinced great teaching is a form of channeling—requiring little more than an agreement to be the vessel of information, be it hypothesis, fact or truth. Sarah recently sent me this book about it..." She paused to search Bessie's face. "Does that sound crazy?" she asked with a chuckle. "I suppose it does."

She leaned forward and kissed Bessie's cheek. "That should give the neighbors something to talk about."

"Too bad Miss Adams didn't live to see it," said Bessie. "She would have been apoplectic."

Miss Amelia Madeira and Miss Bessie Sweeney were unalike in nearly every imaginable way, yet together they launched an unusually talented group of students from an unlikely little burg. And, for those who chose to remain in Prospect after graduation, their influence continued to affect the community for decades.

By 1950, Amelia's life had become so fully engaged she began to anticipate early retirement. Although accumulating only a modest savings, she dreamed of traveling abroad—including a visit to the Azores, the birthplace of her father's ancestors. Though "dear Emily" said one could travel by simply closing her eyes, Amelia was ready to experience the real thing; she told herself she might have already done so had it not been for Karl.

Because she'd never learned to drive and depended on others for transportation, she'd visited him only sporadically over the years. When Sarah divorced him and sold the house in Potosi, he was inconsolable. Her visits were often cut short when he fell into blame-filled accusations. 'It's your fault I'm in here. You poisoned her against me!'

His self-victimization and tortured rants reminded her of Fredo, who rarely took responsibility for his circumstances. It was during a visitation to Farmingdale in late January of 1950 that she was summoned to the administrative office. As always, Bobby Allenby had driven her there. He went on ahead to visit Karl.

"Dr. Murray will see you now," said the receptionist. Dr. Aloysius Murray was Farmingdale's new chief administrator.

"Let me get right to the point," said Dr. Murray, a diminutive man, who exuded an arrogance that immediately set her on edge. "Care for your brother has been provided by the taxpayers of Missouri since 1930. Twenty years. I have carefully reviewed Karl's case, and he appears totally benign. Therefore, I see no reason for keeping him here. He might well benefit from being with his family, and I believe that would be you."

"Yes, but are you aware he suffers from tertiary syphilis... which, according to some authorities, may yet contribute to his further mental decline?"

"I am not inclined to wager on whether or not someone's mental condition will deteriorate once they leave this facility; however, I am fully qualified to state that your brother seems most capable of functioning outside the confines of a taxpayer-supported hospital. And, as of next Friday morning at 9 a.m., he will be released to your care."

She started to protest, but it was obvious the decision was final. "Could you possibly make it Saturday? I have classes all day Friday and, as principal, I'm in charge of the building for Friday night's ballgame."

"Perhaps you could take a personal day," he suggested, unmoved. "After all, he is your only brother...is he not?"

This was a day she had long dreaded, but she hadn't anticipated the devastating psychological impact his return would impose. In truth, she hoped he would never be released.

Bobby Allenby agreed to pick up Karl, drive him back to Prospect and stay with him until she returned home later that evening. He had maintained contact with Karl through the years and remained a loyal friend.

"Bobby, promise me you won't buy him any liquor," she said, matter-of-factly. "I know you've snuck it into him for years, but now that he's coming home, I'm asking you to please stop."

In anticipation of his return, she decided it was time to have Fredo's monument removed from the shed. For three decades, she'd contemplated having it hauled off to the city dump, but fear it might revive memories of his defaced statue of St. Michael and the controversy it sparked, she'd postponed the inevitable. She hired a crew, headed by a former student employed at the Iron County Granite Company, to have the limestone statue relocated to High Ridge Cemetery—replacing the modest headstone on Fredo's grave.

Other than a few obelisks and several smaller angel statues Fredo had carved decades ago, grave markers at the local cemetery consisted of simple granite and limestone headstones, none more than a few feet tall. In comparison, his statue was embarrassingly large—towering. With the lofty seraph's hands and lower set of wings missing, it now resembled an ancient relic, desecrated by conquerors of a fallen city. Knowing the back-fence clamor it would create, she wished she'd had it destroyed.

Friday morning, Bobby found Karl waiting in his room, a small suitcase resting at his feet. After two decades of confinement, it saddened him to see everything he possessed contained in one tiny valise. "Hey, buddy, ready to go?"

"You kiddin'?" he answered, without expression. Karl's gray hair was closely cropped—leaving him looking hollow-eyed. A threadbare patch still covered his left eye. Over the years, his voice had changed; it was now gravelly. He sat, brooding, most of the trip, but when he entered the Prospect city limits, he finally spoke, with a terseness reminiscent of Fredo's.

"Look at the roads. Gravel last time I saw 'em." The words

escaped slowly, medication deadening any emotion.

"Nearly every street in Prospect's paved," said Bobby, "...'cept the ones on the outskirts. Lots of things have changed. People you knew are gone...businesses, too. There are two lumberyards now and four gas stations."

"Pharmacy still there? Need my medicine."

"Street's Drugstore is what they call it. They still have a soda fountain, but it ain't like the old Prospect Pharmacy. They carry over-the-counter medicine, but you'll have to get your prescriptions filled from ol' Doc Carlson."

The very mention of Carlson's name seemed to agitate him. "That quack still around?"

Bobby thought he could hear Karl grinding his teeth. Knowing how many times he'd blamed Carlson for young Millie's death, he attempted to change the subject. "Hey, maybe we can go to some ballgames. Prospect and Potosi's got two of the best teams in this part of the country, and they play for the conference title next Friday. Remember how much we loved playin' ball? Those were some good times."

Karl stared straight ahead. After nearly a minute, he spoke.

"Max Nixon hung himself...in the room next to mine."

"That was a long time ago. Don't go diggin' up the past now, ya hear? There ain't nothin' back there but a bunch of ol' bad memories."

"Couldn't get over things. Things he saw in the war. Things he did...and didn't do. What thanks did we get? Farmingdale! Prisoners! Prisoners of war!"

"Like I say...that's history."

"To *you*, maybe...'cause *you didn't fuckin' go!*" He spit out every word—stabbing the air with pointed resentment, his voice strained and angry. The surge of adrenaline appeared to animate him. He folded his arms over his chest and stared out the window.

"Stop by Corkey's so I can get me some smokes and a bottle, will ya? I'm gonna need it..."

THIRTEEN

> *A wounded Deer—leaps highest—*
> *I've heard the hunter tell—*
> *'Tis but the ecstasy of death—*
> *And then the Brake is still!*
>
> *The smitten Rock that gushes!*
> *The trampled Steel that springs!*
> *A Cheek is always redder*
> *Just where the Hectic stings!*
>
> *Mirth is the mail of Anguish—*
> *In which it cautious Arm,*
> *Lest Anybody spy the blood*
> *And, "you're hurt" exclaim!*
>
> *~E. Dickinson*

Dearest Emily,

Only those who have suffered greatly know how pain can inspire greatness. Like a wounded deer, you defied the hunter's victory as your words leapt off the page and emblazoned themselves in our hearts and minds. I can only hope my words and deeds may have inspired in others what yours aroused in me, dear Sister.

It has been my guiding principle to keep separate my personal and professional lives, allowing the pain of one to inform the other. How successful I've been, I'll never know.

Of late, the struggle has increased. Karl's disease has devoured whatever remained of goodness and is slowly ravaging every last cell and molecule, leaving behind a fetid monster, who, by comparison, has transformed Papa into a saint. Nightly, I lock every lock on my bedroom door, quietly sliding each bolt, one by one, into place in hopes that the cold, metallic "clack" will not infuriate the one who was formerly *meu irmão*.

At his worst, Karl was never cruel, though losing dear Millie drove him to the edge of sanity's abyss. Now, the alcohol ignites his buried anger and this dread disease has transformed a once beautiful boy into a gargoyle—a living, breathing "*lusus naturae.*"

In her last letter, Sarah describes it as "an outward manifestation of his inner turmoil." I only know that it is a trial I can no longer bear. He threatens not only my physical being but also my very sanity. I fear what will happen when he discovers his precious gun missing. I keep it under my pillow so as not to fall victim to his impulsivity...and, frankly, to afford protection in case the locks do not hold.

Like you, I had a chance at love...and like your own, unrequited it remained. Yet, passion's embers smolder still. What kind of God offers up a love that would appropriate my one, true destiny:

that of Teacher? Had I lived two generations hence...a pedagogue and paramour, perhaps.

"Miss Dickinson," <u>you have been my greatest teacher</u>! Never venturing forth, you managed to reach beyond your prison walls to teach the power of words, the awesome freedom of creativity and the spontaneity of genius that refused to be stifled by any oppressor—be he father, brother or lover. In my darkest moments, your verse shone the light of truth, lifting me from despair, and bringing a measure of comfort and peace.

Still, I wonder if you were able to love those who hunted/haunted you—knowing the heights you attained were a result of their attempts to bring you low? I do aspire to that noble station, but too often fall short, I fear.

Muito Amor & Respeito,
Amelia Irmelinda Madeira

*　　　*　　　*

Many a night Chester O'Malley waited for everyone to exit the school building so he could revisit, like a pilgrim seeking an ascetic's tomb, Miss Madeira's classroom. There he would take his seat, third from the front, in the row nearest the window. Hoping she had left a poem on her blackboard as she so often did, tonight he was surprised to find two. Some part of him knew she left them there, knowing he would see them, hoping he would read them. Under both, she had written the name: Emily Dickinson.

The first, he recognized:

You left me—Sire—two Legacies—
A Legacy of Love

A Heavenly Father would suffice
Had He the offer of—
You left me Boundaries of Pain—
Capacious as the Sea—
Between Eternity and Time—
Your Consciousness—and—me—

The second, he also recognized…as one of her own:

Could I buy back those tender days—
With coins of rectitude—
Or cleanse my Heart of dark despair—
With Life's own Solitude—

He remembered the poem and the circumstances under which she had originally sent it to him in college as a post-script to a letter, a letter written in hopes he would reciprocate. He responded neither to her letter, nor to her appeal to communicate. Instead, he froze her out as she had him at his most vulnerable—rejecting his love and denying her own.

Thirty-four years ago!

He spoke the words aloud: "Could I buy back those tender days with coins of rectitude?" 'A rectitude of judgment? The rectitude of her motives? Would we be together now had I been able to respond? Would I have ever turned to Harris Butler for solace? Would I have killed my father…or sought comfort and strength in her arms?'

He wondered if she ever imagined him here where he sat all those years ago communing with their love of words, at first dreading, then welcoming her questions. He remembered another poem she had written just for him. He recited it from memory:

"I felt your Pain as if my own, Your Sadness cleaved my joy. 'Twas if a mirror reflected now, An essence of my Self." She had written it on the blackboard the day after he first revealed himself—opening to her, sharing his heart. It was then he realized

she felt as he did, that she loved him as much as he loved her.

For several months after he took the janitorial job, they rarely exchanged more than polite conversation and furtive glances; however, in the past few years, they often engaged in lively banter and fell into lengthy discussions about the state of literature. Each knew how much the other cherished those talks. Several months ago, she had invited him to join the Delphi Book Club, based on his essay entitled, "Alienation: The Appeal of *The Catcher In The Rye* To Today's Rebellious Teen."

He wondered if she also knew he sat, nightly, at her desk, picked up her pen, opened her books and let his fingers skate over the smooth pages, tattooed with her diacritical marks and notations, as if they were her skin. Did she purposely leave a handkerchief in her middle desk drawer, one with the lace edges and the blue embroidered "M," redolent with the soothing fragrance of lavender— knowing he would respire her very essence?

He moved to the blackboard and added a familiar Dickinson quatrain:

> *Remorse—is Memory—awake—*
> *Her parties all astir—*
> *A presence of Departed Acts—*
> *At window—and at Door—*

He hoped when she saw his addition, all doubt would be removed; she would know with certainty.

Tonight, however, he needed something more. Tonight, shrouded in the darkness of the new moon, he longed to see Amelia in a setting of domesticity: to watch her cook, set the table, or sit reflectively in the antique rocking chair by the front window. Tonight, on Thanksgiving eve, he proposed to do just that. Chester descended the stairs to the basement, grabbed his coat from the furnace room and headed for West 6th.

As was her custom, Amelia arrived home from school around six o'clock. Relieved to find Karl passed out on his bed, she was horrified to discover he had been rummaging through the dresser drawers in her bedroom, its contents strewn everywhere.

My journals! She rushed to the spare room at the end of the upstairs hall. The door remained locked. Dozens of journals were stacked, untouched, inside the storage closet.

'I can't continue to live this way?' Karl was no longer her brother; this was a walking affliction. 'Whatever happened to that darling boy who once was my constant loving companion?'

It had taken nearly three and a half decades for the tertiary syphilis to manifest. It began with a stiffening of his joints. For the last year, he'd complained of increased spinal pain and in the past few months, developed a shuffling gait. In addition to blinding headaches, he bemoaned the reduced sight in his one good eye. Even more disturbing, tumor-like masses of inflammation had begun to appear all over his body and, most recently, on his face—one on his left temple and another large gumma obscuring his right cheekbone. The physical signs were frightening, but they were nothing compared to his violent mood swings—bordering on psychotic outbursts.

Doc Carlson said his condition indicated an insidious form of heart disease and to expect him to either suffer a fatal aneurysm or complete heart failure. *But when?* To send him back to Farmingdale at this stage of his life seemed particularly cruel; however, his intemperate and disturbing behavior left her little choice.

When he failed to appear for supper and remained asleep at 7:30, she called Sarah to inform her of her decision to have him recommitted. "You can't imagine what he's like now. It's worse than it's ever been. And, his face. Remember how handsome he was? These insidious tumors have turned him into a—"

"Who you talkin' to?"

She turned to see him hunched over in the doorway. He'd removed his eye-patch—revealing an orb, matted with a catarrhal discharge, like a distempered dog.

"I have to go now," said Amelia—slamming the handset down on the cradle.

"Talkin' to Sarah again...wasn't ya? *Tell me!*"

"No-o-o," she said, her voice trembling.

"*Liar!*"

"You're sick. You need someone to look after you and I can't do it anymore."

"Not going back to that goddamn hospital!" he snarled—shuffling towards her. "Never going back there...*never!*"

"*Stop it*...you're frightening me!"

She shoved a chair towards him and ran for the stairs.

"Never let you send me back there!"

He lunged towards her—knocking over the chair. As it crashed to the floor, he suddenly dug his fingers into his face and staggered backwards—colliding into the table. An excruciating pain spiked through his left eye. Clawing furiously at his scalp, he emitted an agonizing wail as he sank to his knees.

When she reached her room, she quickly bolted all the locks on her door. *The prudent carries a revolver. He bolts the door.*

She heard the phone ring. *Sarah! Please call the police!*

From his vantage point behind the large Spirea bushes fronting the house, Chester moved quickly onto the front porch. He could see Karl crawling, slowly. As he reached the doorway by the foot of the stairs, he, once again, grabbed his head in agony. With great effort, he struggled to his feet. Out of the corner of his eye, he spotted a face staring through the window. His head recoiled and his bulbous face contorted in disbelief.

Chester froze.

Suddenly, another lightning bolt exploded in Karl's brain—propelling him backwards. He crashed into the pot-bellied stove—striking his head. He collapsed, unconscious.

Upstairs, Amelia heard the ringing phone go silent.

Through a light snowfall, Chester rushed back to school and made an anonymous call to the county sheriff.

FOURTEEN

For the past several years Bessie and Amelia had accepted an invitation from Supt. Meeker and his wife, who began a tradition of inviting the school faculty to a large Thanksgiving potluck luncheon at their home. Though they had originally planned to go together as was customary, Amelia called early that morning—saying she wasn't feeling well and asking Bessie to extend her apologies.

"Guess there'll be enough food without my chicken and noodles."

"I've known you for thirty-five years," said Bessie. "In all that time, we never talked about the turmoil you went through with your father. And now…"

"My father? What are you saying?"

"*Karl*," she said. "What are you going to do about Karl?"

There was no response.

"I'm terribly afraid for you, dear. You know I would never say anything under normal circumstances, but I saw the sheriff and Doc Carlson at your house last night. I'm so worried."

"Bessie…*dear* Bessie. You have been the most faithful friend to me, even when I haven't always been the friend I should have been to you."

"Nonsense."

"But there are just some things I can't discuss. Things for which there are no words."

"Well then, I'm going to tell you the same thing you told Mary Logan almost twenty years ago when she came to you about her father." There was a lengthy pause. "Amelia...?"

"I appreciate what you're trying to do, but there is a difference. Mary Logan came to me needing help, seeking advice, and I gave it to her."

Again, there was silence.

"I love you, dear," said Bessie, tenderly. "You know I'm always here if you need anything."

"Yes...and I do love you, too. More than you know."

As Amelia hung up the phone, she thought she heard Karl stir. Normally, he slept until mid-morning, long past the time she departed for school, but the events of last evening—resulting in a visit from the county sheriff and nearly ending in his arrest—made it imperative their paths not cross, not this morning.

She had refused to press charges—explaining to Sheriff Everett Bowers that she and Doc Carlson would make arrangements with the state hospital to readmit him this coming Saturday. Sheriff Bowers had wanted to lock up him overnight, but Carlson administered a heavy sedative that quickly subdued him.

"I'll check on him in the mornin'," he assured her. "If you need me before then, call and I'll be right over."

"He appears to have suffered a mild stroke, but he doesn't seem to be physically impaired; however, mentally, he's a danger to you and to himself."

She had no idea how long the sedative would last or how much he would remember about the events of last evening, but she had no desire to encounter him. Therefore, she hurriedly slipped on her coat. Reaching for her purse, it suddenly struck her that Bessie's concern was not only genuine, but also one she shared. As quietly as possible, she climbed the stairs to her bedroom, removed the revolver from under her pillow and shoved it into her purse. *If people only knew!*

Before leaving, she hurriedly scribbled a note. '*Food in icebox. Please eat. Gone to Meeker's—spending day. Doc Carlson will check on you. Happy Thanksgiving, brother. ~Love, Amelia.'*

Knowing Bessie might see her if she walked straight to school, she headed west and circled the block. There was only a light dusting of snow on the ground, nothing like the storm they'd predicted.

Spending a holiday at school was not that unusual for her, but it was a first for Thanksgiving Day. In spite of what had become a hellish existence with Karl, she was thankful for so many things: her job; her associates; the school and county libraries; her students, past and present; literature; her garden; her health, though she had experienced severe migraines of late; and her writing: journals filled with reflections, observations and poetry.

She was eternally grateful she and Chester had reestablished a relationship whereby they could share their love of words and ideas. Above all, she was most thankful for a career that now spanned three and a half decades.

She could finally acknowledge, just as Sarah had once predicted, that the love she had sought throughout her life was to be found in the students who afforded her the opportunity on a daily basis. Even on her worst days, while observing a student struggling, having an epiphany or joyfully expressing an idea, she could actually feel her heart opening, feel the flush of that powerful energy. More than anything, those moments kept her going.

She spent the day reminiscing; walking down the hallway, she paused in front of each class picture—recalling students she hadn't thought of in years. Continuing past her room, she entered the library, expanded through her solicitation of donations from area businesses and the many contributions of her former students. Had she not enjoyed teaching so much, she would have been content being a librarian, full-time. She loved the heft of a book, the pungent smell of pulp and glue and the sensuousness of its ragged deckle-edge signatures.

There is no Frigate like a Book...to take us Lands away...

In her worst moments, she had always had books to lighten the burden, to ease her suffering. Books were portals to other worlds, and 'what kind of a world would there be without them?' she wondered. She was certain one of her greatest accomplishments was turning her students into lifelong readers.

She moved from the library to her classroom. There, she spotted the Dickinson quote Chester had left. Regret...*it's the Past—set down before the Soul and lighted with a match!'*

She picked up the chalk and added the final stanza:

> *Remorse is cureless—the Disease*
> *Not even God—can heal—*
> *For 'tis His institution—and*
> *The Adequate of Hell—*

She surveyed the room. A deluge of memories engulfed her. A pang of sadness, like the sharp pain she sometimes felt in her chest, shook her. The realization produced an audible cry...a keening lamentation. She brought both hands to her mouth—as if to hold the sorrow in.

'Six more months. Inconcebível!' Six month before she relinquished her classroom to a successor. It was almost impossible to imagine never setting foot in it again. She steeled herself.

"No more regret, Chester...no more remorse," she said aloud. *Apesar de tudo...a vida continua!* 'In spite of everything...life goes on!'

For a long time she sat in silence. Finally, exhausted from the emotional catharsis, she let her mind wander. In retirement, she would continue to serve on the board of the county library. As long as she found it rewarding, she would maintain her position as president of the Delphi Club. And recently, she'd entertained the idea of publishing some of her own poetry.

But first, she would travel: to California and Cincinnati to visit cousins she'd never met; to England, to the Azores and back to America—first to Camden, New Jersey to see Walt Whitman's cottage; next to Concord, Massachusetts and Walden Pond, then on to Amherst and her beloved Emily's home, to view her handwritten poems in the Amherst College archives.

She asked Bessie to travel with her. Though she briefly entertained the idea, Bessie said she had no intention of retiring anytime soon. "You have your gardening and your poetry. What would I do with myself? No, I'm afraid I'll teach 'til I drop. Nothing would make me happier than to one day just keel over on my desk. Of course, not in front of the children."

She'd even thought of asking Chester to join her—knowing how much he loved Dickinson and Whitman, before acknowledging with a sigh, 'What am I thinking?'

She walked to the window and peered out at the warped wooden birdfeeders, once belonging to Miss Orton. She recalled her low opinion of her predecessor, one that age and wisdom would now revise to include: survivor. 'Dear Miss Orton…what trials did you endure in your personal life, unbeknownst to anyone?' She could not remember the last time someone had uttered her former teacher's name.

"Forgive me…for my impertinence and my willful bearing," she whispered prayerfully.

It suddenly occurred to her how new generations of students come along with no knowledge of the teachers, whose dedication and sacrifice helped create the culture of the school and of the community that endures decades beyond their tenure. *Soon…that will be me!*

That thought seemed trivial when she remembered the predicament still facing her at home. Though forced into the decision to send Karl back to Farmingdale, she felt terribly guilty. In spite of the abuse, the boy she remembered had once been her sole companion and protector.

That was the brother she loved.

She set out for school early Friday morning. With the help of Doc Carlson, Karl was to be transported back to Farmingdale on Saturday. 'One more day…then a return to normalcy…or, at least liberation from the growing anxiety and dread.' She was grateful for the two-day holiday. It couldn't have come at a better time. No students. No faculty. A chance to get work done without interruption.

I do hope Chester will be in today. Like her, he often spent holidays at school. She had recently purchased a copy of Faulker's *The Collected Stories*, and though she had been saving it for his birthday, she decided to surprise him with it a few weeks early. Knowing how, in the past, he railed at the obfuscation of what he referred to as 'Faulkner's often convoluted and purple-tinged prose,' she looked forward to the many discussions it was certain to stimulate. And, in anticipation of his potential criticism, she bookmarked the introduction with a sprig of lavender—hoping he might appreciate her humorous gesture.

Due to the holiday, she'd been unable to deposit school funds on Thursday. She opened the safe, removed a satchel containing monies collected for yearbook deposits and the annual senior trip—counting it twice before departing the school at 8:44. Tiny flakes, like bits of ash, swirled in the frigid air. The yellow-gray sky appeared ready to dump a foot of snow.

At 8:56, she entered the law office of "Wm. R. Stevens, Attorney-at-Law."

"Miss Madeira…so nice to see you. Are you here to see Mr. Stevens?" asked Jennifer Johnson Stewart, (class of '44), who seemed genuinely surprised to see her former teacher.

"Miss Madeira? Is that you?" echoed a voice from an inner office.

"Go right on in," said Jennifer.

Amelia smiled. "I like your hair, Jennie."

"Why, thank you. Tom hates that I bleached it," she said— referring to her husband, Thomas Stewart (class of '43).

"It's very…modern. You tell Tommy I remember when he used to slather his hair with pomade 'til it fairly dripped," she said— starting down the hall.

"I surely will," said Jennie, laughing at the thought.

Amelia stopped at the first office on the right. Attorney William Stevens, (class of '30) sat behind a large mahogany desk.

"Come in, Miss Madeira. This is a pleasant surprise. What brings you here this morning?" he asked—rising to his feet.

"Billy, I need to make out my will."

"You know…only you and my mother still call me Billy."

"Would you have time to do it now, I wonder?"

"Depending on how involved it is, I think we could accomplish that now. Please, have a seat."

At 9:59, she thanked Billy and said goodbye to Jennie, who had typed the will and sealed the envelope, and headed up the street to the Bank of Prospect. She entered through the heavy glass door and got in line behind Daniel Dundon, (class of '40) who was writing a check at the teller's window. Cashing the check was Jean Lynn (Jones) Gunderson, (class of '27) wife of G. R. Gunderson, bank president.

"Miss Madeira," said Daniel. "Haven't seen you in a coon's age."

"The junior class play wasn't it? How've you been, Danny? How's Marguerite (Donaldson), (class of '42)?"

"Couldn't be better, thanks. You know we just had another baby girl."

"No, I hadn't heard. How many is that now?"

"Three."

"Three girls…how *wonderful*."

"You might like to know we named her Bessie Amelia."

Amelia started to respond, but failed to find the words.

"It was Marguerite's idea. Can't tell you how many times we've said if it wasn't for you two, we'd have hated school. Well, me more than her. She was always a better student than me…than I."

"You were a fine student, Danny. Remember the Globe Theatre you built for English III? I still have it."

"No foolin'?"

"Use it as an example of what a good project should be."

"I spent weeks on that thing…before and after school. Daddy thought I'd lost my mind. Gave me a hard time about it.

Can't believe it hasn't fallen apart by now. Well...'spect I better be goin'. She's probably finished shopping at Rainey's. Better get down there before she stops in at The Clothes Horse and puts us in the poorhouse. Be sure and tell Miss Bessie about the little one."

"Of course...and give her my best."

"I'll do that. Take care now, Miss Madeira."

She smiled at Danny as he departed, and then plopped the satchel down in the teller window.

"Good morning, Miss Madeira. Looks like we have a sizable deposit today."

"$967 if I counted correctly. Yearbook and senior class trip."

"Senior class trip. Remember *ours*? First time any of us had been on a train. A bunch of hooligans. Don't know how you put up with it."

"Was that to St. Louis...or Memphis?"

"Memphis. We all stayed one night at the Peabody Hotel...with the ducks that walk through the lobby."

"Was that your class, Jean Lynn? Anymore...I get them confused."

"It was. You know, Gil and I went back there on our honeymoon. Joked about you not letting us hang out on Beale Street after dark. 'Too dangerous,' you said."

"I was afraid some of you girls would be snatched right off the street. I was on edge the whole time. Debauchery lurked everywhere."

"Probably so...but we were too young and foolish to realize it."

"Sometimes, I think I'm getting too old to sponsor another trip."

"Nonsense. Learned more history on that trip than I did in any history class. Besides, who else would do it?"

"Well, it won't be long before it will fall to someone else. Retirement is beginning to look very enticing."

"*You*...retire? Never. What would Prospect High be without

our Miss Madeira?"

"The same thing was once asked about my predecessor, Miss Orton. You remember her?"

"Not really. Mother had her, I think."

"See? Life goes on..."

As Mrs. Gunderson counted out the money, Amelia spotted the bank vice president, (class of '25). "Gilbert Ray, might I have a word?" She quietly explained she had just come from Steven's Law Office, where she'd named him executor of her estate. She held up the large manila envelope containing her will. He noticed she'd written 'Call Sarah Jamison Moore, Little Rock, Arkansas' on the front. He said he was honored to serve as executor. She gathered up the satchel and the deposit receipt and bid the Gunderson's good day.

At 10:14, she paused in front of Street's Drugstore. Staring through the large, plate glass window, she spotted Alberta Conrad Street, (class of '31). She waved to Alberta and headed back towards school. A light snow was once again falling.

By the time she reached school, large wet flakes were piling up on the teeter-totters, swings and the merry-go-round. A senior boy, Mike Henderson, (Class of 1953) honked as he drove by in his father's light blue Ford station wagon. She waved back; perhaps that's why she didn't notice the footprints as she entered the building at 10:27. Or, perhaps she saw them and believed they belonged to Chester.

Chester thought he heard the front door open and close. Earlier, he'd heard the door chain rattle and assumed it was Amelia returning from her daily run to the post office. As soon as he had a chance to mop the boy's dressing room, he planned to slip upstairs and say, 'Hello.' Having just read a new book of literary criticism on the concept of imitation, he was anxious to discuss it with her.

Chester was in the lower hall, near the door to the gymnasium, when he heard the fatal gunshot.

Epilogue

Chester O'Malley died of heart failure in March, 1962. Following Miss Madeira's death nearly a decade earlier, he finished out the school year; however, he resigned the following June. For many years, he frequented the county library, though by 1960, his health had declined and he often failed to appear for days at a time. Former teachers said that when the old school building was raised in the spring of '61, Chester was so dispirited they feared he might take his own life. If absent more than a week, Phyllis Jenson would stop by to check on him. It was on one such concerned visit she discovered his body, slumped in a chair. In his hands, she found a book entitled, *Janus.*

Upon his death, Mrs. Jenson produced a notarized, handwritten document wherein Chester had donated his large personal library and 'all its contents.' When she and an assistant came to claim the books at his home, they discovered countless journals and manuscripts—including two completed novels and three decades of various literary periodicals containing short stories and poems published under his *nom de plume*, S. A. Moon. In addition, they were shocked to find the daybooks and diaries of Amelia Madeira, who had willed them to him. All were transported to the Iron county library, where they were archived in four large filing cabinets.

Months later, while pouring through Chester's journals, Phyllis read accounts of his undying love for Miss Madeira and his turbulent relationship with Prof. Harris Butler, whom he described as "yet another failed father figure," in addition to the events that led to his suicide attempt while at Washington University.

She also came across an epic poem, reminiscent of Tennyson's *In Memoriam*, in which he revealed his love for boyhood friend, Willie Stansbury, who died of complications from pneumonia at only twenty-nine years of age. It closed with this octet:

> *Oh, noble friend whose features fair*
> *Locked in repose forevermore*
> *Needless knock on Heaven's door*
> *Your throne and crown await you there*
> *And I, resigned, long to be free*
> *Of censored love and human fears*
> *My heart cries out with anguished tears*
> *'Til Death unites my Soul with thee*

The poem, along with an unsent letter of condolence, an apology for being unable to attend Willie's funeral, was tucked in an envelope addressed to his wife, Sandra.

All of these stunning discoveries were minor compared to Chester's detailed account of finding his mother dead, and the horrifying description of how he murdered his father. Thinking no good could come from that disclosure, Mrs. Jenson considered destroying the journal, but in the end, she reported the incident to Sheriff Bowers, who released a statement published in the *Prospect Banner*. A blurb from the article found its way into the *St. Louis Post-Dispatch*.

Believing nothing could top that revelation, she continued to devour the journals. Two months later, she happened upon two yellowed newspaper clippings, folded and paper-clipped to a shocking journal entry.

The first:

Suicide Verdict Returned
At Madeira Inquest

Eight Witnesses Appear Before an Inquest Jury to Tell of Final Acts of PHS Principal and Teacher

A coroner's jury last Sunday evening ruled the death of Miss Amelia Madeira, Prospect high school principal, as suicide. The jury report, as written by Marion G. Howard, who served as foreman of the group, stated: "It is the unanimous verdict that Miss Amelia Madeira destroyed her life by her own hand."

The inquest was called by county Coroner, C. N. McNabb and Prosecuting Attorney Thomas Liggett, following the discovery of Miss Madeira's body in the Prospect school building last Saturday morning. Held in a special session Sunday evening at Prescott's Mortuary, the first witness called was Chester O'Malley, who discovered the deceased's body at 7 a.m. last Saturday. O'Malley, school janitor, explained he saw a light on in the principal's office. Thinking someone left the light on all Friday, O'Malley opened the door and discovered the body of Miss Madeira slumped on a couch in the office lobby. He said that he immediately went to the nearby home of Supt. Charles Meeker and told him that the PHS principal and long-time teacher had shot herself.

Trooper J. B. Kline, Ironton investigating officer of the tragedy, was the next witness. Trooper Kline testified that he arrived at the office and discovered what had happened. The state patrolman told the jury that, in his opinion, the death was a suicide, since a brown envelope was found on Miss Madeira's desk and the words "Last Will and Testament of Amelia Madeira" were typed on the envelope, which remained sealed.

Trooper Kline stated that there was not a note left in the office, other than the words, "Notify Sarah Jamison Moore, Little Rock, Arkansas," which had apparently been written in longhand on the envelope by Miss Madeira. He identified the envelope as brown in color and bearing the logotype of Atty. Wm. R. Stevens, Prospect Attorney. The patrolman said the bullet from a WWI British service revolver, engraved: Webley MK VI, penetrated Miss Madeira's right temple and went completely through her head and dislodged behind her left ear. He said he was unable to locate the bullet believed to be an usual caliber.

Had Been Ill

Supt. Charles W. Meeker was the third witness before the inquest jury, and he told panel members the PHS principal had been ill for some time. He said she suffered from severe headaches for many months. He said the last time he saw the high school principal was late Wednesday afternoon, following school dismissal for the two-day Thanksgiving holiday. When Meeker left he said he told her, "Miss Madeira, you had better go home before you get snowed in." He said she smiled but did not answer him as he left the school office.

Dr. Albert Carlson, Prospect physician, was called to the witness stand, and he told the jury members he found Miss Madeira in a half-sitting and half-reclining position on a couch in the high school office. He said the antique revolver, which he believed to be of WWI vintage and of English origin, was in her lap and her right hand was on the gun. He said Miss Madeira was examined and no pulse or heartbeat was detected.

Atty. Wm. R. Stevens, Prospect, was the fifth witness before the jury. He testified that at about 9 a.m. last Friday, Miss Madeira entered his office and asked that he write her will. He said he noted nothing unusual in her actions, and that she appeared to be perfectly rational. He said after a little discussion, G. R. Gunderson, President of the Bank of Prospect, was named the administrator of her estate. G. R. Gunderson was the next witness, and he testified that Miss Madeira had entered the Bank of Prospect Friday morning and deposited monies into the school account as per her usual custom. As the bank was closed for observance of the Thanksgiving holiday on Thursday, she had been unable to make her normal deposit until Friday morning.

The next witness was Alberta Street, Prospect, who said she saw Miss Madeira stop and peer into Street's Drugstore window at about 10:15 a.m. Friday morning. Mrs. Street testified that it was Miss Madeira's custom to stop by the Drugstore after depositing school funds. However, Friday she merely looked in the window, waved to Mrs. Street and continued on towards school. She said she now realized that Miss Madeira had not stopped by to say hello but goodbye.

The final witness was Sheriff E. C. Bowers, Ironton, the other investigating officer at the scene of the tragedy. Sheriff Bowers said he called a Mrs. Sarah Moore, former sister-in-law of Miss Madeira's, at Little Rock, Ark. after reading the request of Miss Madeira, which had been written on the envelope containing the will. In answer to a question from the jury, the county peace officer said he found no powder burns on the hands of Miss Madeira. (underlined in pencil).

In less than five minutes after the jury was instructed to return a verdict of suicide or death from other causes, the verdict of self-inflicted death was returned last Sunday evening by the 6-man panel. The inquest was then adjourned by Prosecutor Liggett.

The second:

Second Suicide Shocks Prospect Community; Plan Double Funeral

Brother of Miss A. Madeira Had Been Scheduled For Return To Farmingdale

Karl Madeira, 56, brother of PHS principal and teacher, Miss Amelia Madeira, was found dead in the Madeira home, early last last Saturday morning, according to investgating officers, Patrolman J. C. Kline and Sheriff E. C. Bowers. Mr. Madeira, who was believed to be in declining health, was scheduled to be returned to Farmingdale State Hospital, where he was a patient for many years, according to Dr. Albert Carlson.

The body was found hanging from the transom in Miss Madeira's bedroom. For the past several years, she had cared for him at the family home on West 6th St. As there was no note, the county coroner, C.N. McNabb, was unable to determine if Mr. Madeira hung himself prior to or following the suicide of his sister (as reported elsewhere in this newspaper). It is believed that both suicides occurred within an hour or two of each other last Friday.

Mr. Madeira was born in Cincinnati,

Ohio. He was an outstanding athlete at PHS and still holds many school and county records. He owned and operated Madeira Lighting and Electric for several years. He was preceded in death by his parents and a daughter.

Phyllis removed the clippings to read:

25 December, 1952
(the loneliest day of the year)

It has taken the time it has taken for me to be able to record my feelings about the tremendous loss of Amelia Irmelinda Madeira...only one month ago—a lifetime! Of all the misfortunes I have suffered, her death has been hardest to endure. I blamed myself for not anticipating the worst. I knew the situation with her brother had reached its nadir. Clearly, the anxiety over Karl's deteriorating condition affected her health. She was ravaged by severe migraines and her mental state was taxed. No one knew the agony of her home life, the abuse she suffered at the hands of that monster.

When I came to claim her journals, I counted six locks on the inside of her bedroom door; it was obvious from the condition of the oldest, entry had been forced on more than one occasion. The Inquest was a sober affair. I was the first witness called. I said what they wanted to hear—no more, no less. It was evident from the start the authorities wanted no revelations. I overheard Supt. Meeker say 'nothing good' could come from unearthing unpleasant details. That's when I knew the truth would not emerge from the hearing.

What is the truth?

The truth is I have loved Amelia Madeira for thirty-five years. Even when I refused to communicate with her, after she rebuffed me, I never stopped loving her, though for years, I convinced myself otherwise...

Odi et amo. Quare id faciam, fortasse requiris?
Nescio, sed fieri sentio et excrucior.

(I hate and love. Why do I do this, you ask? I know not, but I feel it happening and I am tortured.).

Reading her journals, I realized her refusal to acknowledge her feelings for me hinged on her understanding that choosing to be with me would have forced her to forfeit her teaching career. Her poems revealed a torment equal to my own. How sad to know our destinies were determined by circumstances beyond our control. How different our lives might have been.

Knowing how she selflessly cared for Karl—following his release from the State Psychiatric Hospital in Farmingdale—people speculated that the shock and the shame of his suicide overwhelmed her otherwise impeccable judgment. Within days, however, rumors began to grow like apples on a poison tree.

It was a most difficult decision to allow this tragedy to be recorded as a suicide, as if such a thought would ever have entered her mind. I have never known anyone who valued life more than she. And, having read her journals many times now, I know she was the ultimate survivor. Would that I had a fraction of her fortitude and determination!

For years, I have regretted taking revenge on my father for murdering my dear mother. I have felt the deepest remorse. Because I judged him to be guilty of utmost cruelty, I chose a Sophoclean patricide. True suffering would have been allowing him to live, sober, with the memory of his heinous crime. Instead, I meted out justice as I saw fit. It took many months before I realized the error in judgment; my contrition led to my own attempted suicide. In time, I prostrated myself before the Most High—acknowledging my guilt and resolving then and there, given the same circumstance, I would forego retribution and let the courts decide his fate.

Permit me to state here that the Universe has a deliciously perverse sense of humor...for Fate, once again, provided me with an opportunity to test my resolve.

Having heard the gunshot, it took almost a minute to reach the principal's office. When I entered the doorway, I nearly collapsed at the sight. Amelia was slumped over on the sofa and blood was seeping from a hole in the side of her head; even so, she was still breathing. I slipped in beside her and held her in my arms. There was no gun in sight.

From the blank look in her eyes—the dazed look of a wounded deer—it was obvious she was in shock. I sat holding her for another minute, and then I whispered, 'My dearest love...I must call Doc Carlson.'

As I started to pull away, she fumbled for

my wrist—gently squeezing it. Then, her grasp loosened, her breath shuddered...and she died there in my arms.

My Miss Madeira was gone!

As I continued to hold her, I could feel rage slowly building within me. How well I remembered that volcanic reaction; it was comprised of the same passion and ardor I once experienced when I discovered my mother's slain corpse. Once again, I was faced with a choice, and the choice seemed clear.

I gently repositioned her body as I'd found it. I descended the steps to the basement and entered the boiler room. In an old metal case, I retrieved a hammer, my father's trusty helve. I slipped it through the belt loop in my coveralls and headed for West 6th. Luckily, no one saw me enter the Madeira home, though, at the time, I made no effort to conceal my intention or myself.

Inside, I discovered a skillet on the stove. She had apparently left breakfast for Karl. I glanced in towards the downstairs bedroom. His bed was unmade; he was nowhere in sight. On the dining room table was a note: 'To school early. Home by 6:00. Breakfast on stove. ~Amelia.' Next to her note, a gun and another note; the scrawl read: 'She was the greatest love of my life!'

Overhead, floorboards groaned. I picked up the antique revolver, still reeking with the after-burn of gunmetal, and headed towards the stairs. As I reached the top landing, I could hear sobbing. He had thrown himself onto her bed. In his clenched fist, he held a rope—the noose coiled around his neck.

I raised the revolver. "You sick bastard," I

said.

"Yo-o-u," he uttered. How grotesque he had become, his bloated face bulged with tumors; his eye-socket was sunken and his eye, scabrous and matted.

"You killed the one person I ever truly loved," I confessed. "The best person I have ever known."

Stupefied, at first he said nothing. "Go ahead then...pull the trigger!" he begged.

In that instant, I realized Amelia had protected him all these years. Would she want him remembered as her murderer? Would a murder prompt an investigation—revealing all the sordid details she hoped to suppress?

"Get up! Bring the noose!"

Standing in the hallway, I held the gun on him as he tied the rope over the transom and secured it with a knot. He stood trembling before me on an old railroad conductor's stool.

"Pull it tight! Tighter!"

"No one...will ever know...how much I loved...my little Sis, minha irmã cama,' he blubbered, tears rolling down his pustulous cheeks.

"That wasn't love," I said—placing my foot on the stool, ready to shove it out from under him. Something stopped me. Remembering there was no atonement in the role of executioner, no matter how impeachable the offense, I removed my foot. "Do it...or don't!" I said. "Either way, you're a dead man."

As I descended the stairs, I heard the stool scoot across the hardwood floor. I glanced up through the railing. His body was writhing, the tips of his shoes barely brushing the floor. For a moment, I had the urge to cut him down; instead I blessed him: *Ut crimen, suus iustus remuneror!* (To the guilty his just reward!).

On my way out, I grabbed the note containing his declaration of 'love'—crushing it and stuffing it in my pocket. On a sideboard, I spotted a drinking glass, etched with a giant Ferris wheel and the inscription, "St. Louis World's Fair 1904." I took it as a reminder of the glorious childhood memory Amelia had once shared with me. It sits here now on my writing desk.

Knowing Supt. Meeker would be out of town until late Friday evening, I chose to wait until Saturday morning "to discover the body." I hoped the extra day would make it more difficult for the county coroner to determine the times of their deaths. I wiped the gun clean of fingerprints before placing it in her hand.

What concerned me most was the absence of powder burns on her hand. At the Inquest, when Sheriff Bowers referenced it, I held my breath, shocked no one challenged the discovery of this damning piece of evidence, until I saw Bowers exchange glances with Supt. Meeker and with Miss Bessie Sweeney, who served on the six-"man" jury.

As people were leaving the inquest, Supt. Meeker summoned me to his office. He handed me a book. "I found this on the counter under Miss Madeira's will."

It was a copy of William Faulkner's "Collected Stories." Inside, a stem of lavender bookmarked an inscription: 'To My Dear Chester, whose love of words and whose facility for language know no equal. I look forward to reading

your stories someday soon. With the greatest love
and admiration, Amelia.'

Those were the words I had longed to
hear! Those are the words that have sustained me
whenever I have wanted to be free of this tortured
existence.

I thanked him and took the book with me.
Rarely a day goes by that I do not lovingly press it
to my anguished heart.

Remembering the uproar created by the discovery that
Chester had murdered his father, Phyllis was reluctant to surrender
this new information to the authorities, no more so than Sheriff
Bowers was to receive it. Once again, he issued a statement, but not
before deleting major portions of the journal entry.

In time, former students were relieved to know their dear
teacher had not chosen to take her own life. Realizing she had been a
long-suffering victim of abuse, restored her reputation—even among
those who remembered her as being "mean."

Responding to the numerous "letters to the editor," calling
for special recognition of Miss Madeira's life and accomplishments,
Mrs. Jenson created a memorial fund in her honor. In addition to an
annual scholarship given to an outstanding Prospect High School
senior who pledged to pursue a career in education, the fund was
used to purchase a small headstone for her grave. At first, the Delphi
Club chose Emily Dickinson's poem, *Death is the supple suitor*, as
an inscription. However, after some debate, Alberta Street
convinced the others to use one of Amelia's poems instead:

> *What recompense—my Soul—*
> *No Refuge find—escape the Mind—*
> *No bride of Heaven be—*
> *In Innocence a dark reward*
> *In Memory all doubt restored*
> *What now—Eternity—*

The inscription was carved by Frederick Hoffman, grandson

of the late William Hoffman, of Missouri Red Monuments.

In the intervening years, hundreds of people have made the pilgrimage to High Ridge cemetery to honor Miss Madeira, some who knew her only by reputation. None left without commenting on the large sculpture that loomed over the Madeira family plot.

In the 1980's, a curator from the St. Louis Art Museum, built as the Palace of the Fine Arts for the World's Fair, came to view the hand-carved seraph. Impressed by the magnificent carving, he photographed it and included it in a coffee table edition entitled, *Classic Art of the Midwest*.

Next to Elephant Rocks State Park, renowned for its granite "pachyderms," the Madeira gravesite and statue remained the most visited attraction in Iron County, Missouri until it was vandalized and toppled in 2008 by several teenagers—one, the great great-grandson of former Madeira student, Billy Patton.

When Miss Bessie Sweeney died in 1984 at the age of eighty-eight, a framed picture of the young Amelia Madeira, reading in her garden glider, was found on her bedroom nightstand. It sparked rumors the two may have been lovers.

In a cabinet of the break room at the Iron County Library sits a drinking glass commemorating the 1904 St. Louis World's Fair. No one knows its origin, but the consensus is that it's probably a cheap replica issued during the 2004 Centennial celebration.

To make room for a bank of donated computers, four ancient filing cabinets containing scores of literary magazines, hand-written manuscripts, old yellowed notebooks—and the revelations they contained—were recently hauled off to the city dump.

A book of poetry, *Nosegays For Emily,* by Amelia Madeira (edited by C. F. O'Malley) can be found, located between tomes by Archibald MacLeish and Edgar Lee Masters. And, in the fiction section, a single copy of a self-published novel entitled, *Janus,* by S. A. Moon, remains shelved—still awaiting the opportunity to impact the life of that first curious reader.

Acknowledgments

I am grateful for the many friends who gave encouragement along the way. The first, Jean Lenihan, who, having read the (original) prologue and first chapter, insisted, "You must write it!" Then, to the many readers who read and re-read the various drafts— chief among them, Dan Dundon and Drew Larson, whose names were given, in gratitude, to characters. My gratitude goes to other readers: Jon Henderson, Terry Lay, Lori Freeman, Leslie Shew, Susan Maedor, Anita Beth Anderson, Molly Hueffed, Garth Reeves, Ricki Newman, Karen Yoe, Lindsey Reeves, Chelsea Calvert, Wally Turner, Kye Fleming, Vicki Nienaber, Tenilla Sheehan and Leslie Patheal. Thanks to Susana Martins for correcting my Portuguese, and to Mary Logue and Nancy Wick for their editing expertise. I'm most appreciative for the assistance I received from the Gentry County Library.

I also want to acknowledge my former colleagues at Highline Big Picture High School for the important work they do. Most of *Miss Madeira* was written from 4:30-7:30 a.m., before assuming my Advisor role at the school. Let me also praise former colleagues at Franklin High School (TN); Middle College High School (TN); and Overton High School, Nashville (TN)—where I taught for the past eleven years—especially those who expend super-human energy engaging the forgotten, bored, ignored and needy. It's time to stop saying teachers are underpaid and remedy the situation. In an "enlightened" society, this disparity would never exist. (Forgive me for channeling my inner-Madeira).

Special recognition to Dr. Sheila Rhodes, the best teacher I ever had. She said "fuckupta" in the basement of New Chapel and was fired.

Special thanks go to my beloved partner, Brad Wilkinson, who designed the cover art and my website, and endured my need to read the manuscript aloud. To my amazing children, the wonderfully talented Rachel Rockwell (award-winning stage director) and Jeremy Spencer (FFDP drummer extraordinaire)—thanks for making me so proud. And to grandson, Jake Helm, whose first word was 'light'— Papaw loves you!

Lastly, to super agent, Marly Rusoff, who guided *Miss Madeira* from its infancy to its completion, I remain forever in your debt.

I drew inspiration from two books for this novel. First, *A Wounded Deer: The Effects of Incest On The Life And Poetry Of Emily Dickinson* by Wendy L. Perriman. It was the title that first gave me the idea to try to create a parallel between the lives of Emily Dickinson and Amelia Madeira. Secondly, *The Poems of Emily Dickinson*, edited by R. W. Franklin, the first and foremost edition of Dickinson's original poetry ever assembled (impeccable). Also, I referenced James Cavanaugh's *Book of Poetry, Some Men Are Too Gentle To Live Among The Wolves*, which I read at a time of personal crisis in 1975. And, lastly, thanks to WashingtonMo.com for its plentiful information about the 1904 St. Louis World's Fair.

About the Author

Austin Gary has lived various lives as a teacher; newspaper editor; copywriter; director of T.V. & Radio broadcast; actor/performer; creative director; music producer; BMI award-winning songwriter and intuitive numerologist (as Gary Heyde).

He is a gourmet vegetarian cook; remains tied (after 47 years) for 10th in single-game assists (18) in the Missouri High School Sports Records; survived to the 5th round of the U.S. Senior 9-Ball Championship (1998); and caddied for Judy Rankin in the 1975 U. S. Women's Open. Forced to give him an "A," his former college creative writing teacher added, "I truly pray you never have anything published. I'd hate for people to be influenced by your profane ideas!" (Her prayers were very nearly answered).

He currently lives in Port Moody, B.C., (City of the Arts).

www.Austin-Gary.com

Published by Deckle Press